A NEFARIOUS ENGAGEMENT

LYNN MESSINA

potatoworks press
greenwich village

COPYRIGHT © 2019 BY LYNN MESSINA
COVER DESIGN BY JENNIFER LEWIS

ISBN: 978-1-942218-29-6

This is a work of fiction. Names, characters, places and incidents either are the product of the author's imagination or are used fictitiously. Any resemblance to actual persons, living or dead, events or locales is entirely coincidental.

All Rights Reserved

Published 2019 by Potatoworks Press

Without limiting the rights under copyright above, no part of this publication may be reproduced, stored in or introduced into a retrieval system or transmitted in any form or by any means (electronic, mechanical, photocopying, recording or otherwise) without prior written permission of the copyright owner and publisher of this book.

The scanning, uploading and distribution of this book via the Internet or via any other means without the permission of the publisher is illegal and punishable by law. Please purchase only authorized electronic editions and do not participate in or encourage electronic piracy of copyrightable materials. Your support of the author's rights is appreciated.

*To Jill Smith, whose gorgeous narration gives
life to Bea and her duke*

CHAPTER ONE

If Beatrice Hyde-Clare had thought for even one moment that securing the affections of a lord of high standing would inure her to the consequences of exposing a murderer at a glittering society event, she was immediately disabused of that notion by her aunt, whose mortification at her niece's audacity was so acute, she could barely keep her gracious smile in place.

She did, of course, effecting wide-eyed elation as she quietly berated Bea for the insupportable breach of etiquette. As appalled as she was by her relative's scandalous behavior—following a gentleman onto the balcony to have a private word, accusing him of an immoral deed, exposing herself to a violent attack—she was more horrified by the prospect of the *ton* sensing her disapproval. It would never do for anyone at the Larkwells' ball to suspect how cross she was with her niece.

Oh, but she was very cross indeed!

How could the wretched girl do this to her family *again*? It was bad enough that she had unmasked a killer in the villain's own drawing room only a few months before. Such a flagrant want of discretion to claim your host bashed a fellow guest over the head with a candlestick in the dead of night! An assertion of that nature should be levied in private or, better yet, not at all, for making it was a shocking violation of the basic rules one agreed to follow at a house party.

But no, her capricious niece leveled the accusation in front of everyone, including the perpetrator's husband and son. Was she lacking in all sense of propriety?

Obviously so, for she now had revealed the Marquess of Taunton's misdeed in the middle of Lady Hortense's come-out.

Vera Hyde-Clare felt positive Beatrice knew better.

Although, to be fair, Vera had not thought to include a ballroom on her exhaustive list of places where it was not quite *comme il faut* to unmask a killer. She had mentioned the front parlor, naturally, and the dining room, as well as the library, study and rose garden if tea was being served outside on an especially pleasant day. The failure to cite the ballroom in particular had been naught but an oversight, one that should have been offset by her insistence that revelations of murderers should be confined to the stables and, in extreme circumstances only, the kitchens.

Accepting the omission as an unfortunate lapse she would correct as soon as they returned to their carriage, Vera could not bring herself to believe it would have significantly altered her niece's actions. Even if she had been thorough in her catalogue of locations, Bea would still have behaved as she wished. Her niece, who had been quiet and biddable for the first six and twenty years of her life, had of late exhibited an inexplicable refusal to heed any advice but her own. Her family, unable to attribute her obstinacy to any sort of internal fortitude, assumed her mind had been slowly unraveled by recent horrifying events, such as stumbling across a dead body in a darkened library, being trapped in an abandoned shed far out in a field and discovering that the love of her life, a lowly law clerk from Cheapside, had died violently in a carriage accident.

Bea, who knew exactly what thoughts were running

through her aunt's head, for she had been liberal in sharing them in the past few months, tried to arrange her features into a sufficiently contrite expression. Aunt Vera felt deeply aggrieved by her conduct, and allowing her the pleasure of being disappointed in her charge was the least Bea could do.

As sincere as Bea's efforts to show remorse were, however, they were all for naught because she was simply too giddy to do anything but grin hugely.

Minutes ago, moments ago, Damien Matlock, Duke of Kesgrave, had consented to be her husband. The Duke of Kesgrave! The most glittering prize on the Marriage Mart, who had every advantage to his favor—appearance, status, wealth—loved her, middling Beatrice Hyde-Clare with the drab features and bland personality.

'Twas the most extraordinary thing to have ever happened.

And yet she also felt it to be remarkably mundane, for now that he'd declared his feelings, there was a sort of wild inevitability about it.

For weeks she'd wallowed in her room, calling herself every kind of fool for falling for someone so high in the instep as the Duke of Kesgrave. It was an absurdity beyond anything to hope for even one moment that the imperious lord would unbend enough to realize the strange compulsion he felt to be in her presence—a compulsion he had plainly owned to her with confusion—was in fact love.

She'd spent all those hours nursing her misery while the duke, having already recognized the truth of his emotions, made every attempt to declare his feelings.

Well, she thought humorously, not *every* attempt. If he'd sought some means other than conventional letters and morning calls, they would have sorted this matter out ages ago in the comfort of her own home rather than on the Larkwells' balcony in the presence of the murderous Lord Taunton, whose thwarted attempt to snuff out her life had ended with his hair on fire.

Recalling the scene, she let out an errant giggle, for the episode hardly seemed real to her now: Taunton on the ground in a faint, her sitting on his chest to restrain him, Kesgrave clutching her shoulders as he declared his love.

That the duke had handled the situation with wry amusement—kissing her tenderly without concern for the unconscious form starting to awaken, accepting her proposal, which was really more of an announcement—only increased her delight, as it had been his sense of humor that had drawn her to him in the first place. For all his pomposity and pedantry, Kesgrave possessed the startling ability to poke fun at himself. Although elevated by rank and breeding, his gaze was nevertheless firmly placed at eye level and he could see everything clearly, including himself.

Having credited him with such admirable clear-sightedness, Bea had naturally assumed it could not extend as far as the selection of a wife. With generations of Matlocks at his back demanding perfection, he would dutifully provide it, choosing a paragon of grace and beauty to produce impeccably cherubic children whose elegantly docile features would lend refinement to the family portrait gallery on the second floor. This diamond of the first water would bring not only faultless poise to the union but also a large plot of land and an irreproachable pedigree.

The transactional nature of the connection Kesgrave would inevitably forge disgusted Bea, but she could not fault him for falling in line with expectation. He was the sixth Duke of Kesgrave, after all.

Ah, but that was *precisely* the aspect of the situation she'd been unable to comprehend despite the many times he'd patiently and portentously explained it to her. He was indeed the sixth Duke of Kesgrave and would make no decision that did not please himself.

With every option available to him, he chose her.

It was a staggering idea to grow accustomed to, and Bea thought it was rather unlikely she ever would.

Fortunately, Aunt Vera was giving her plenty of time to settle into the notion, for the other woman would allow no interruption of her soliloquy. Uncle Horace had made two unsuccessful attempts so far, both of which were quelled by his wife's refusal to yield the floor, and their fellow guests were far too polite to intrude on what appeared to be an intimate family moment. Mrs. Hyde-Clare feigned happiness with such conviction, even Bea was taken aback by the tenor of her dissatisfaction as she switched her attention to her niece's appearance.

"The deplorable state of your dress!" Vera exclaimed, dropping her voice lower even as her smile grew wider. The expression did not reach her eyes, a cloudy shade of gray that seemed perpetually on the verge of rain, and her nose, always a bit off center, widened in disgust. "That is the second one you have ruined in a matter of months, and I can only assume it met the same violent end as the other one. Must you keep getting yourself into scrapes with angry gentlemen? Really, Bea, how can you be so remiss? I was full of sympathy, was I not, when you got yourself trapped in that dilapidated hut in the Lake District? I looked at you in your torn dress and bruised face and knew at once you had been grossly misused by the feckless Skeffington heir, who shoved you inside and locked the door. Appreciating the gravity of the situation, I took him to task on your uncle's behalf. And when you were assaulted at Mr. Davies's funeral, which you should never have gone to, I tended to your bruises. But now it has happened for a third time, and I wonder just how much compassion I'm expected to have. Should it be without limit? Clearly not, for it seems only to embolden you to create further contretemps."

After this lengthy critique, Aunt Vera paused for breath, and Bea glanced at her uncle to see if he would try yet again to say his piece. Unlike the overly bright expression on his wife's face, Horace's smile seemed to be genuine and sincere. No doubt he was thinking of all the lovely blunt he would save once he foisted her onto the duke, she thought cynically. Although he had never been particularly generous with his purchases for her, always making sure she got the lesser version of everything on offer to hold on to a few extra shillings, he believed himself to be quite profligate on her behalf. Her relatives' ability to consider themselves liberal while withholding money and affection was perhaps their most remarkable achievement.

Uncle Horace, deciphering the meaning of Bea's look a moment too late, opened his mouth to speak just as his wife resumed her lecture, railing now against Bea's impertinence in suggesting *she* cared more about issues of justice than Vera herself.

"Just because I do not go about society lodging lavish charges against my betters does not mean that I approve of illicit behavior. Am I deeply troubled by Mrs. Lambert's repeated efforts to skint the fishmonger? Of course I am. The fishmonger cannot provide me with the mackerel I require if he doesn't have enough money to buy supplies. But do I publicly berate her and expose her to the censure of her peers? Heavens, no. Society cannot function if we all live in deathly fear of our peccadillos being discussed as freely as the weather."

Bea was hardly surprised her aunt equated parsimony with murder, as she measured the severity of a transgression by the societal discomfort it engendered. What did take her aback, however, was the vehemence with which Aunt Vera purported to know the duke's feelings on the matter. As they aligned with her own—conveniently, Bea observed with wry cynicism—she was able to clearly articulate the extent of his mortification at the prospect of marrying a woman who would identify murderers in between the waltz and the quadrille.

"No man wants a wife whose sense of decorum is so compromised, she scours the private business of other men in hopes of discovering their secrets," her aunt said soberly.

Although an impish impulse tempted Bea to assure her

relation that the duke had no issue with her investigative activities, she decided against provoking the other woman further. Alas, Aunt Vera needed no provocation and continued to fulminate unabated, progressing smoothly from lamenting Kesgrave's misfortune to bemoaning her own.

Nabbing a duke was a feather in Bea's cap, to be sure, and Vera could not blame her for seizing the opportunity to secure her future while increasing her stature, but it would have been much better for everyone concerned if she had allowed him to proceed with the grand and glorious match his grandmother had arranged. Lady Victoria was far better suited to a duchy, with her raven locks, centuries-old name and large tract of land that marched along the Matlock estate's northern border.

Such an arrangement was exactly what a marriage should be—the ruthless yoking together of two ancient families.

The Hyde-Clares, Vera explained, were not great. They were good, yes, indeed very good, with their modest-sized family seat in Sussex and humble motto, "*Si non est molestum*" ("If it's no trouble"). But an essential aspect of their family's goodness was embracing their limitations, and as such they took immense pride in keeping their eyes turned down and never daring to tilt them up to the dizzying height of greatness.

And now Bea had ruined everything by thrusting herself upon a duke.

Thoughtless baggage!

Had she not considered what her engagement would mean for the rest of her family? It would upend their existence, for people would now begin to expect things from them. They would be required to turn themselves out in the first stare of fashion—to wear the finest silks, to drive the fittest horses, to host the fanciest parties.

Good God, she would have to invite his grandmother to tea!

At the discovery of this fresh horror, Vera's smile dipped for the first time as she imagined the famously formidable dowager in her own drawing room stroking the worn damask of the settee with finely wrought contempt.

The fabric would need to be replaced as well as the curtains, which had been unevenly faded by the sun. And the condition of the rug was far from pristine.

Vera blanched as she counted the many faults of the drawing room and realized how much it would cost to replace everything—and by everything, she meant every piece of furniture in the London house.

The dust had barely settled between Bea and the duke, and already the adequate comfort with which the Hyde-Clares lived was insufficient. Clearly, their situation would only continue to devolve until they were forced to live in luxury and splendor.

As her aunt bewailed the oppressive obligations of home improvement, Bea laughed. It was not Vera's typically excessive response that amused her, although she felt positive the chairs in Uncle Horace's study were safe from the dowager's censorious eye. Rather, it was the unmitigated absurdity in believing she, quiet and docile Beatrice Hyde-Clare, had spent any portion of time thinking about what it would mean to be a duchess. Not even at the beginning of her first season, when she was an eager young sprig fresh from the schoolroom and convinced the spray of sprinkles across her nose lent her visage a whimsical charm—hopeful days before the spiteful Miss Brougham, seeking either a victim or a foil, called her drab—had she ever contemplated aligning herself with anything but a second son.

Unable to see any mirth in the situation, as the price of satin was quite dear indeed, Vera forgot herself enough to scowl at her niece. Likewise misperceiving the source of his niece's amusement, Uncle Horace stiffened his shoulders, for if there was anything he resented more than an unnecessary expense it was the cavalier treatment of an unnecessary expense.

Several hundred pounds in refurbishments was no trifling matter!

Bea knew the moment needed to be defused before the interested bystanders who waited for their chance to curry favor with the soon-to-be Duchess of Kesgrave realized her aunt's happiness was only a facsimile of the honest emotion she was expected to feel, but her mind was oddly blank. The events of the past half hour—confronting a murderer, averting a violent death, discovering the duke loved her, being accosted by well-wishers, submitting to her aunt's displeasure—had impaired her ability to think quickly. Indeed, in this moment when an intelligent retort was required to soothe her relatives all she could think about was her increasingly severe thirst. Her terrifying confrontation with Taunton had left her curiously parched, a condition that had worsened the longer her aunt spoke. Now she desired a glass of ratafia with the frightening intensity of a traveler lost in the desert for several hours.

And a quiet spot in which to consume it, she thought, well aware that the conversation with her aunt would not be the last one of the evening.

Even if she somehow managed to avoid the attentions of her fellow guests, she could not leave without exchanging a word or two with Kesgrave's grandmother, a far from welcoming prospect. Aunt Vera's concerns, while overblown, were not entirely without merit, for Beatrice had already been looked over by the discerning dowager and found wanting.

And of course she could not evade her cousins, whose effusive felicitations she had yet to receive, as the irrepressible pair would accompany her home.

Picturing their unrestrained glee at her achievement, for they were both quite in awe of the duke, she settled on a ruse she felt confident would distract her relatives.

"You must remember Flora," she said.

As her beloved daughter was never far from her thoughts, Vera took slight offense at this command not to forget her now. "Flora?" she asked, her shoulders stiffening.

"Being cousin-in-law to a duke will be hugely advantageous to Flora, allowing her to make a brilliant match," she explained before recalling the depths of her aunt's aspirations. At once, she amended the statement. "That is to say, a *good* match. Our family's connection to Kesgrave will provide Flora with every opportunity to meet suitors of moderate social standing, and I know she is far too thoughtful a young lady to disappoint you by overreaching as I have."

Although Bea knew this statement to be false, for her younger cousin, though certainly kind, was hardly the sole of consideration, Aunt Vera was a fond mother and instantly agreed. Uncle Horace found the sentiment to be accurate as well, and the pair began to lavish compliments on the head of an imagined suitor whose relations would never stoop to notice the condition of the upholstery.

Grateful for their absorption in a topic unassociated with herself, Bea turned her attention to solving her next problem—alleviating her thirst without being waylaid by society matrons and their daughters inviting her to tea. She had already received a dozen such offers and could not bear the thought of having to evade a dozen more.

Six seasons of comfortable obscurity had little prepared her for the prominence of being a duke's wife.

Kesgrave—damn his insolence—had known this would happen. He had warned her of the very thing the moment before she'd spun on her heels to return to the party and found herself swarmed by a parcel of London hostesses begging for her favor. The duke herded the group back into the ballroom before any of them caught a glimpse of Lord Taunton's unconscious form on the terrace and then summoned a servant to send for a Runner. Bea had yet to receive an update on how the marquess's apprehension was progressing, but she fully expected to be called to present her case against him before the evening was over.

In the meantime, the refreshment table beckoned.

Alas, it was on the other side of the dance floor, which put it just beyond her reach, and rather than risk getting swarmed anew, she asked her uncle if he would be so kind as to procure her a glass.

Bea thought it was a benign enough request, but both Horace and his wife turned to stare at her in shock. Aunt Vera even gasped.

"Putting on airs already?" she asked archly.

It was a patently ridiculous charge, and yet Bea understood exactly why her aunt lodged it. In the twenty years since she'd been left on their doorstep as an orphan to be raised by her father's brother, she'd made distressingly few requests. Thrust violently into the unknown by her parents' tragic drowning, she'd been repeatedly told by well-meaning family retainers to be biddable and silent, advice with which a terrified Bea had ardently complied, for she did not want to be left in the care of unknown villagers in the nearest cottage. That she would dare to ask for something now must seem like the grossest impertinence.

"Oh, dear, I fear I am," Bea said with an exaggerated concern she in no way felt. "What a shameless creature I must be. I trust it goes without saying that I'm relying on you and my uncle to keep me humble. You must be ruthless with me, Aunt, and not let your affection corrupt your good judgment."

Although Bea frequently made satirical comments without Aunt Vera noticing anything untoward, the notion that she had ever allowed affection for her niece to influence any decision was too outlandish for even her to accept. Wary of being teased, she narrowed her eyes and examined Bea's tranquil expression for signs of mockery. Finding none, she huffed impatiently and suggested Bea fetch *her* a glass of ratafia whilst seeking her own refreshment.

"Yes, exactly like that," Bea said, smothering a laugh that could be misconstrued as contempt, which it wasn't. She genuinely admired her aunt's ability to be consistently unkind. "I can feel my ego shrinking by the second. Really, you are too good to me."

Vera dipped her head graciously while Uncle Horace promised to make an equal effort to keep her self-regard in check, and Bea, unable to bear her thirst any longer, excused herself to procure drinks for both of them. She had barely taken a dozen steps before Miss Petworth looped her arm through hers as if they had been friends since they were in leading strings and insisted she tell her *everything*.

"There's no need to be shy, my dear," she said with conspirational relish, "for there mustn't be any secrets between us."

Oh, indeed there must be many, Bea thought, as amused as she was astonished by the audacity of the girl, for never had they exchanged a single word before this moment. She imagined the young lady would be at a loss to describe a single thing about her, except perhaps the color of her hair and then simply as a lucky guess. Despite the absence of a relationship, Miss Petworth beamed at Bea, her eyes gleaming with anticipation as she tried to coax the former ape leader into disclosing an interesting on-dit that she could immediately begin to circulate.

"I won't tell a soul," Miss Petworth promised with brazen dishonesty. "Anything you say will remain *entre nous*. I am in alt for you, my dear, simply in alt. I always knew you would accomplish something spectacular, not like my mother, who did not quite believe you existed when Mrs. Alcester told us the wondrous news. She thought her friend was making a joke at her expense because naturally she had hoped the duke would form some kind of an attachment to me. But why would he look at a plain old thing like me when you're in the room?"

As Miss Petworth was an exceptionally beautiful woman—large gray eyes, chestnut curls, rose-blossom cheeks—this observation was at best thoughtless and at worst cruel. She was a contemporary of Flora's, having made her bow to the queen within the very same month and had, to her cousin's annoyance, instantly drawn the attention of all the handsome young bucks. Her fortune was reasonable, being large enough to excite interest and yet not so immense as to attract fortune hunters. She had a low, husky voice that required one to lean in closer to conduct a conversation, and a lively wit that was pointed but not tendentious.

Flora, whose straight auburn hair and hazel eyes lent her an appealing prettiness, could not abide her. If Miss Petworth had been just a little bit older than her own twenty years, she would have revered her wholly, as she felt an innate respect for people who excelled socially. But the Incomparable's accomplishments felt a little too much as if they'd come at the expense of her own.

Knowing how strongly her cousin resented the other woman, Bea wasn't at all surprised to see her marching toward them now with precision and purpose, a stormy expression on her face as she noted the intimacy of their pose. She could only imagine how absurd she looked, tethered to Miss Petworth like a kite on a string, and tilted her head to express her amusement. She found no answering humor in Flora's gaze. If anything, her cousin's ire grew deeper, and she coiled her arm through Bea's other limb and tugged fiercely as if to force a separation. The abrupt movement caused Bea to totter and Miss Petworth to stumble, and Flora heroically supported them both as they struggled to regain their poise.

"My dear Miss Petworth," Flora said with persuasive concern, her eyes drawn together as if genuinely troubled, "I fear you are suffering from an instability complaint. How terrible for you. You must sit down immediately until it passes. Can you make it to a chair without falling down or shall we find someone to escort you? Lord Dawlish appears unoccupied. I'm sure he'd be thrilled to lend his assistance."

Before either Bea or Miss Petworth could respond, Flora called to the septuagenarian, who relied on a cane to ensure his own balance, and insisted he save the poor girl before she collapsed entirely. Convinced of her own stability and noting the slight wobble with which the earl crossed the floor, Miss Petworth fervently protested the plan, which caused Flora to decry her rudeness in depriving Dawlish of the pleasure of providing her with support. His lordship, who had only a moment ago appeared peeved by the request, immediately owned himself insulted, causing Miss Petworth to stammer out an apology while Flora urged her to accept his arm, which was shaking slightly from the effort of being extended in her direction. The young beauty blanched as the elderly peer quivered, and Flora all but pushed the pair away in an effort to eject them from the conversation, as if Dawlish had also tried to cajole his way into Bea's confidence.

It was a horrifying spectacle from beginning to end, and Bea, mortified by her cousin's behavior, realized that her engagement to the Duke of Kesgrave, a seemingly positive event in the lives of the Hyde-Clares, who had been trying to unload her onto an unsuspecting suitor for almost a decade, had somehow undermined the sanity of her entire family.

CHAPTER TWO

After twenty years of listening to her aunt prattle with seeming incessancy on subjects such as how to use an embroidery hoop and why puce is an inappropriate color for young ladies with ginger hair (an apparent non sequitur of such specificity, her niece still found herself wondering at its cause several years later), Beatrice assumed she could endure anything. During one particularly grueling session in the drawing room at Wellsdale House, Aunt Vera had held forth on the variation in lace patterns in the court of Elizabeth I. The lecture ostensibly discussed the superiority of needle lace over bobbin lace but in reality addressed the inadequacy of female rulers.

Trapped inside on what was inarguably the first beautiful day of spring, the air so brimming with the sweet scent of lilacs and sunshine she could almost smell them through the heavy curtains, Bea, her hands folded demurely in her lap, had ruthlessly smothered whatever impatience she'd felt to smile calmly and serenely for hours.

And yet now, as Aunt Vera added an eighth footman to the catalogue of servants her niece would be obliged to oversee as the mistress of a large ducal estate, Bea realized her fortitude was not as great as she'd supposed.

The list, which had begun in the kitchens with a temperamental French chef whose fondness for complicated sauces required several assistants, was so disconcertingly long, Bea couldn't quite believe her aunt wasn't making up fairy stories just to frighten her. Surely, the eighth footman was no more real than the forest witch who ate poor lost children.

Unfortunately, Bea knew her aunt lacked the imagination necessary to implement such a scheme. Indeed, Aunt Vera's sincerity could not be doubted, for with every new retainer she listed, her own composure seemed to slip a little more, as if she herself might one day be called on to manage such a distressingly large staff.

No, Vera's only intention was to provide her niece with a correct accounting of the servants soon to be under her command, and Bea, in possession of all the information she could handle, jumped to her feet before the wretched woman could add a ninth footman to her assortment.

"Good gracious, Beatrice!" her aunt said, gasping in horror at the abrupt movement. "A future duchess does not jump up like an amphibious creature onto the bank of a pond. She rises to her full height with grace and calm, her shoulders so languid and determined you scarcely realize she's moving." As if aware of the impossibility of the challenge she had just set forth, Vera shook her head and sighed with regret. "I wish more than ever that Mr. Davies hadn't been so remiss as to step in front of that carriage. How well suited you are to be the wife of a law clerk!"

Although Aunt Vera frequently lamented the untimely death of Bea's supposed former beau—"supposed" because the man in question, a Theodore Davies of Lincoln's Inn, was naught but an invention devised to elicit confidences from a young lady Bea had suspected of murdering her own father in the Lake District—this was the first time she had done so since the advent of her niece's engagement.

The irrationality of her aunt's complaint, that the lost

opportunity of welcoming a lowly law clerk into the family was a true deprivation, tickled Beatrice, and she felt some of her apprehension fade.

"'Tis a tragedy, to be sure," she agreed briskly, "but do recall Mr. Davies was married with two beautiful children at the time of his accident. It was not the carriage that prevented that happy union but his wife."

As reasonable as this point was, her aunt would not concede it, for surely true love could overcome anything save death.

Disheartened by the impossible obstacle, Vera sighed deeply and, determined to cheer herself up, returned to her original purpose, which was providing her niece with an accurate assessment of her prospective obligations. Her intent was not to dissuade the girl from wedding the duke, of course, but it would be horrendously disingenuous to pretend the option didn't exist.

"You must not think anyone will judge you harshly if you decide to reconsider your answer," Aunt Vera added in a comforting tone. "I'm quite certain they will think better of you for not taking advantage of what must have been a moment of weakness on Kesgrave's part. If I understand it correctly, he felt some concern over your physical safety after your interlude with Lord Taunton and acted impetuously."

Bea paled at once as the ugliness of the *ton*'s pernicious gossip washed over her. She wasn't a naïf or a fool. She knew very well that society could be quite cuttingly cruel in its opinions, but not since her first season had she been subjected to its judgments. Spinsterhood, for all its discomforts, had shielded her from the harsh glare of the beau monde, as a woman who had failed in her purpose was but a phantom.

Now, suddenly, she was visible again.

Kesgrave's attention had given her shape and form.

The pressure on her chest grew from painful to unbearable as she began to wonder how many people believed as her aunt did—that she had dishonorably exploited the situation to improve her standing.

Unable to breathe, Bea pivoted swiftly and strode to the door.

Inexplicably confronted with her niece's departing back, Vera called after in confusion. "But where are you going? We have yet to touch on the various maids you will encounter. There are so many: upper housemaids and lower housemaids and scullery maids and laundry maids and kitchen maids and dairy maids."

As quickly as Bea swept out of the room, she could not outrun the litany of maids nor escape the fact of their existence. Unlike the eighth footman, she knew they were real. At one time or another she had relied on the skills of each—not in a single weekend or even a single week but in a narrow enough slice of time to know such a full complement wasn't unusual.

She darted to the staircase to hide in her bedchamber, but she had barely taken two steps before she realized she couldn't stand the prospect of being confined in the compact space.

Beatrice needed air.

Without pausing to retrieve her reticule, she marched to the front door and stepped out into the March day, which was slightly cooler than the bright sun had indicated.

No matter, she thought, arriving at the end of the stone path and considering her options: left or right? It felt strange not to have a direction, and standing there, she realized she'd never left the London house without a purpose already in mind. It was simply not how one behaved in the city, wandering the streets with the aimlessness one applied to a country park.

She needed a destination.

But where could she go?

The image of the researchers' room in the stately Montague House, with its green leather chairs, frescoed ceiling and rich woods, popped into her head. How calm she had felt there, exploring the history of the knife she believed had killed the Earl of Fazeley! The well-heeled dandy had dropped dead at her feet as she was leaving the offices of the *London Daily Gazette,* and although her intervention was not required by the authorities, she had been compelled to follow up on a suspicion she'd had about the weapon.

Kesgrave had been at the museum, too, inserting himself into her investigation with baffling frivolity that she only now recognized as undeniable attraction. The fact that she associated the room with his comforting presence explained its appeal, for she longed to feel close to him by being in a place where they had once laughed together.

It was only natural, she thought, somewhat defensively.

The events of the night before had been so wildly bizarre, so outlandishly abnormal, a tiny part of her wondered if they had truly occurred. She knew the Marquess of Taunton had actually tried to kill her because she had the scrapes on her back from where he'd raked her body against the stone balustrade. And black char marks on her dress definitively attested to the fact that she had escaped his deadly grasp by wielding a torch in his face. But there was no tangible evidence that Kesgrave had kissed her, and she had nothing to rely on but her memory of the episode, which seemed to grow more implausible the longer she considered it.

The only incontrovertible proof she had that her engagement was real was her aunt's insidious attempts to undermine it. The older woman would have no reason to make such an effort if the betrothal were a mere figment of Bea's imagination.

If only she'd had the opportunity to speak with Kesgrave once more during the evening! Surely, then, she wouldn't be rattled by this unnerving sense of uncertainty. Alas, after sending her off with the horde of fawning matrons, he had disappeared into a room with their host, emerging only once, briefly, to fetch Lord Hartlepool from the ballroom. Fleetingly, her eyes had met his across the dance floor, but no words were exchanged, and she remained ignorant of the discussions being held in private.

Bea had tried to linger at the ball to learn something of Taunton's fate, but Aunt Vera, worried that the excitement of the evening had further weakened her niece's already fragile mental state, insisted they leave immediately following supper. Although this perceived frailty was a fiction created by Vera to explain her previously biddable niece's newfound intransigence, Bea was genuinely too exhausted to argue the point and submitted meekly to her aunt's instructions. She would have made more of an effort to remain if she'd thought she could find out useful information from her hosts or Kesgrave, but it had become clear to her during the long meal that the only thing she would discover that evening was that future duchesses have little opportunity to eat their meals in peace. Snide comments about her appearance—only half of which addressed her dishevelment following her confrontation with Taunton—warred with questions about her courtship of the duke. Everyone had failed to notice a relationship developing, and they deeply resented the oversight, for which they somehow held her responsible.

Oh, you clever girl!

It was not said as a compliment.

Bea, hoping to draw some attention to Taunton's perfidy, for surely his offense was greater than her own, tried to explain that her dress had been damaged in an altercation with the marquess, but nobody would listen. The general assumption seemed to be that she had gotten herself into some mischief with one of the torches on the terrace, and Taunton had come to her aid.

'Twas a most infamously galling assertion.

Even the Countess of Abercrombie, a former suspect in the Fazeley affair who had lent Bea a hand in her investigation of the marquess and could usually be relied upon for an intelligent reply, had turned doltish at the news of her engagement. Only an hour before she had been chastising Bea for failing to assist her in a very important matter, and now she was preening fatuously and assuring everyone within earshot that the arrangement was due to her specific machinations.

It was absurd, to be sure.

Yes, her ladyship had provided consolation when Bea despaired of the duke ever returning her feelings, but to imply she had actually brought about the match was entirely without merit. Indeed, Lady Abercrombie had assumed the case to be hopeless and offered an investigation as a distraction from her misery. She had certainly never given her any reason—

Bea froze as she repeated the word to herself: distraction. That was exactly what she needed, and there was nothing better than solving a puzzle to provide her mind with a useful focus.

At once, she turned to the left and walked determinedly toward Lady Abercrombie's residence in Grosvenor Square, happy to have a purpose. And not just any purpose—one she excelled at. Although nobody would expect a gently bred lady to succeed in the occupation of identifying murderers, least of all her, it was a task for which she was somehow perfectly suited. Years of quietly observing her family had given her a keen eye for detail, and her prodigious reading habit had provided her with all sorts of arcane knowledge that proved to be surprisingly useful.

She'd discovered her aptitude during the house party in the Lake District, when one of the guests was brutally attacked in the library in the middle of the night. She certainly had no business inserting herself into the unpleasantness, but the Duke of Kesgrave's decision to have the death ruled a suicide left her no choice but to intercede. Having resolved that situation in a satisfying if highly awkward manner (she did not need her aunt's lecture to know the comfortable elegance of the drawing room ill befitted revelations of murderers), she found herself confronted yet again with a piteous corpse in the form of the fallen Lord Fazeley. The next time she examined a dead body—a former opium smuggler recently returned from India—it was not mere happenstance. Her expertise had been expressly sought by one of the guests in the Lake District who had recognized her ability to sift through evidence and piece together a story.

And now Lady Abercrombie was to provide her with yet another intriguing mystery to scrutinize. An investigation was the perfect way to divert her mind from Aunt Vera's endless chatter about footmen and defenseless dukes.

The beautiful widow swept into the drawing room, an extravagant affair decorated with ruthless precision in the Oriental style, and Bea, noting her appearance was as ravishing as ever, was instantly reminded of the first time she'd met her. Then, as now, her ladyship had appeared lavishly turned out in a low-cut gown that displayed her many attributes—brooding eyes, fulsome lips, glossy black curls, generous bosom—to great effect. Kesgrave, who fondly called the countess Tilly, had immediately adopted court manners and made a leg, which Bea had mocked as soon as they'd returned to the carriage.

Recalling the scene made her think affectionately of the duke, and she smiled warmly at Lady Abercrombie.

"Oh, my dear, I'm so elated you called," her ladyship said, grasping Bea by both hands and drawing her to the settee. "Morton is bringing tea and cakes so we can have a proper coze. Now you must tell me everything. I want to hear every single detail. What a triumph! Not since the Gunning sisters took the town by storm has the beau monde been more surprised by the engagement of a duke. Your mother would be beside herself with joy, I'm sure of it. And not *just* because his rank is so impressive, although I don't doubt that would please her to no end, but because he is so well suited to you. Only someone of his sterling character and imposing bona fides would look past your seemingly obvious limitations. Even admiring him as I do, I did not think he had the mettle. You are to be commended, my dear, for bringing him up to scratch. I had long known you were remarkable, but this feat proves it. Now do stop being coy and tell me everything."

As her hostess had not paused for breath from the moment she'd entered the room, Bea hardly thought the charge of coyness was fair, but she knew better than to protest. She was also too sensible to take offense at Lady Abercrombie's observation that Kesgrave's attaching himself to her required great reserves of courage. Although the choice of words struck her as overwrought, she herself had had little faith in the duke's ability to rise to the occasion. She, like the rest of the ton, had been unable to look past *his* seemingly obvious limitations.

Fortunately, they had all been wrong.

"I appreciate your enthusiasm, but I'm here on a more pressing matter," Beatrice said smoothly, determined not to be swayed from her purpose. She knew how easily distracted her ladyship could be, especially as she had set for herself the particular goal of arranging the young lady's future. Out of affection for Bea's late mother, who had been the countess's dearest friend, she had taken Bea under her wing, adopting her as a sort of protégé and resolving to find her a husband by the end of the season. To that point, she had drawn up a list of prospective suitors that contained several respectable candidates, though none so high-flying as a duke.

"More pressing matter?" Lady Abercrombie repeated softly, her brow furrowing as if struggling to comprehend a very puzzling idea. "My dear, you have just achieved the most brilliant match of the season. What matter could be more pressing than that?"

Amused by the sincerity of her confusion, for Bea imagined a brilliant match was precisely the sort of thing that swept all other matters from her ladyship's head, she said, "Your investigation."

Far from clarifying the issue, this information only deepened the widow's bewilderment, and she tilted her head slightly to the side as she sought understanding. "My investigation?"

Given how sternly the other woman had chastised her only the night before for failing to follow through on her promise to help her investigate a pressing issue, Bea couldn't smother the laugh that rose to her lips. How utterly lost the countess looked!

"Yes, my lady," she said with a smile. "Your investigation. You originally broached the subject in the carriage ride home from the Red Corner House when you asked if I accepted referrals and raised it again last night. If you remember, you were quite cross at me for failing to call on you to discuss it as we'd agreed. I am, per your orders, calling on you now to have that discussion. You seemed quite troubled that the matter had yet to be resolved."

"But that was last night," her ladyship said.

"Yes," Bea said agreeably. "I myself just observed that the conversation happened last night. I'm reassured to know you recall it as well."

"Yes," the countess said, although with a shake of her head that seemed to indicate no. "Last night *before* your engagement."

Although Lady Abercrombie clearly thought this clarification explained everything, Bea could not comprehend the distinction she sought to make. The only thing in her life that her engagement had irrevocably altered was her ability to cross a crowded ballroom unnoticed by the *ton*. "That is correct. We discussed it before I had my incident with Lord Taunton on the terrace. But you were quite insistent that I address the matter immediately and rightly so. I said I would help you and failed to live up to my word. I'm here now to correct that oversight, so do tell me what the problem is."

Her ladyship stared at her a moment as if aghast and then let out an awkward laugh. "You wretched girl! I know you are teasing me."

Now Bea stared, taken aback at the charge. She had

done nothing but comply with the widow's instructions. "With all due respect, my lady," she said slowly, "but I fear *you* are teasing *me*. I am here solely at your request. If you no longer desire my aid, then please have the courtesy to tell me so."

Perceiving her guest's earnestness, Lady Abercrombie gasped in horror. "You can't mean to continue to solve mysteries now that you're engaged to the duke!"

Struck by the depth of her dismay, Bea realized she had no idea what she meant to do now that she was engaged to the duke. Aside from the joy of having her affection returned and the anxiety of possibly overseeing a vast household staff that included eight footmen, she hadn't considered at all what it would mean to be Kesgrave's wife.

Naturally, it entailed a significant improvement in her circumstance. She had never visited his London home—although she had, of course, seen it looming over Berkeley Square, for it was impossible to miss—or his family seat in Cambridgeshire but felt confident both contained large libraries that she could bury herself in for days. And the duke had access to unlimited funds, which, although never a driving concern of hers before, indicated she could finally get a decent mount and learn to ride properly. She'd always admired their coachman's skill with horses and would relish becoming an accomplished whipster herself. And rout cakes! If she was in charge of a dozen housemaids, then surely she could have rout cakes whenever she wanted them, perhaps even on a daily basis if she was so inclined.

But did regular access to her favorite pastry mean she could no longer use her wits to identify murderers?

Obviously, it was an absurd question, for dead bodies didn't just fall into one's path demanding that their murderers be identified. Yes, it had happened twice to her in the recent past, but those instances were shocking anomalies. She had had no way of locating a third corpse until Mr. Skeffington very thoughtfully provided her with one. Certainly, an event such as that would not happen again.

The fact that she was sitting in Lady Abercrombie's drawing room because the event had indeed happened again did little to persuade her that being presented with cases would be a frequent occurrence. This was merely another anomaly.

Ultimately, then, she wasn't giving up anything by agreeing to her ladyship's statement and saying that, no, she did not mean to continue to solve mysteries now that she was engaged to the duke.

Oh, but the thought of making such a concession did a very strange thing to her composure, she thought, as agitation immediately overtook her at the prospect of being that other Bea again—the one who didn't identify murderers, the one who couldn't think of a retort to even the most banal query, the one who fetched her aunt's mob cap several times a day, the one who quietly accepted her uncle's indifference.

Kesgrave had never known that Bea. She had disappeared the moment her gaze met his over the cooling corpse of Mr. Otley in the library of the Skeffingtons' Lake District manor house. The terror she had felt in that instant, when she expected him to murder her with the same ruthless ease with which he'd ended the spice trader's life, had awakened an inexplicable fearlessness. No longer could she be content to glare at him with impotent dislike or imagine throwing fish patties with olive paste at his supercilious head. No, this newly emboldened Bea confronted him directly, calling him to account in front of her relatives and his friends.

'Twas beyond anything.

Her aunt had yet to recover.

Neither, to be honest, had Bea.

And now, before she had truly regained her footing, she was engaged to be married to his august person. Suddenly, she found herself overcome with a pair of conflicting fears, for she was at once scared that she would revert to that compliant ninny and terrified she wouldn't. Which would his grace prefer?

Even before she finished asking herself the question, Bea knew she could not let the answer matter. To conform to his expectations would be to betray the person she was now, and she was particularly loath to do that.

Stiffening her resolve, she took a deep breath and answered the countess. "I cannot speak of future mysteries, as I expect they will be hard to come by, but at the moment, I'm here and eager to address your concern. Do tell me the details so that we may begin."

Although Lady Abercrombie did not immediately speak, her stern displeasure with this answer conveyed itself clearly. She pursed her pouty lips and wrinkled her nose as if smelling something distinctly unpleasant. Finally, she sighed as if surrendering. "Very well, my dear. If you insist. It's a locket."

"A locket?" Bea repeated, leaning forward.

"Yes, a locket. I lost it and could desperately use some assistance in finding it," she explained.

Bea greeted this information skeptically, as their last conversation on the subject had included a victim, one whom she'd assumed had been dead for a while given the countess's lack of urgency. Nevertheless, she asked her to describe the piece of jewelry.

"It's a gold locket," she said. "Yes, gold. Quite lovely, although not very precious. Its value is mostly sentimental. It was a gift."

"A gift," Bea said thoughtfully. The raven-haired beauty's husband had died on the Peninsula almost a decade ago, and in the interim she had taken many lovers. It was her affair with Sir Walter Heatherton, the famous collector whose assortment of antiquities filled an entire hall at the British Museum, that had brought Bea into her house the first time. Recalling that encounter, she asked if the gift had been presented by Heatherton.

Her ladyship's eyes flickered in surprise before she said, "Yes, it had. It was indeed a gift from dear Sir Walter. An antique, yes, from his travels. I'm desolate to have lost it. As you know, he died tragically in a volcanic eruption. It was the last thing he gave me. I will not rest until I find it again. I cannot thank you enough for your willingness to help, especially now when you have so many more important things to think about such as your trousseau. I hope you will let me help you with that, as I think we can both agree that Vera Hyde-Clare cannot be trusted to turn a young duchess out in style. We will visit my modiste. She's quite ingenious with a needle and will know precisely how to create a gown that will give you a figure. I assure you, she quite invented my bosom for me."

Amused by this observation, for her ladyship's generous décolletage appeared to be a naturally occurring phenomenon, Bea thanked her for her gracious offer. "I would like that. But before we pay a call on your seamstress, why don't you tell me what the actual mystery is, rather than this nonsensical canard you made up on the spot to distract me. We both know Sir Walter did not give you a locket. During our first meeting, when Kesgrave and I interviewed you with regard to the Fazeley affair, you made it abundantly clear that he routinely gifted you with daggers, not jewelry. Every time you turned around, you said, there he was with another dagger."

Astonished to be called on account with such precision, the countess stared at her for several long moments before making a moue of disgust. "You really are a wretched girl, and you will make a vile duchess if you cannot allow people the dignity of their polite fictions. Yes, yes, of course. You're correct. There is no locket," she said impatiently. "I was just trying to stop you from embarrassing yourself and the duke. Was last night not enough for you? Accosting the Marquess of Taunton on the terrace and then returning to the ballroom looking like a bedraggled waif! I cannot begin to know what you are about. You are very fortunate the Larkwells' cared enough about your reputation to put out the story that Taunton's quick thinking saved you from hurting yourself in an accidental fire. You are very capable and no doubt object to being portrayed as the victim, but there's nothing to be gained by your becoming the veriest quiz."

Although Bea appreciated knowing the source of that exceptionally inaccurate and personally offensive on-dit, she could not say which idea she found more risible: that Taunton had been turned into the hero of the piece or that some quarter of society did not already consider her to be the veriest quiz.

Because she could decide, the countess groaned loudly and shook her head. "I wish I had never mentioned that miserable referral. I only did as an act of mercy, for you were so desolate over Kesgrave, and I thought it would distract you from your hopeless passion. I see now there's no value in trying to do a good deed. You will forget this nonsense and allow me to have the pleasure of seeing you garbed in appropriately strong colors. Do have some tea while I ask Morton to send notice to Madam Bélanger that we shall be there within the hour."

Not wanting to be an entirely disobliging guest, Bea accepted the cup of tea and took a delicate sip as she contemplated the excessive splendor of the drawing room, with its rich silks, lotus-shaped chandeliers, gilded serpents and trompe l'oeil wallpaper. She had originally taken the room as proof of the countess's frivolity, but further acquaintance revealed that her ladyship felt compelled to decorate extravagantly to evade the boredom of her rarefied existence.

"You recently told me a lady must have a hobby," Bea reminded her. "Partaking in investigations is mine."

Lady Abercrombie was unswayed. "You can afford to decorate now. Kesgrave is so plump in the pocket you could refurnish Prinny's pavilion in Brighton without him missing a farthing. Here, do have a cake. There's only so much a modiste can do to give one a figure. At some point, you do have to take an interest."

Although she wasn't hungry, Bea accepted the proffered slice and politely nibbled at the corner. It was sweet and lemony. "I will take your suggestion under advisement when I have access to Kesgrave's funds," she assured her hostess, "but for the moment I'm still just the impoverished Miss Hyde-Clare. Now, if I'm remembering our conversation correctly, you indicated that there was no pressing need to investigate. That makes me think that the victim has been dead for a while." She watched the countess's face carefully for an indication that her reasoning was correct. The other woman did not flinch at the mention of a victim, so Bea decided she was right in assuming the mystery involved another fatality. "A little while? No, I think not. More than a little. I'm not even sure what that means. Months perhaps? Or years?"

"You will stop this at once, for my patience is at an end," she said testily. "The Duchess of Kesgrave will not run around town solving mysterious deaths. Clara would not want that."

Bea thought it was a rather dirty trick to use the mother she barely remembered against her, and she stiffened because it hurt her afresh to realize she didn't know anything about what her mother would want. Her parents had drowned together in a boating accident when she was five years old, a tragedy that somehow weighed heavier on her heart now that she had met someone who had known and loved them. Her uncle, whose relationship with his brother had been severed long before his death, had withheld details out of either a miserly impulse to deny his brother the dignity of being a cherished memory or a genuine indifference to his niece's welfare. It wasn't until Lady Abercrombie expressed astonishment, still keenly felt all these years later, at the unlikely fate of someone with her father's remarkable boating skills that she discovered he was a yachtsman of some note. Uncle Horace had never said a word, and her aunt—

The air seemed to disappear from her lungs as a wildly outlandish idea struck her.

No, no, she thought with agitation, shaking her head

as if trying to dislodge the notion. No, it wasn't possible. It was absurd. It was the height of preposterousness. It didn't bear consideration.

But no sooner had the idea sprouted in her head than it began to grow roots and firmly embed itself in her psyche. It wasn't just Lady Abercrombie's shock at the way her parents had died. Even the most accomplished sailor could find himself overwhelmed by events that spiraled out of control until nothing he did could save him, not even his skill. No, it was also the letters, the ones from her mother that her ladyship had been rereading of late. She had dug them out of whatever drawer or chest they'd been hiding in for twenty years so that Bea might have them. And there were diaries, too, she recalled, kept by the countess and contemporaneous to her parents' deaths. Lady Abercrombie had resolved to peruse them to refamiliarize herself with the details of the time, so she could tell Bea everything.

How had she put it? Bea wondered.

Oh, yes: *I will prattle about your remarkable mother to such an extent, you will beg me to stop.*

Had revisiting these matters twenty years later with fresh eyes revealed something overlooked two decades before?

Again, Bea scoffed at the outrageous implausibility of her theory, and yet she couldn't stop herself from gathering more evidence. Her ladyship's referral, for example, which had struck her as such an unlikely proposition she'd originally assumed it was a trick to stop her from scrutinizing further crimes or an attempt to pair her with an eligible *parti*. The referral made complete sense, however, if it pertained to Bea's own parents. Lady Abercrombie was unconventional, to be sure, but even she would not go around dropping murder investigations into the laps of unmarried young ladies. Only the connection to her parents would spur her into taking such an improper step.

Additionally, Bea could not dismiss the very lack of urgency in pursuing the matter, which had confused her from the beginning. Clearly, there would be no need for swift action if the murder had happened over twenty years ago. And her ladyship had responded irritably only a few minutes before when Bea wondered if the interval since the death could extend into years. The widow might have just been annoyed that Bea had dismissed her directive to try her hand at decorating or she might have been unnerved by how close her friend's daughter was getting to the truth.

It was the latter, she thought with conviction. Lady Abercrombie was just conventional enough to feel genuine glee at Bea's coup in nabbing a duke and would do nothing to undermine the accomplishment. If she hadn't gotten engaged to Kesgrave last night, she and the beautiful widow would be in the midst of a very different discussion.

Bea, whose entire life had been consumed by convention and conformity, understood her stance perfectly, for she herself trembled at the thought of harming her association with Kesgrave. 'Twould be so easy to compliment the cook on her scrumptious tea cakes and discuss the colors that would best suit her pale complexion. Aunt Vera had shown little interest in anything but the price of her wardrobe for so long.

But she could not do it—turn her back on the parents who had never asked her for a single thing. They'd loved her. As vague as her memories were, she could still recollect the shocking change from hot to cold, the harsh breeze that had greeted her as she stood on the doorstep at 19 Portman Square. The weather had been warm but still the air was chilly.

She could not betray that love by walking away because it might cause discomfort. Either Kesgrave would understand or he wouldn't. The question of which Beatrice he would prefer was now immaterial.

Slowly, Bea raised her eyes to look at Lady Abercrombie, the teacup rattling against the saucer as she returned both to the table with shaking hands. "I'll accept your referral," she said, curling her fingers into a ball because she couldn't bear the trembling. "I will investigate my parents' murder on your behalf."

CHAPTER THREE

To Lady Abercrombie's credit, she did not cavil or stammer or insist her guest was an absurd child who believed in fantastical stories about fairies. She didn't sigh loudly to announce her displeasure or even pull her lips together in severe disapprobation. Rather, she acknowledged the comment with a curt nod and rang the bell for the butler.

"Ah, there you are, Morton," she said when the servant finally appeared in the doorway. "Please ask Beth to fetch the diary and packet of letters on my bedside table and do bring us a bottle of champagne from the cellars too. Two glasses, of course, as we will both be indulging."

"Very good, my lady," he murmured before leaving the room and closing the door gently behind him.

"We might as well toast to your good fortune while it lasts," her ladyship explained as she reached for a tea cake. "I cannot believe Kesgrave will condone your behavior now that it reflects on the Matlock name. His grandmother, for one, is a high stickler and frowns at any hint of impropriety. I imagine the reason he has not called on you yet today—and I make that assumption based on the fact you were free to visit me—is the dowager summoned him to Clarges Street to take him to task for his rash decision.

No doubt she is devising a way to extricate him as we speak. Don't be surprised if he's suddenly called away to the country on a most consuming errand."

To say that Beatrice felt no spark of alarm at these words would be a lie, and she was far too honest with herself to deny the obvious. Her position with Kesgrave was tenuous, and if the Dowager Duchess of Kesgrave decided to bring an end to her grandson's engagement, she would do so swiftly and irrevocably.

How fleeting it all felt now—those moments of unmitigated joy on the terrace when Kesgrave, with all the pedantry in his meticulously ordered soul, put the labors of Hercules in their proper sequence. No two people could have been in more perfect accord, and she would not have believed their bond could sunder so easily.

And if it could, then it wasn't a bond but a wisp, and surely she wasn't foolish enough to regret the snapping of a wisp.

Brave words, she thought.

Nevertheless, Bea would not let fear dissuade her from the matter at hand. According to Lady Abercrombie's calculations, her looks, age and lack of social success already made her objectionable to the dowager. Adding inappropriately inquisitive to the list of unappealing traits would do little to increase her inadequacy.

While Bea stiffened her resolve, the countess finished her tea and returned the cup to the table. Morton, entering in the company of the housekeeper, directed her to lay the tray in front of her ladyship before placing a leather-bound volume and a collection of letters next to a pair of empty conically shaped glasses.

Lady Abercrombie picked up the diary and flipped thoughtfully through it as she spoke. "I have no one to blame for this contretemps but myself. If I had believed for one moment that Kesgrave could return your regard, I would have held my tongue. But he was courting Lady Victoria, whose dark good looks cannot fail to please, and your feelings were unremarkable, for a dozen girls fall in love with him unprompted every season. I had no cause to think you were any different." Her tone turned sullen, indeed almost accusatory, as if she had been misled or deceived by a deliberate trick. Then she shook her head and smiled ruefully. "I should have known better than to pity Clara Leighton's daughter. Now, are you very sure?" she asked, cradling the book in her arms, as if reluctant to let it go.

"Yes," Bea said quickly, without hesitation, sliding forward a little in her seat to accept the items. There could be no other answer, for it was impossible to settle the future without first resolving the past.

And there was always the possibility that her ladyship was wrong about her parents' deaths, Bea reminded herself as she clutched the small stack of envelopes addressed in her mother's hand. Just because she suspected something nefarious happened did not mean that something nefarious actually happened.

With a firm nod, the countess filled both glasses with effervescent champagne and handed one to Bea. Then she raised her own high in the air before her and said, "To a most unlikely duchess and my dearest friend's daughter. I underestimated you once and will never do so again. May you have all the happiness you deserve. I know your mother and father would have been so proud, and I hope that if you ever need a parental surrogate, you won't hesitate to call on me. To you, my dear."

Bea was expecting a perfunctory toast, and the warmth of the sentiment forced her to blink back tears lest she start weeping on the elegant red silk of Lady Abercrombie's lavish Oriental-style settee. She took an overly long sip of the champagne to give herself a moment to regain her composure, then lifted her hand to say something equally flattering in return. Before she could think of the right words, her ladyship said, "Your father was a spy."

Astounded, Bea stared at Lady Abercrombie as if she

had suddenly grown a second head. She wanted to laugh because the claim seemed so incredible and then a moment later she felt a strange desire to cry, for she had no idea of the credibility of the claim. In her head she had pictured her Uncle Horace, his heavy-lidded eyes hidden behind a black mask, his rotund frame crouched behind a whisky barrel as he eavesdropped on a conversation. But that was all wrong, of course. The two brothers were nothing alike.

"Not a real spy," her ladyship immediately amended. "He did not work for the foreign office reporting on the movement of French troops. Napoleon had yet to rise to power, and the Frenchies were still killing each other at an alarmingly high rate. No, your father was performing a service for the prime minister, William Pitt, whom he knew from his years at Cambridge. It was just a silly schoolboy game, pretending to be a cobbler to infiltrate a group of tradesmen who advocated for the right of all men to vote. It was called the English Correspondence Guild, and, according to your mother, who supported your father's work wholly, they mostly met just to discuss political treatises. Clara went to a few meetings in disguise and thought it was the greatest lark. That's why I didn't take her concerns seriously."

Bea, who had read Charles Wreston's biography of the younger Pitt, knew the group of tradesmen who formed the English Correspondence Guild numbered well into the thousands. If she was remembering correctly, its membership nearly topped three thousand at the height of its seven-year existence. As her ladyship said, it was primarily concerned with parliamentary reforms—increasing representation in the House of Commons and opening up the field of who was allowed to vote—but Pitt, one eye turned steadily toward France, feared revolution. He found the organization and others like it so potentially damaging to the stability of the kingdom that he passed a series of acts that made them illegal.

Having been only a small child during the Reign of Terror, Bea had little firsthand experience with the fear that swept through the British aristocracy at the frequent beheadings of their French counterparts. Even so, she couldn't help but think Pitt's response to the lower orders organizing for political change was a bit overwrought. He should have been more concerned about the bread riots that were breaking out across the country due to bad harvests, and supporting a bill that ensured workers earned a minimum amount of money for their labors would have gone a long way toward solving the problem.

Instead, however, he had sent her father in to infiltrate the guild.

Her father.

Bea wondered how it was possible to feel such disappointment in a man she could not remember.

"You say my mother participated in this spying as well?" Bea asked softly.

"Oh, yes, she had a love of adventure, Clara, and was always ready for an escapade," Lady Abercrombie said with more than a hint of admiration. "There was nothing she wouldn't try once. But she also had a flair for the dramatic. Your father and she would have a slight disagreement over the most minor thing, such as the placement of a portrait in the gallery, and she would insist that her marriage was over. *Richard cannot abide me anymore! I shall take to my bed and sink into a decline!* It was all nonsense, of course, which is why I put no stock in her concern that someone in the English Correspondence Guild had discovered their secret and might wish to harm them. Indeed, I forgot about it almost immediately, for then she told me she was in the family way, and that was by all accounts the more interesting news. And then soon after they were both dead and I could not think of anything but my own devastation for months. It's only now that I reread her letters and my own diary entries that I wonder if I was remiss in dismissing her concerns. Your father was also anxious in the end, which was unusual because he had such an inexhaustible gaiety about him."

Although she heard the countess rattle on, Bea remained permanently stuck at *in the family way*. If the timing of the disastrous excursion had worked out only a little differently, she could have suffered the Hyde-Clare's benign indifference in the company of a younger sibling.

"How far along was she when she died?" she asked.

"Three months," Lady Abercrombie said, "maybe four. Ah, she was so excited because it had been very difficult both times to become enceinte. Your father was thrilled, too, as naturally he wanted an heir. He could not bear the thought of his priggish brother getting everything."

Bea recalled her sparse childhood, with its rough fabrics and inferior designs to spare unnecessary expenses. Even the gown she had worn last night, charred now from extinguishing the fire in Lord Taunton's hair, was of mediocre quality and two years out of fashion. If there was an inheritance to hoard, it certainly had not passed to her.

"What did 'everything' entail?" she asked, her fingers gripping the glass of champagne so tightly her knuckles were white.

"Investments," her ladyship said. "Stocks, mostly, in businesses that were just getting started or devising innovations on previous inventions, such as the Phillips steam engine, which improved upon the Watt steam engine. I had forgotten, my dear, how enthusiastic Clara could be about Richard's latest discovery. She would marvel about every little detail: fuel costs and cylinders and rotary power. La, she could be so very tedious! You will see for yourself in the letters, particularly when you get to a treatise on something called the sun and planet gear. I quite wanted to shoot myself in the head rather than continue to read, a sensation I recollect now I'd felt the first time I'd encountered it."

Every sentence Lady Abercrombie uttered contained so much new information about her parents, Bea felt awash in it and wished she could pause the other woman's words like one ceased the ticking of a clock. She had barely digested the idea of her father as a shrewd investor before she had to absorb the notion of her mother as the author of complicated technological dissertations.

And underneath it all, just below the surface of her cognitive deliberation, was the thought: What had happened to the investments? The ancestral home, Wellsdale House, she knew, had passed into possession of her father's younger brother, who was grateful to have a country seat in addition to his London home, and her parents' belongings had been sold off to pay for Beatrice's upkeep. But nobody had ever mentioned stocks. Could Uncle Horace not have used the profit from the sale of those certificates to offset her expenses and allow her to hold on to a few cherished mementos of her parents?

Or did he have another use for the money?

A deeply sinister thought flitted through her head as she wondered if her uncle had amassed a large debt that was conveniently settled by the death of his brother. He did, after all, have a fondness for speculation, as her aunt had lamented more than once, and a penchant for top-quality snuff.

But no, Bea thought, squashing the idea, unable to believe that either of her humble relations would rise to the presumption of murder.

"Your father was an experienced yachtsman," the countess announced.

"Yes, you have said," Bea replied, for Lady Abercrombie had made the observation several times in her presence. "But even the most experienced seamen run into situations they are ill equipped to handle. The HMS *Royal George*, for instance, sank while moored at Portsmouth. It wasn't even out to sea and yet 800 people died as it took on water in the gun ports. Rear Admiral Richard Kempenfelt himself had been aboard and could not save them."

Lady Abercrombie laughed at this account and said,

"My goodness, you are *just* like your mother. She, too, had the disconcerting ability to call up inconsequential facts from her memory at a moment's notice. Yes, I understand your point and have most likely read the same volume on maritime disasters as you. But it wasn't his ability to command a vessel that I was making reference to. It was his decision to go out onto the River Medway in the middle of a rainstorm and to take the skiff he'd use for fishing rather than the yacht. A parsley-head who didn't know an anchor from an anchovy might make that novice mistake but not Richard Hyde-Clare. I would bet my life on it."

It was strange, Bea realized, how little she knew of her parents' deaths

. All her life, she'd been told they'd drowned while boating, but nobody had mentioned the circumstances. The oddity of their choices had never once been remarked upon. Had anyone else noticed the peculiarity of Richard and Clara deciding to brave the elements in a paltry rowboat?

Recalling how easily the constable who had been summoned to examine Mr. Otley after his fatal altercation in the library in the Lake District had been swayed by the duke into believing the death was self-murder, she knew it was futile to wonder. The man called to attend to her parents would have had no cause to suspect something nor any incentive to do so.

"Did you voice your concerns to anyone?" Bea asked.

"My dear child, I didn't have any concerns," her ladyship said with dismissive condescension as she raised her glass to take a sip. "I had only the jolt of surprise at the news, which I voiced to you as soon as we met. Their death by drowning was a shock then and it's a shock now, but it's only with the rereading of dear Clara's letters and my own diary from the time that I have concerns. As I said, I'd completely forgotten about Clara's anxieties about the English Correspondence Guild. But with the clarity that comes from the passage of years I can readily see what happened. Clara's fears were justified, and one of the members of the guild, discovering that Richard was indeed passing information about its activities to the prime minister, killed your parents. I cannot imagine how he contrived it or why he felt it was necessary to murder your mother as well when she was merely an innocent bystander. I leave that for you to figure out, as you are the clever one here."

Bea thought it was rather remarkable how Lady Abercrombie managed to make a compliment sound like a curse. "Yes, I'm the clever one," she agreed softly, unsure where all her cleverness would take her. She had done nothing save ask the countess a few questions, but already it felt different, this investigation. It was not merely a matter of intellectual curiosity or the intriguing challenge of piecing together a puzzle. It was deeply personal and unnervingly compelling.

"It's not too late for us to reverse our course," her ladyship said with sudden vehemence. "Forget all about this unpleasantness and focus on something truly important like my missing gold locket. The story might have a few incongruencies now, but I promise to smooth them out and have the appropriate item of jewelry hopelessly lost by the end of the day. You have a bright future with Kesgrave, my dear, and you are not obligated to imperil that for anyone, even your parents. Indeed, especially your parents. I spoke the truth when I said Clara would not want that. She would have been beside herself with joy at her daughter making a love match."

Although the offer was sincere, Bea knew it had not been made with a genuine expectation of its being accepted. Lady Abercrombie knew she would not be content with a child's game of hide-and-seek. But it was lovely that she cared enough to propose it, and acting on impulse, she did something she rarely did, something as a child in a house full of indifferent relatives she never got a chance to do—she reached her hand across the table and grasped the other woman's. "Thank you," she said warmly.

Lady Abercrombie squeezed her hand in return and considered her with a fond look for a moment. Then she pulled back with a merry laugh and topped off Bea's champagne even though she had had but a few sips. "Now, my dear, do stop being an inscrutable sphinx and tell me everything about your courtship of the duke. You may start with why you went into seclusion for two weeks. I assume it was because you thought all hope was lost—a necessary step in any romance, although sometimes, tragically, the last. I trust you followed my advice and arranged yourself languidly on various mourning couches throughout the house."

Beatrice had in fact spent the two weeks lying on her bed trying to interest herself in various narratives that under any other circumstance she would have found thrilling and interesting. As it was, she'd stared her way through a biography of Johannes Kepler without actually reading a single word. Nevertheless, she assured her ladyship that she had followed her advice to the letter, even sneaking into her aunt's sitting room to take advantage of every divan in the house.

"That unpleasant fish! I'm sure she never lay languidly on anything in her life," Lady Abercrombie sneered disapprovingly.

Although Bea refused to share many details of her relationship with Kesgrave—more out of desire to cherish them privately than a fear of scandalizing her ladyship—she did condescend to give her a very broad outline. With the widow's persistent interruptions, the account took twice as long as she had anticipated, and she was surprised to see how late it was when she finished. A hasty departure, however, was not possible, for Lady Abercrombie insisted she visit first with Henry, the lion cub she had adopted as a pet as a way to ward off ennui.

"He absolutely adores you," the countess said fondly as the lion licked Bea's chin.

Bea wasn't entirely convinced it wasn't a display of hunger, not affection, but she cooed softly to the cub, who was by any measure adorable.

"You will keep me abreast of your investigation, of course," Lady Abercrombie said as she bid her visitor goodbye. An offer to take a carriage back to Portman Square had been roundly rebuffed by Bea, who welcomed the opportunity to order her thoughts during the walk home.

"Yes, if there's something to know," Bea said cautiously, for she had no idea how the investigation would progress.

As it was much later in the day, the air was cooler than before, and Bea shivered as she stepped outside. Nevertheless, she was in no rush to see her aunt again and kept her pace steady but slow. The first thing she did was make a list of the actions that needed to be taken. Obviously, she would start with her mother's letters and then move on to Lady Abercrombie's diary. Then she would have to find out everything she could about the English Correspondence Guild, for she could not remember many details about it from Wreston's tome. She recalled its size, of course, and that it had lodged itself in Mr. Pitt's side like a particularly nasty thorn. But the specifics of the group escaped her.

She would also make an effort to speak to some of the former prime minister's colleagues to see if they remembered anything about her father's assignment. Perhaps she would be able to locate men who worked alongside him.

Or surely there were men whom he considered his friends. They were likely to know something about his activities.

Yes, she thought, turning right to walk up the path to number 9, there were several steps she could take to further the investigation. She could even question her aunt and uncle, for they were certain to know something of use.

She'd never probed the source of the brothers' rupture.

She had never probed anything, she thought sadly, entering the house.

"Beatrice!" her aunt screeched the moment she saw her. Standing next to her in the hall was Uncle Horace, who was in the process of shaking the Duke of Kesgrave's hand.

His grace's face lit with pleasure as he turned to smile at her, and Bea, taken aback by how handsome he looked—his golden curls glistening, his blue eyes sparkling, his square jaw endearingly set—felt an uncomfortable warmth creep up her cheeks. Embarrassed, she wanted to turn away but his gaze was too compelling.

Beside her, Aunt Vera buzzed anxiously, her voice unduly deep and portentous as if to compensate for the squealishness of her original greeting. "Beatrice, how marvelous you have returned. I was just telling the duke that you were at the lending library, and look, you have a book with you, so it was absolutely the truth." It was an unintentional slip, to be sure, and she laughed awkwardly in hopes of drawing attention away from it. "Such a proper activity for a young lady. My niece only does proper activities, your grace. You must have no concern on that score. She will not don an inappropriate outfit to attend a funeral she wasn't invited to. Never think that! She will make you an excellent wife. Most excellent. She has many wonderful qualities to recommend her such as…"

But here the woman's ingenuity failed her, for she couldn't think of a single positive trait to list, and she turned to her husband with a meaningful glance, as if imploring him to supply a few.

Or just one.

Alas, he too fell short of the task, and after sputtering clumsily for a few seconds, announced, "Kesgrave came to discuss the settlement."

Bea, who had been amused by her relatives' predicament, recoiled at this news and felt her face turn white. It was a nonsensical response, she told herself angrily, for surely nothing followed the betrothal of a duke so certainly or so swiftly as a discussion of the settlement. It was the only way to ensure a sensible distribution of monies and properties in the case of widowhood or children.

Perhaps that was the cause of her shudder, she thought, the speed with which the exquisite lightness of love could turn into the mundane business of succession.

"Actually," Kesgrave said smoothly, "I came to see you, and in your absence, agreed to discuss the settlement with your uncle. Going forward, the solicitors will take care of it. But now that you are returned from your errand, I would like to revert to the original plan and have a tête-à-tête in the front parlor."

Although the invitation contained within it the request for a private conversation with his betrothed, Aunt Vera ignored his desire for intimacy and owned herself delighted with the scheme. "We will have a cup of tea and discuss your family," she said, leading him to the settee. "Tell me, how did your grandmother receive the news? Was she very disappointed? My heart goes out to poor Lady Victoria. How well you two looked together."

Resigned, the duke assured her that his matrimonial plans had no bearing on the Tavistock heiress as he darted a searing look, full of impatience and longing, at Bea. Her stomach curled in response, and she felt her color rising again. Unable to bear the intensity, she tilted her head down and examined her hands, now grasping her mother's letters so tightly their delicate edges were crumpled.

Despite Aunt Vera's attempts to dominate the conversation, Kesgrave managed to address several questions directly to Bea. They were banal enough—what book she was reading, how she enjoyed her visit to the library—but she discovered herself incapable of answering them intelligently. Curiously shy to be in his presence after the rapture of the Larkwells' ball, she resorted in most cases to just yes or no.

The timidity of her performance horrified her, for in

a matter of minutes she had reverted fully to the creature she had once been, the impotent orphan who sat quietly across from the duke that first night at Lakeview House, fantasizing about pricking his superiority by throwing coffee custard *à la religieuse* at his head.

Remarkably, she had managed to puncture his ego—but with words, not edible projectiles.

And now she was silent.

It was a worrying development, for it now seemed inevitable that she would return to her previous state, especially in light of the eighth footman. How could she not? She had been fearless for a few months and fearful for decades.

After a half hour that included a disconcertingly in-depth conversation on the benefits of beetroot, sparked by her aunt, who considered a fondness for the vegetable to be one of the points upon which she and the duke were most in sympathy, Kesgrave announced his departure. He was engaged that evening to eat at his club with Hartlepool but hoped he might see Bea later at Lady Bebington's musicale.

Even if Bea weren't exhausted from the day's travails, she would have still cried off from attending the musical event, an interminable evening showcasing her ladyship's five daughters that she had dutifully graced in previous years. Today, however, she did not have the fortitude necessary to smile blandly at performances that were at best mediocre and at worst the equivalent of two cats fighting over a rat's carcass in an alleyway. Additionally, she wanted to begin the investigation into her parents' deaths. The letters clutched tightly in her grasp seemed to vibrate with impatience to be read.

Before Bea could tell Kesgrave she would not be going, her aunt jumped in to explain at length how excited the family were to attend. She gushed about the pleasing sound of Lady Marjorie's dulcet tones and Lady Diana's command of Italian and Lady Sarah's ability to project her voice to such a remarkably far distance you could hear her singing on the front path outside. With each fresh musing of the evening's offerings, Bea became further entrenched in her decision to abstain. She did not say anything, of course, for she knew Aunt Vera would object. Far better to simply feign a headache as the others were leaving.

As her aunt's appreciation for the Bebington daughters' musical gifts seemed inexhaustible, Bea was forced to interrupt with a reminder that Kesgrave had an appointment to keep. Recalled to her duty, Vera leaped to her feet and again slipped her arm through Kesgrave's to escort him to the door, thwarting once and for all any opportunity for a private moment between the newly engaged couple.

If Bea hadn't been so relieved to avoid the awkward revelation of her lackwittedness to her betrothed, who would almost certainly regret his impulsivity in tethering himself to her, she would have been mortified by her aunt's gross obtuseness. But as she had yet to recover her composure and was greatly afraid she never would, she welcomed her aunt's interference and, following the other woman's lead, said goodbye to the object of her deep and abiding affection with a brusqueness that bordered on rude.

As soon as the duke took his leave, Aunt Vera looked at the clock and confirmed that there was just enough time to finish their conversation from earlier, recalling that they had left off at dairy maids. "A vitally important role that I will catalogue in detail if you would just return with me to the parlor."

For a moment, fleeting and fulfilling, Bea imagined—in the words of her young cousin Russell—landing a blow on her aunt's jolly nob, before following her into the parlor and submitting silently to another dispiriting lecture.

CHAPTER FOUR

Nothing in Beatrice's life had prepared her for the exquisite torment of reading her dead mother's letters. She'd expected the well of sadness, the keening hole in the center of her being where maternal affection should be, but she hadn't imagined the intense waves of regret at not getting to know this charming, warm, vibrant woman whose words practically danced off the page. It was an unnerving sensation, she discovered, to find yourself yearning for something you'd long resigned yourself to doing without.

Although the letters were purported by their author to be "solemn depictions of domestic life and strife," as Clara had written in February 1793, they were in fact playful and irreverent descriptions of a happy marriage between two people who knew their own minds.

"Very well, then, I said to him, if you want foie gras, then you shall have foie gras!" Clara wrote in a letter dated April 23, 1793. "Nothing is too culinarily daring for the man who holds my heart! But of course I instructed Cook to make the ice cream with apricots because they are far more suited to dessert and I quite adore them, and when it was served after the meal, the deliberately enormous meal of all his favorite dishes, he was far too full to have more than a bite. And the expression on his face! So confused, my darling. His brow wrinkled! His nose jumping like a bunny's! Then he tried it again and, noting the flavor, asked who had the temerity to feed the goose apricots. Our current investments were drawing nicely, he said, but not so well as to support apricot-eating geese, and he immediately barred the purchase of the fruit."

The missives, which were far more helpful than the scribbled half-finished thoughts in Lady Abercrombie's diary, were deliberately brimming with gossipy tidbits, as they were written to entertain the countess during her sojourns to the country with her husband and children. Requisite mentions of the Duchess of Devonshire's latest exploits mixed with lavish accounts of extravagant parties and visits to Vauxhall Gardens. Mutual friends were discussed in detail: Mrs. Farnsworthy, whose fondness for peacock feathers threatened to bankrupt her husband; Lady Swingdale, whose inability to hide her growing affection for Lord Rushden had started to raise eyebrows; Thomas Thelwall, Earl of Wem, Richard's oldest friend and sparring partner, who seemed determined to earn Clara's approval ("Assured of my continued sufferance, for in his absence I would be forced to fence with my husband, a prospect as daunting as it is potentially tragic, Wem swears he will settle for nothing less than my eternal devotion").

Richard's investments were discussed in varying degrees of detail. As Lady Abercrombie had mentioned, Clara devoted several paragraphs to the technological advances of the Phillips steam engine. The highly anticipated opening of the rebuilt Drury Lane theater, however, merited barely a sentence.

Her husband's involvement in the English Correspondence Guild was referenced only in passing at first, as Clara described it in May 1793 as a favor for the prime minister. The particulars weren't revealed until four months later, when she included with her letter a pamphlet from the political society. "You must not be put off by the assertive earnestness of their prose," she wrote in company of the booklet, which Bea assumed had been discarded long ago. "Richard assures me there's nothing to be done about the intensity of their beliefs. He has tried to imbue their dreary meetings with a note of levity and been asked to either hold his tongue or return when he feels more respectful of the struggle."

Having freely disclosed the pertinent details of her husband's activities, Clara belatedly requested that they go no further than her reader. "Richard is insistent nobody find out about the covert assignment. His starched brother would be horrified by the association with radicals, even if it has the imprimatur of the Crown, and Wem would cluck anxiously, for he hovers over us like a mother hen."

Clara went to her first meeting of the guild in November 1794. Donning her husband's clothes to escape detection, she seemed to feel the same freedom Bea had the first time she had dressed up as a man to visit the Earl of Fazeley's town house. "Scamp! Rogue! Scoundrel!" her mother had effused as she described the sensation of looking at herself in the mirror.

She recorded her first fissure of alarm in February of the next year, reporting that Jeffries, who was identified as the group's founder, had looked at her askance at the previous evening's meeting: "I will not call it a prickle of alarm, for that would be overstating my concern, but perhaps a tickle. Does that sound appropriately worrying to you, my dear? Just a tickle. Or maybe I mean trickle. I suspect we will never quite know the correct term."

The next time Jeffries appeared in a letter, it was spring. In May, Clara wrote: "The trickle prickle has become a pickle, for the situation can now be described as difficult. Jeffries knows something in the state of Denmark has rotted, but he appears unable to pinpoint exactly what. But, oh, how he tries, staring a hole into me and my husband as if determined to dig up our innermost selves with his eyes. If only he knew what Richard was writing in his reports to Pitt. What tedious tales! What yawn-inducing yarns! Truly, my dear, guild meetings are efficient and orderly, with none of the fomenting one would expect from a radical organization. The members discuss political tracts and debate the best way to accomplish their goals. If I were Jeffries, I would be grateful that someone was thoughtful enough to report the congeniality of my meetings to the prime minister, for nothing they do is beyond the bounds of the law. A colleague who is also there at the bidding of Mr. Pitt—a peer, no less—cannot bear that low-born agitators such as these are allowed by the Crown to go about their business and advocates for inciting violence to justify an official response. Richard finds his pugnacity worrisome and his temperament dangerous, but I'm convinced it's only talk, for no gentleman could be so unprincipled."

Then in August, a mere three weeks before she died, Clara reported feeling genuinely menaced by Jeffries's attention. And it was no longer just the founder of the group who worried her but two of his confederates as well, for the three of them would sit in a corner whispering to each other and looking at the pair accusingly. "Do they know we're spies?" Clara wrote to her friend before providing the answer. "I'm fairly certain they do, and I worry increasingly about how violently they will respond. They are rough men but do not appear to be brutal, and yet sometimes, just below the surface, I feel the roil of anger, as if only so many treatises can be written to keep them calm before they burst to the surface like Poseidon from the sea."

The letter of August 15 was the last one Clara sent. She and Richard would be returning to their home in Sussex soon and she would write again once they were settled.

Bea placed the letter on top of the stack and noticed her hands were shaking. She could not pinpoint the exact cause of the apprehension. Some of it had to be grief, for in two hours she had gotten to know her mother better than in twenty years and everything she'd learned made her sad. But what were the other components? Impatience, she thought, to read the letters again and glean more information about both her parents. Eagerness, perhaps, to begin the investigation, the first step of which would be by identifying Jeffries and his confederates and arranging interviews to interrogate each. Fear, possibly, that Kesgrave might object to his wife investigating unlikely deaths.

No, she thought, as the trembling in her limbs grew stronger. It was not *might* object but *definitely*.

Previously, he had supported her efforts, exploiting his standing to help her gain access to suspects and documents and working alongside her as if they were colleagues. But that was before—when she was just a strange curiosity, a disobliging spinster with a knack for solving mysteries. Now she was to be his wife, which had to alter the equation somewhat, for what one accepted in an associate differed from what one tolerated in a spouse. A relationship between partners striving toward a common goal required a level of respect that a husband was not required to extend: An associate's compliance had to be sought, whereas a wife's could be demanded.

Kesgrave had tried to halt her efforts once before by gaining her solemn promise not to investigate any more murders. She had evaded the prohibition by making what she herself knew to be a semantically questionable distinction. Nevertheless, she *had* sworn to stop investigating dead bodies that fell into her path and Mr. Wilson's corpse had been placed there by Mr. Skeffington. As dubious as her reasoning was, she thought it only fair, for the duke had had no right to curtail her activities.

And now he did.

It was perfectly reasonable for a duke to expect his duchess not to skulk in dark corners and unearth the secrets of their fellow members of the *ton*.

Agitated by the predicament, for she could see no way forward that didn't end with her heart shattered, she closed her eyes and took a deep, calming breath. She didn't have to pursue the matter, she told herself. Her parents would certainly not hold it against her if she chose the surety of a brilliant match over the uncertainty of a hazardous investigation. Indeed, it would most likely be exactly what they'd expect from their child, having raised her to be successful and sensible.

But they didn't raise me, she thought with a surge of anger, as if they had contrived their own deaths at the hands of Jeffries or one of his cohorts. Maybe they hadn't, but in dying they had abdicated the right to have any opinion about her behavior.

She knew she was being ridiculous, formulating responses on behalf of her dead parents only to then take offense at her own arguments, but it made her feel as if she were talking to them.

Our first quarrel, she thought in amusement, and laughing softly, felt the disquiet in her bones begin to subside. It didn't matter anymore what anyone wanted—not Lady Abercrombie or Kesgrave or her parents or even herself. The truth had its own gravity, and it pulled her toward it. For twenty years, she had known one inexorable fact about her own existence: Her parents had drowned. Now the countess had added a skiff and a rainstorm, and Bea couldn't bear to spend the next twenty not knowing if her parents had simply been so reckless as to risk everything on a single sodden, madcap adventure.

Had she truly been of such little importance to them?

Resolved to her course, she opened her eyes and there he was—the Duke of Kesgrave slipping into her bedchamber.

"When taking a suitor to task for not demonstrating sufficient impatience to declare himself so as to scale the wall outside your bedchamber and enter your room through the window, which, you will recall, you did last night," he said with conversational ease as if arriving to take tea in her sitting room, "it's commonly accepted courtesy to have a window through which he may enter. In the absence of just such an aperture, I was forced to sneak into the house through the front door."

Her heart leaped.

Oh, how it leaped.

It was not the sight of him, though, certainly, that was something to behold—his athletic form shown to advantage in meticulously tailored evening clothes; his blue eyes dancing in the candlelight, so amused by the scene and his particular place in it—but rather his words, the beloved pedantry with which he'd wooed her. That afternoon, when they had met in the hallway, he had seemed vaguely foreign, a sensation made worse by her own self-consciousness and mortification. Now, however, he was wholly familiar.

"Sneak, your grace?" Bea asked, raising an eyebrow in feigned disappointment. "That is all I get? A single-word description of your adventure? Are there not dozens of tedious details to share? Minutiae on the challenges of unlocking the front door? A lecture, perhaps, on the best method for creeping up a staircase undetected? Come, Kesgrave, don't tell me you're going to turn concise now."

It was a properly provoking speech, brimming with disrespect and humor, and the duke, unable to withstand such a charming display of affection, sat down next to her on the bed.

"I would offer to share my knowledge of locks, which, despite your mockery, is actually quite considerable, in a private tutorial, but I fear your aunt would insist on joining that as well," he said, taking her hand and raising it to his lips.

Now her heart fluttered.

Her thoughts, however, remained clear, and she regarded him curiously. "Is that why you have taken the extraordinary step of sneaking into the house? To avoid Aunt Vera? She would be devastated to hear it, for she takes such a particular interest in your welfare."

"Aha!" Kesgrave exclaimed.

As much satisfaction as the triumphant glee in his tone conveyed, the interjection itself was still nonsensical and Bea tilted her head in confusion. "I wonder, your grace, if you are taking your newfound fondness for concision a little far. Perhaps you can find some compromise between lengthy exposition and abrupt outbursts."

"I knew something was wrong this afternoon when you were not at home to receive my call," he said.

Bea could not help but laugh at this display of ego. "Naturally, as your betrothed, it's my duty to sit on the settee, stare at the clock and await your visit. How very selfish of me to presume to go about my life as if everything had not been fundamentally altered by our engagement. Fear not! In the future, I will plant myself in the drawing room until you condescend to appear. Tell me, your grace, am I allowed to read a book whilst I keep vigil? Or does your vanity require monotony?"

"Brat," Kesgrave said fondly, not in the least offended by her satirical reply. "I would never expect you to twiddle your thumbs while waiting for me to arrive, but I did think you would be at least a little curious about how matters with Taunton were settled. I seem to recall a particularly accusatory look aimed at me across the ballroom last night. Perhaps I have you confused with someone else?"

Bea colored slightly as she realized how thoroughly the Marquess of Taunton and his crimes had slipped her mind in the wake of Lady Abercrombie's revelations. "Oh, that was me, all right, although I think *disgruntled* is a more accurate description of the look. The next time we get engaged, you may do the polite with every society matron in London while I have the pleasure of watching the authorities drag off Taunton. Did he struggle with the restraints so that the Runner had to handle him roughly? Do say yes."

When Kesgrave did not respond immediately, Bea

gleaned a reluctance and began to speculate, for she had realized all had not gone to plan when she learned Larkwell himself had circulated that ridiculous story about Taunton rescuing her. "He was not dragged away at all, was he?" she asked, not at all surprised, for Lady Skeffington had eluded punishment by wielding her influence with the local authorities. It was shocking how easily the aristocracy could get away with murder, and yet not shocking at all. "Let me guess what happened: He stood on his consequence, and the magistrate, cowered by the presence of a Very Great Man, deferred to his marquessate. There is no evidence of his crime against Mr. Wilson, so freeing himself from that charge was easily arranged. But how did he overcome his attempt on my life, which you witnessed firsthand?"

The duke opened his mouth to reply, but she forestalled him with a lift of her hand, for she recalled quite clearly something Taunton had said moments before he'd attacked her. "A romantic tryst gone awry? I sent him a look that bid him to follow me onto the terrace, but having attained my goal, I suddenly suffered an attack of conscience and he was only collecting his due. No," she said thoughtfully, "not an attack of conscience. He wouldn't credit me with one. The opposite in fact. Rather, I perceived a greater prize—you, of course—and changed my mind. Indeed, I arranged the entire scene on the terrace to maneuver you into rescuing me, and like a sap skull you promptly fell in line. How does it feel, your grace, to have a London magistrate consider you to be the veriest of fools?"

"Not a magistrate," Kesgrave corrected with a cynical smile. "Lord Larkwell. He insisted on taking over the matter, as it was his house and his ball. Unlike Skeffington at Lakeview House, he did not yield when I exerted my authority. He and Taunton are old cronies, having won and lost fortunes together at the hazard table during their salad days. He denied entry to the Runner, refused to hear a word against his friend and assured me that nobody would look twice if I denied an engagement had taken place. Taunton, not comprehending the depth of my affection, offered to swear on a stack of Bibles that you had enlisted him in your evil scheme, a scheme that failed to prosper because he revealed everything to me and we worked together to thwart it. Naturally, you resisted our efforts, and somehow in the ensuing tussle you were just enough of a pea goose to light your own dress on fire, which Taunton heroically extinguished. I trust it goes without saying that I declined his offer."

'Twas infuriating how easily the marquess had slipped the yoke of responsibility. Lady Skeffington, at least, had to escape to the Continent and suffer the indignity of living among foreigners. For Lord Taunton to continue in his existence as if nothing ghastly had happened was beyond the pale, and Bea at once began to wonder if there was a way to hold him accountable that did not involve the Crown. She knew nothing of his finances, but Kesgrave had not a minute before mentioned a proclivity for gambling.

"Is it possible to arrange a game—hazard, perhaps, or vingt-et-un if it better serves our purpose—with extremely high stakes," she said slowly as the idea began to take shape in her head, "and then induce Taunton to lose? Yes, yes, there are rules against cheating at cards. I know you gentlemen take it very seriously—one's honor and all that. But surely it's more dishonorable to end a man's life?"

"An ethically murky area, to be sure," Kesgrave said, "but one that we are not required to plumb, for Taunton has obligingly gotten himself into substantial debt without our manipulations. As of eight o'clock this evening, I am in possession of all his vowels and have made my expectations known. He has four and twenty hours to leave London and another four and twenty to remove himself entirely from the country. If he shows his face in England again, his wife and children will know nothing but abject poverty for the rest of their lives. If I hear a hint of gossip about you and the terrace, his wife and children will know nothing but abject poverty for the rest of their lives. Perceiving at last the depth of my affection, Taunton agreed to my terms and is even now frantically throwing articles into a suitcase so that he may depart at first light."

Hearing how well the duke had settled matters, Bea felt a mix of relief that some measure of justice had been meted out and delight at how closely aligned their thoughts were. "Well done, your grace," she said with warm approval.

At her complimentary tone, he stiffened his shoulders and said with alarm, "Do not go soft on me now, Miss Hyde-Clare. I got engaged to a harridan and a harridan I expect you to stay. Otherwise, I will be forced to take your aunt's advice and carefully extricate myself from this unfortunate situation."

Bea wasn't at all surprised to discover her aunt had made the suggestion to the duke himself. No doubt she felt it was her duty to present him with every option, lest he go through with the marriage out of a sort of lethargic absentmindedness. Nevertheless, she winced in mortification.

"Aha!" Kesgrave said again.

Although she had no more understanding of the exclamation now than before, she found the gleeful triumph in his voice endearing and realized he had every reason to be concerned, for she did indeed seem to be going soft on him. "Another revelatory insight, your grace?"

"An addendum to the original," he said. "I knew your aunt must have said something to unsettle you, for there could be no other explanation for your uncharacteristic reticence this afternoon. I have never known you to remain quiet when there is an opportunity to roast me. I made up five types of beetroot on the spot—no meager accomplishment, by the way, for unlike you I am not accustomed to inventing persons and things—and arranged them by size specifically to get a rise out of you and you didn't look up once. Desperate for your attention, I even scrambled the order of the British ships that fought in the Battle of the Nile."

Bea's heart quivered again, for few things could reveal the depth of his affection more than a blatant disregard for the dictates of maritime tradition. "Moving the conversation from beetroot to naval battles could not have been a smooth transition."

"One of my fictitious varieties was called the 'audacious,' and it was easy enough to manage from there. Your aunt was momentarily confused—no doubt unnerved by my flagrant break with naval custom," he said.

"A subject about which she feels quite passionately," Bea asserted wryly, although her aunt would immediately take an interest if the duke indicated that she should.

"As any feeling person would. But she was far too polite to correct me," he explained with a teasing smile, for Beatrice had yet to pay him that courtesy. "Now that we've established your level of distraction, I would like for you to tell me what she said that you found so unsettling. It was about the servants, was it not?"

Astonished by how easily he identified the source of her anxiety, Beatrice gaped at him. She had long known him to be astute, but this ability to accurately gauge what was in her head bordered on sorcery.

The duke chuckled at the confounded expression on her face. "I should allow you to believe I'm all knowing, for I suspect it would give me a much-needed advantage in our union, but I cannot misrepresent myself so thoroughly. Your aunt talked at length this afternoon about my impressively large staff and what a daunting task it will be for you to oversee it. It was no great feat to deduce she had treated you to the same discourse. Obviously, I'm not surprised her words had an effect. I have been telling you since we met that I'm very impressive, and it's only right that you finally believe it," he said teasingly.

Bea appreciated the lighthearted note in his voice because it was true: For months he had tried to cow her with his consequence, to intimidate her into stepping aside and allowing him to resolve matters to his satisfaction. She'd paid him no heed, preferring time and again to skewer his self-regard.

Now, alas, she felt at its mercy, for it didn't matter how Kesgrave perceived himself. It was the world's opinion of him that she would be held to—a terrifying notion somehow embodied by the dreaded eighth footman.

She could wallow in it, allow the prospect of an unwieldy staff to undermine her confidence as exhaustively as Miss Brougham's spiteful comment had during her first season, or she could trust Kesgrave. He had every advantage of wealth, breeding and status, and still he had chosen her. That was a not inconsiderable testament to her appeal.

And he was there, in her bedchamber, offering comfort and reassurance because he had known something was wrong.

Aha!

"It was not your impressiveness that gave me pause, your grace, but rather the opposite," she explained, determined to match his light tone, "for only a man greatly lacking confidence would require eight footmen to prop up his importance."

Kesgrave quirked an eyebrow at this communication. "Eight footmen?"

"In the London house alone," Bea added. "Presumably there are several dozen at the country estate. I can only assume your large staff is compensating for some great personal deficiency."

At her observation, the duke rose abruptly to his feet, and Bea feared she had given actual offense, for she had indeed meant for the comment to be slightly suggestive. But then he reached for her hand and tugged gently. "Come," he said, "stand up."

Bea eyed him warily as she slid off the bed. "Why? What is wrong?"

"So many things," he said softly, brushing a few loosened tendrils away from her eyes. "You are adorable. I want to kiss you. We are not married. There is a bed nearby. Should I go on?"

As affecting as his words were, it was the look in his eyes that made her legs unsteady. "That is not necessary. I begin to perceive the problem. Would it resolve the issue if *I* kissed *you*?"

"Given how ardently I responded the last time you initiated—in the carriage ride home from Lord Taunton's, if you recall—I fear that will only exacerbate the problem," he said, his hands caressing her shoulders as he slid them lower.

"Coward," Bea said tenderly. "Craven. Faint of heart."

His fingers rested at the base of her spine. "Are you trying to provoke me into kissing you?"

She grinned at the charge and leaned forward until her mouth just touched his. "How am I doing?"

"Terribly," he breathed before capturing her lips with his own.

Bea had barely a moment to revel in her success before the heat of longing overtook her, and she was incapable of basking in anything except the wonderful sensation of the duke's body against hers. How solid he felt, how sturdy, how strong. Craving more of everything, she wrapped her arms around his body and pulled him closer.

It wasn't enough.

Indeed, it was nowhere near enough.

Murmuring incomprehensibly, she moved her hands along the edge of his shirt, determined to remove the offending fabric.

The moment her hands touched skin, Kesgrave groaned as if in pain, broke off the kiss and took one very firm step away from her. "I have never been so terrified of anything in my entire life as I am of that bed," he said, his voice as low as his color was high. "That warm, soft, welcoming bed. You did well to run away after the incident in the carriage, for I wanted to devour you then as ferociously as I want to devour you now. We will be married by special license by the end of next week at the latest. Your aunt suggested a long betrothal, but your uncle, fearing the fish might wiggle off the hook, agreed there was no reason to wait. I trust that is enough time to resign yourself to the fact that you will be overseeing only three footmen."

It was a very gratifying speech in many ways, not least in its clarity at conveying his impatience to finish what they had so enticingly started, but when Bea looked at the bed all she saw was her mother's letters arranged in a neat pile next to the pillow.

Now, she thought, tell him now.

But even as she ordered herself to admit the truth so he could decide for himself if he wanted to proceed in the engagement with the slightly altered circumstance, she couldn't get the words out. The moment was too lovely to ruin.

Coward, she thought. Craven. Faint of heart.

Sensing her disquiet, he rushed to assure her that he was only teasing. "Of course you don't have to oversee anything. I have many competent people in my employ who ensure my estates run smoothly, and you do not have to do anything if you don't wish to. The general assumption is you will make changes to suit yourself, but if everything is already to your liking, you may retire to the library and emerge only twice a day for meals."

Bea felt buried by the remarkable understanding this speech conveyed and, unable to bear the weight of it, opened her mouth to make a clever retort about how only he could manage to turn domestic competence into an accomplishment worthy of boasting. And yet when she spoke, it came out all wrong.

"I love you," she said.

The pleasure that washed over his face was brighter than the midday sun and, unable to control himself, he took one bold step forward and pressed his lips against hers for another devastating kiss.

This time when he pulled away, he put the width of

the room between them. "You will not provoke me again, my love. I will maintain my dignity, damn it!"

The peevishness of the statement made her lips twitch. "Maintain your dignity whilst sneaking out of the house via the same route you sneaked in? Or do you have another method in mind for a decorous exit? Sliding down the banister, perhaps, in full view of the servants and my family?"

Now he grinned widely. "You are right, of course. I surrendered my dignity the moment my eyes met yours over the corpse of that unfortunate spice trader in the Skeffingtons' library, and I have never regretted the loss of anything less. Good night, Beatrice," he said, pausing with his hand on the doorknob. "One last thing before I attempt the banister. My grandmother extends an invitation to tea. She expects you tomorrow afternoon at four."

The thought of sitting across from his stern relative, who had personally selected a beautiful heiress with title and lands for her grandson, chilled Bea to the bone. Lady Victoria was everything she was not—a wealthy Incomparable whose family owned property that bordered the northern edge of the Maitland estate—and it was generally agreed by the *ton* and Aunt Vera that she would make Kesgrave an ideal wife. Although Lady Victoria's pea-widgeon-ish brain might appear to put her at a disadvantage with the eighth footman, Bea knew her pliability more than compensated for the defect.

Annoyed at her churlishness, for it revealed a daunting lack of confidence in herself, she said, "A command appearance is her notion of an invitation?"

"You have no cause for alarm," he said with insufferable insight.

Bea, who had spent six seasons with a studiously bland expression plastered to her face so that no one would sense her crippling discomfort, resented how easily he could read her. "I'm not alarmed."

"Of course not," he said smoothly. "I merely meant to say that my grandmother looks forward to getting to know you better. She doesn't object to the match if that is your concern."

"I have no concerns," she snapped sharply, then inwardly grimaced, for nothing made one's concerns clearer than the waspish denial of them. "Rather, I thought your grandmother might appreciate a little time to come to terms with her disappointment over Lady Victoria."

"While I'm sure my grandmother would appreciate the consideration, she had no need for it. Despite the *ton*'s determination to see the two families joined, there was never an agreement. My attentions were simply to help bring the young lady into fashion during her first season," he said.

Although Bea did not doubt the truthfulness of his explanation, she nevertheless found it patently absurd. "Lady Victoria is beautiful, wealthy, titled and in possession of acreage. She does not need to be brought into fashion. She *is* the fashion."

"Fortunately, my grandmother isn't as easily impressed as you—nor am I, for that matter. It seems as though you are the one who needs to reevaluate her standards," he added with an infuriating smile. "Now, as flattering as your attempts to stall my departure are, I really must request that you allow me to leave before your family return home. Having endured Lady Marjorie's singing for twenty minutes, I cannot believe anyone would remain for the full program. Adieu, my love."

Kesgrave swept out of her room with the same careless grace with which he'd strolled in, and she stared at the door through which he'd passed like a besotted fool for several minutes before shaking herself free from her stupor.

"Recall, if you will, your dead parents," she muttered irritably, "for they were of import to you only a little while ago."

Sighing with purpose—and perhaps a little bit of regret—she gathered the letters from her bed and sat down at the escritoire to compile a list of actions to take in the investigation of Clara and Richard Hyde-Clare's murders.

CHAPTER FIVE

By the time Bea managed to find an address for the English Correspondence Guild, she was thoroughly out of patience with her troublesome engagement, which, far from strewing her path with rose petals, had provided her with a seemingly endless barrage of new obstacles.

Leaving her house dressed in men's clothing to hide her appearance, while always a fraught endeavor, was almost impossible now, for her presence was constantly sought by family members desiring a word. Flora, convinced that her cousin was withholding important details regarding the incident with Taunton, bedeviled her with questions about the events on the terrace, trying to ascertain just how she had managed to catch her dress on fire when she'd never been a particularly clumsy person—awkward and tongue-tied, yes, but not clumsy. Russell, who, at two and twenty, was the ideal age to be in awe of a Corinthian like Kesgrave, pestered her for information about the duke's habits so that he might convincingly ape them. Aunt Vera wanted to talk about bedsheets.

"Bedsheets?" Bea had asked as she finished her plate of eggs during breakfast.

"Bedsheets, yes," her aunt had said firmly, "and linens

more generally. I can only assume the number of items you will be the custodian of reaches well into the hundreds, but we will commence with the bedsheets and proceed from there."

Although she had determined to begin her day early in order to make significant progress in her investigation before tea with the Dowager Duchess of Kesgrave at four, Bea did not contrive to leave the house in Russell's clothes until after ten-thirty. Before she could sneak through the kitchens and slip out the servants' entrance unobserved, she had to come up with an acceptable explanation for her absence and, realizing her aunt would not consider the lending library to be a legitimate reason to miss a lecture on tablecloths and towels, settled on a visit to the Countess of Abercrombie, who had offered to help her select her trousseau. Nothing Beatrice could say could have distressed her aunt more, for Vera instantly blanched and noted that her ladyship's taste was quite above their touch.

Irritated to be off her schedule before she'd even started, Bea was further annoyed by the fissure of alarm she'd felt stepping into the Addison, a coffeehouse with a repository of old newspapers. It was not the shop itself that caused the sensation, for the Fleet Street establishment was tidy and clean, with long rectangular tables and a bar for ordering, but, as a few pairs of male eyes inspected her absently, a new sense of vulnerability. Previously, if Miss Hyde-Clare was discovered to be dressed as a man, it would hardly have raised an eyebrow, for few people would have any idea who Miss Hyde-Clare was. Those who did know of her would consult the situation and decide she was precisely at the age when an unmarried female's mind started to unravel.

Now, however, she'd gained a measure of notoriety as Kesgrave's betrothed, and any unmasking would not only raise eyebrows but wag tongues as well. It would also expose the duke to no end of humiliation, something she was remarkably reluctant to do.

The look of irritation the clerk gave her when she

requested a dozen issues of the *London Daily Gazette* from 1795 did little to increase her comfort. Although he would be well compensated for his trip to the cellars—the older the paper, the more expensive its retrieval—he clearly resented the effort, and hoping to assuage his temper, she ordered a coffee. Having never partaken of the drink before, she was ill prepared for its bitterness and exclaimed in surprise. It was surely the first time a dearly felt *blech* had been uttered within those walls, and everyone in the room turned to look at her. Bea, worried that her features were a little too delicate, straightened her shoulders, which her aunt had long identified as her most masculine attribute. She dipped her nose into the cup, careful not to let any of the brew touch her lips, and kept it there until she was sure all the men in the room had returned to their business.

Conversation around her resumed, and she impatiently looked at the clock as she waited for the clerk to deliver her newspapers. It was still early, of course, not yet noon, but her freedom was severely curtailed by her visit with the dowager duchess. She had to return to Portman Square not only with enough time to arrive in Clarges Street at four but also to change into her best walking gown and arrange her hair in a presentable fashion. That would require at least an hour, and finding information about a defunct London society in a year's worth of newspapers would be no simple task. Indeed, locating a needle in a bundle of hay seemed far more likely.

Ten minutes later, the clerk delivered the requested broadsheets to her table, and looking at the thick stack, Bea decided that visiting the Addison on an afternoon when she didn't have endless hours to scour the newspapers was a wasted effort. She would just have to do it all again tomorrow but at greater risk to herself, for having allowed her to escape their grasp today, her family would tighten their grip tomorrow.

"No doubt the dowager will order me to attend nuncheon," she muttered sullenly, opening the first newspaper.

Despite her dire prediction, Bea found what she was searching for in little less than an hour. After reading several articles on the organization, including one that provided Mr. Jeffries's personal history in great detail and decried the activities of the English Correspondence Guild as "almost certainly treasonous," she came across a story that provided the location of the society's offices.

"Mr. Jeffries, along with his band of ruthless agitators, undermine the peace and prosperity of the kingdom from a tidy building in Whitefriars Street—number 39, to be precise," the newspaper reported. "If you are in the vicinity, especially in the company of your precious wife or dear children, give it a wide berth, lest the English Correspondence Guild's godless principles weaken the moral bedrock upon which you have built your life."

Whitefriars Street, she thought, delighted to have a starting point for her investigation. It was unlikely that anyone from the society still resided there, as it had disbanded seventeen years ago after a parliamentary act made its existence unlawful, but she was optimistic that the current occupant could provide her with some useful information.

Unfamiliar with the thoroughfare, she consulted the clerk on its direction and was gratified to see him scowl in response. Clearly, it was having to interact with patrons in general that he objected to, not visiting the cellars.

She found this oddly comforting.

Ascertaining that Whitefriars was only a few blocks to the east, Bea checked the clock once again and decided she had enough time to pay a call on number 39.

Pleased, she beamed happily at the clerk, then immediately worried that smiling in gratitude was an overly feminine way to react to pleasant news. To cover her confusion, she threw a few extra coins onto the counter as a gratuity and all but raced to the front door.

She kept a brisk pace as she strode past Red Lion Court and Bouverie Street, halting a few minutes later as she arrived at her destination, a narrow redbrick building with a pointed roof. Above the door, arched slightly to accommodate a window, was a sign that read: Jeffries and Sons, Shoemakers.

Bea's heart lurched.

Confoundingly, she felt an intense desire to run away.

It had never occurred to her that Mr. Jeffries would be so easy to find. Indeed, she'd imagined a painstaking process of interviewing one craftsman after another in hopes of finally locating him in a small, dark hovel on the edge of Clerkenwell. Now, however, she stood only a few feet from his threshold and, as she stared at the sign, realized she had no idea how to proceed. Having failed to anticipate her success, she had not taken the time to formulate a plan for extricating information from the shoemaker. Obviously, she could not simply stroll into the establishment and identify herself as the daughter of Clara and Richard Hyde-Clare, for she was dressed in her cousin's clothes.

Nor could she introduce herself as their son because her parents had employed noms de guerre in their work for Mr. Pitt. Her mother had been Mr. Barlow and her father Mr. Piper. They certainly had not presented themselves as a couple.

Who, then, could she claim to be?

The son of one of the two men was the most likely answer, for it would be easy enough to identify Mr. Piper, say, as her father. That gave her an identity, yes, but a reason to interrogate the founder of the English Correspondence Guild still eluded her. Something pressing had to have happened to bring her to his doorstep. A desire to know more about her parent who died when she was very young? That was certainly true. But if Jeffries knew the truth about her parents as Clara believed, then he would know immediately that her claim to be Mr. Piper was a lie.

Her challenge was to discover what the founder knew, and indicating from the onset that she was an untrustworthy person would do little to further that goal.

She had to be someone else, someone who could justifiably ask questions about the group's structure and its concerns regarding governmental spies in a way that would not call her own honesty into question.

That meant keeping entirely away from the notion of progeny, for it was simply too complicated to figure out what Jeffries did or did not know.

What about a reporter, she thought, one writing an article about the effects of the Seditious Meetings Act on the radical parliamentary reform movement? The timing wasn't auspicious, as this year marked the twenty-first anniversary of the law. If it had been an even twenty, then it wouldn't be too much of a stretch to imagine an editor assigning a story to commemorate the anniversary, as it was common practice to reexamine an event a decade or two after it happened.

Ah, but even if the dates had aligned, there would be no way to explain how a reporter for the *London Daily Gazette* knew that Misters Barlow and Piper were in fact Clara and Richard Hyde-Clare. That information had never become public, and the point of the interview was to discover what Mr. Jeffries and his confederates knew about her parents.

No, for the persona she adopted to be truly successful, he would have to have access to secret government information. That mean it had to be someone well-placed in Mr. Pitt's organization.

And then Bea thought with a boldness that even surprised her: Why not Mr. Pitt himself?

Well, obviously not *him,* for even with her broad shoulders and ability to imitate men of unfamiliar professions such as solicitors, she could not pretend to be a forty-six-year-old man who died a decade ago. But if she was writing a biography of Mr. Pitt with his family's support, then she would have read his papers and letters. It was not implausible that those documents would contain the true identities of Misters Barlow and Piper.

Would Jeffries believe it?

Wreston's biography of Mr. Pitt, which Bea had found to be long on facts if not style, was several years old by now. She could not remember the exact year of its publication but was reasonably confident it had followed swiftly on the heels of the prime minister's passing. Even if Mr. Jeffries recalled the earlier tome, it seemed highly unlikely he would question the existence of another.

Very well, she thought, taking a deep breath and striding to the door as an odd, unexpected anxiety overcame her. It was not fear for her safety, for she did not believe the shoemaker would respond violently to a few questions from Mr. Pitt's biographer. Rather, it was apprehension of what she might discover about her parents.

The interior of Jeffries and Sons bore little resemblance to Wood, the fashionable shop in Cornhill that Bea frequented to acquire her own boots and slippers. The room was simple and sparse, a large square with wide planks for a floor and wooden lasts neatly arranged on shelves. There were only two chairs for sitting, indicating that the store was rarely overrun with shoppers, and the counter in the middle of the room was buried under a high pile of leather and fabric. On the floor, in a large bin, were various tools used in the manufacture of shoes, among them pliers and an awl.

Standing next to the overladen counter, one elbow resting on a swath of red silk, was a man in a dark-blue coat. His hair was gray, with the thinning sides brushed forward in a version of the Caesar, and he wore a brown apron around his waist, indicating that, unlike the attendants who waited upon her at Wood, he made the shoes himself.

As he was inspecting a piece of black leather when she entered, it took him a moment to acknowledge her presence. Then he looked up with a pleasant smile on his worn face, welcomed her to his establishment and immediately began advertising his wares.

"You prefer the dref style, I see. Very becoming, sir, very becoming," he said as he stepped away from the counter. "And the quality of leather I can see is very fine. It is not thinned to within an inch of its life. Without question, you are a discerning customer. I have several things that will interest you greatly, and I can assure you that the quality at Jeffries and Sons is as good as or better than what you are used to. I was just this very minute inspecting an order of calfskin leather that arrived today that would be well suited to the dref or the blucher. Or perhaps you are in need of Wellingtons. I can certainly make a very fine pair of boots for you in a matter of days. I can produce them more quickly if necessary, but that is expedited service and is priced accordingly. We have many options at Jeffries and Sons to suit any taste. Just tell me how I may be of service and we will begin."

As Bea hadn't anticipated that the shoemaker would see her as a patron or that he would immediately recognize the superior quality of her cousin's shoes, she was momentarily at a loss as to how to respond to his enthusiasm. Since she considered him the most likely culprit in the death of her parents, she wasn't worried about disappointing him, for his feelings were of no concern to her. She simply did not want him to become petulant when he realized there wasn't a sale to be made. If that was to happen, he might refuse to answer her questions.

Could she pretend to be Pitt's biographer *and* a boot buyer?

Bea pondered the challenge of maintaining two fictions at once and decided that interrogating a man while he measured her foot would undercut the professional impression she hoped to make. It was better to announce her interest forthrightly from the onset rather than approach the matter obliquely from the side. At the same time, she did not want to give up the element of surprise, for Jeffries might reveal something useful in an unexpected moment.

"You are to be congratulated," she observed in the deep

tenor she had perfected during her previous investigations. The most productive disguises were male, and she had discovered a significant amount of pivotal information by pretending to be the duke's steward. "Everything in your store is so tidy and in its place. I did not anticipate such an obvious respect for the merits of organization from the founder of the English Correspondence Guild, as the organization was devoted to upending the social order and stability of the British government."

Keenly, she watched his reaction, knowing he could not be pleased to be confronted by his past while trying to conduct business in the present. She thought his nose would twitch or perhaps his eyes would narrow in suspicion.

Instead, he laughed, a loud, barking sound that filled the sparse room.

"Young man, someone has been telling you impish yarns about goblins and trolls, I see. Presumably, it was your father in an attempt to keep you in line," he said, returning the leather strip to the counter and resting his elbow next to it. "Did you question his authority? Refuse to go back to school? Show compassion for the chimney sweep? Suggest that our system of laws seems designed to make the poor worse off by punishing them for their poverty? Any of these is usually enough to elicit the tale of that wicked radical Jeffries, tried for high treason three times and barely escaped with his neck intact. As you can see, your father's stories are wrong, as is his understanding of the guild's aims. Our intention was never to destabilize the British government, merely to ensure that all men had the ability to participate in it. But power never yields without a struggle. There, some words of wisdom from an old sage. Keep it in mind the next time your father browbeats you for offering a crumb of bread to a beggar. Now I must ask you to be on your way, as this is a business establishment and not a finishing school for boys."

As the lengthy speech was delivered with consistent good humor, Bea did not believe he was offended or angered by her interest. Indeed, his words seemed to indicate that he was frequently visited by young men seeking information or enlightenment from the founder of the old reform society.

Clearly, he was not nearly as reluctant to talk about his history as a radical as she'd anticipated. Perhaps obtaining the information she sought would be easy.

"Although I might appear to be of school age, I assure you I am not so young that my father has any control over my actions. My name is John Wright, and I'm here as a representative of the"—she paused to think of the name of a publisher and then uttered the first one that came to mind—"Sylvan Press, which has commissioned me to write a biography of Mr. Pitt. Naturally, I wanted to speak with you, as his interest in your organization was keen."

Now Mr. Jeffries guffawed. "My lad, if you are going to go about calling yourself a writer, then you must learn how to use the tools of your trade. Mr. Pitt's interest in the English Correspondence Guild was not 'keen,' as you say, but fanatical, frenzied, zealous. Another good word to describe it would be *corruptive*. He was so wedded to his own view of the group that he placed men among the membership to change it into what he thought it already was."

Bea, who had planned to wind her way to the topic of governmental spies in order to lull the shoemaker into revealing more than he'd intended, was dumbfounded by his forthright attitude and had no idea how to proceed. She'd assumed the information about Mr. Pitt's manipulations would come as a nasty shock, but he obviously already knew all about it.

That meant Clara's suspicions were accurate. Mr. Jeffries *had* known who she and Richard were and probably did not take kindly to their presence at his meetings.

How, then, to account for his amusement?

Had he laughed solely for her benefit, to confuse her or calm her suspicions? He would do that only if he'd found something about her untrustworthy. Could he have taken one look at her, with her plain features and drab-colored hair under Russell's beaver, and seen Clara or Richard Hyde-Clare?

No, she thought after a moment, it was not possible. It wasn't merely that she bore little resemblance to her beautiful parents but also that twenty years had passed in the interim. How fresh could they be in his memory? After two decades, the Hyde-Clares would be a flutter at the edge of his consciousness.

If his jovial manner had not been adopted specifically to mislead her, then the truth had to be simple: He was genuinely cavalier about Mr. Pitt's attempts to undermine the English Correspondence Guild.

She decided that if she really were a biographer researching the life of her subject, this sort of candor would thrill her. "You see, Mr. Jeffries, this is precisely why I sought you out. Your firsthand knowledge of the episode in the prime minister's life is unparalleled. Now, these men placed among the membership—they were spies?"

"Oh, yes," he said with relish, "spies, spies and more spies. I would say that at any given time, at least a dozen of our members were spies for the government."

Bea, who had assumed the prime minister's recruitment of her father to spy was a novelty, could not hide her surprise. "A dozen?"

"At least," he explained. "Presumably, there were more, but as I had an organization to run, I couldn't keep track of them all."

She nodded slowly, absorbing the information, which altered slightly the nature of the problem her parents' deaths would have solved. "I must admit, I'm taken aback by your lack of concern. Mr. Pitt's efforts to undermine your organization were quite serious. As you yourself just observed, the Crown brought treason charges against you three times."

The shoemaker laughed again as he asked Bea if she were in fact trying to educate him on his own history.

"Clearly, you are a biographer, for no one else would dare. I appreciate your perspective on the matter and can understand why you have it, especially if you've been studying the issue from Pitt's point of view. To address your question, then, let me assure you I felt no reason to be concerned. Every time a man joined our ranks it was an opportunity to educate him on the right of all men to vote. The vast majority of the men the government sent to spy on the society were won over by the righteousness of the cause. I rely on the companionship of many of them still today. My sister's husband was recruited personally by Mr. Pitt's valet. I bear none of them ill will, not even Braxfield, who tried to incite members to take up arms against the government in order to justify a harsh response. If his attempts to cause rioting and death had succeeded, I might feel differently, but they did not because we were a peaceful organization. Nothing our society did was unauthorized by the law. In fact, our actions were so stridently within the bounds of what was legal, Pitt had to pass several acts to force our dissolution." His smile turned wry as he added, "Those were not the parliamentary improvements the guild had hoped to bring about, but it does prove that it's possible for a small band of tradesmen to alter the laws of the kingdom."

Although she was no longer startled by his evenhanded response to Pitt's machinations, she was still in awe of it. To see an attempt at sabotage as an opportunity to recruit new members required a remarkably sanguine nature few people had.

"Ah, yes, that's very helpful to me, as a biographer," Bea said, wondering how she would direct the conversation to her parents. "I did not realize the men recruited by the government were so pliant in their beliefs."

Jeffries, straightening his shoulders, took slight offense. "I do not like what a word such as *pliant* implies. They were men open to reason and won over by logic. The principles of the guild were solid."

"Did you find recruits across social strata were swayed by your principles?" she asked, pleased her voice remained smooth as she got closer to her point of interest. "Richard Hyde-Clare, for example, who was one of the men Pitt personally placed within your London group. As he was gentry, I'd expect him to be more resistant to your arguments. How did he respond?"

He showed no reaction other than mild curiosity. "Richard Hyde-Clare?"

She could not believe her father was that easy to forget. "Yes, Richard Hyde-Clare. According to Pitt's papers, he joined in May 1793."

Mr. Jeffries picked up a scrap of brown leather as he repeated the name once more under his breath. Then he shook his head slowly. "No, I do not recall him, but it would be foolish to suggest I knew every man in the government's employ. There were probably hundreds of spies over the years, and the group itself was broken up into eighty smaller divisions across the country so that our movements were harder to monitor. It was unlikely I ever met him. But your larger point is well taken and I concede that it was impossible to win over every spy with logic and reason. Braxfield, for example, was a viscount, and although he and I never debated the issue, I could tell he took personal umbrage at the prospect of all men sharing in the vote."

Bea wanted to believe his claim to have no idea who her father was, but she recalled too well her mother's description of Jeffries's hateful glares, his wrathful stares. He and his confederates were rough men, Clara wrote, roiling with anger, seething with a brutality that lay just beneath the surface.

"You would not have known him by his given name," she said, pressing the issue, "as he had assumed a false identity for the purposes of his assignment. I believe he called himself Mr. Piper."

A flicker of annoyance crossed his face at her

persistence. "Even if they regularly attended the meeting in this very building, I cannot claim to have known a Mr. Pip—"

His denial ended on an abrupt shout of surprise as his face turned pink.

No, not pink. Red. Red as bright as a foot guard's uniform.

Bea's entire body turned to ice as she watched the color in his face deepen to purple. That he remembered her father was no longer in doubt. Richard Hyde-Clare had obviously made a profound impression, for here the founder was, horrified twenty years later.

Only something truly awful, Bea thought, could have created such a lasting impact.

Suddenly, it seemed incredibly plausible that he'd disposed of her parents in a violent and thorough manner—so violent and thorough he never expected to be confronted with either one of them again.

And now he had.

How had he done it, she thought, and called up the image of her parents in the pouring rain, the wind whipping around their bodies as they stood next to a small boat. Did Jeffries aim a pistol at her mother to gain her father's compliance? Did Clara plead for their lives? Did she cry? Did Richard grasp her hand and silently assure her everything would be well? Did he think he could handle the boat no matter how rough the waters?

"Oh, yes…he…um…yes, him," Jeffries stuttered as Bea continued to stare, one part of her brain firmly planted in the room with the shoemaker, the other floating beside the river in a punishing storm. "Yes, I do recall the gentleman now. Oh, indeed, I remember him well, as well as his 'friend' Mr. Barlow." He could not have said the word *friend* with more disgust or revulsion. "I had no idea he worked for Pitt. But, yes, that makes sense. He tried to undermine the guild by inserting violent men who would rile us to riot, so naturally he would also try to discredit the guild by placing deviant men, unnatural men, men who weren't fully men, within our ranks. One immorality is as good as another." He pressed his thumb and forefinger to the bridge of his nose and applied pressure, as if trying to dislodge something inside him. "I should not be surprised that a man as ruthless as Mr. Pitt would sink to such a revolting level, and yet somehow I am shaken to the core."

Bea had no idea what he was talking about. Her mind had stepped out of the room, yes, to wander along the banks of the Medway at the moment of her parents' deaths, but only in the loosest sense. In every other way, she was with Jeffries and heard every word he spoke.

Deviant men?

Unnatural men?

Men who weren't fully men?

If they weren't fully men, then what were they? Men who were half-horses like centaurs?

It defied understanding.

Unable to decipher his meaning, she asked him to explain. Alarmingly, his cheeks, which had begun to return to a reasonable shade of pink, flamed scarlet again.

"They were sodomites," he said tersely.

Bea laughed.

How could she not when confronted with a supposition so wildly off the mark as to be not just in another field but in another county altogether? Her parents—a pair of sodomites! What looks they must have sent each other for the founder of the English Correspondence Guild to believe such a thing! What affection they must have displayed!

And it happened right here, she realized suddenly, giggles pouring forth in the most undignified manner, in this very room. Where had her mother stood to evade Mr. Jeffries's disapproving glare? There, toward the back of the shop, near the shelves of lasts? Or did she hide in the corner by the window?

What would her mother think if she knew that far

from suspecting her of being a spy for Mr. Pitt, Jeffries assumed she had engaged in immoral relations with her father? All that anxiety about being discovered—wasted on the wrong concern! Her life was never in peril, only her upstanding reputation as a fine young man.

She would laugh, Bea thought, just as I am.

The idea made her as happy as it did sad because, for the first time in her life she felt as if she and her mother shared something—a joke, a secret, a story to tell her father over tea in the drawing room in the quiet lull before dinner.

Comprehending anew just how much she had lost was an arrow to the heart.

Jeffries glowered furiously at her, and she couldn't help but wonder if this scowl, this mix of antipathy and repulsion, was the exact same one he had directed at Clara twenty years ago.

"It is a terrible thing," he insisted stiffly, "punishable by death."

Naturally, Bea knew this, for sodomy was a very serious offense and as recently as five years ago two men were hanged for its practice and six were pilloried in the Haymarket after a molly house on Vere Street was raided. The shocking affair had been zealously covered in all the newspapers and even written about in a book called *The Phoenix of Sodom*. Having read the reports as well as Mr. Holloway's tome, she understood the severity of the crime, and yet she was far too familiar with the classics of Greek literature to condemn the practice entirely. In the *Phaedrus* Plato argued that love between two men was an ennobling deed that could return a soul to heaven, and Aeschylus wrote convincingly of Achilles' and Patroclus's passionate feelings for each other. Apollodorus, too, in the compendium of myths called the *Bibliotheca,* described Thamyris's amatory relationship with Hyakinthos without censure.

It was true, yes, that Plato's view on the matter evolved, so that by the time he wrote the *Laws* many years later, he stood in staunch disapproval of the practice, but that only underscored to Bea the malleability of such judgments.

She recognized, however, that a measured response would not serve her purpose and regained enough control of her mirth to echo the shoemaker's outrage. "And so it should be! 'Tis a shameful thing indeed, highly immoral and thoroughly depraved, and I'm appalled to discover that Mr. Pitt was of such a low mind as to subject you to it. I knew he had resorted to underhanded schemes to discredit your organization, but I had no idea they were so dishonorable. This information, I assure you, was not in the papers I've been given by the family. Nevertheless, I will be sure to include it in my book, as I plan to correct the record on several points."

The promise mollified him greatly. "I would be hugely in your debt, Mr. Wright, if you would indeed do that. Mr. Wreston got many things about the society wrong, for it seemed to me as if he had a particular story he wanted to tell and discarded all facts that did not align with it."

"A hazard of the trade," she explained with feigned knowingness. "I am resolved to do better."

Jeffries thanked her again and said, "I expect you are too young to properly understand the gravity of the situation, but as the leaders of the group, it fell to me and my lieutenants to preserve the moral character of the men who joined. I could not let honest, hardworking men be corrupted. Some were younger than you and easily influenced. Something had to be done and I resolved to eject them from the society. My lieutenants thought such despicable behavior required a stronger response on the part of the organization, to demonstrate to everyone—the membership, of course, but also the community at large—that we were a moral society committed to upholding decency and wholesome values. While I agreed that ejection was a mild response to such depravity, I felt the members of a society devoted to the principles of peaceful organizing could not yield to violence in matters of personal repugnance. It would be a betrayal of all we held dear. My lieutenants did not agree, and the arguments grew quite heated. It was a very difficult period, and all I wanted was for them to stop coming to meetings. And then, just as I began to despair that the matter would never be resolved, they stopped coming. It was a blessing."

From the relief in his voice, Bea easily believed he considered their sudden absence to indeed be a blessing. The question was, was it an unlooked-for one? The timing, a little too convenient to be mere coincidence, indicated a heavier hand than fortune.

"Why do you think they stopped?" she asked mildly.

The shoemaker lifted his shoulders to indicate uncertainty. "Because God is benevolent? Because Misters Barlow and Piper, despite their depravities, were not entirely lost to decency and knew they didn't belong among honorable men? Because they sensed my ardent disapproval? I did not wonder at the cause then and I do not worry about it now. As long as they did not darken my doorstep, I was content."

In his words and attitude, she sensed a conscience genuinely clear of guilt or agitation. However the matter was arranged, he believed himself without culpability.

Was he entirely without blame or had he wrung his hands about the intractability of the problem and publicly wished for a solution like Henry II grumbling that none of the men in his court would rid him of "one turbulent priest"? Had his so-called lieutenants responded as swiftly and effectively as the king's knights, resolving the matter without the issuance of a formal command?

Clearly, Mr. Jeffries was not the man to answer those questions.

"How very fortunate indeed," she said brightly, glancing at the clock on the wall to consult the time. It was just early enough that she could squeeze in another interview if her second subject's location was as convenient as the first's. "I'm relieved for you that it worked out so well. No doubt the two lost their revolutionary fervor and decided to invest their time in another project. I'm grateful for the information you've given me and hopeful you will provide more. May I return at a later date to ask more questions? My intention in seeing you today was simply to gauge your interest in assisting me with my project."

Jeffries's response could not have been more enthusiastic, and if she were truly a biographer, she would be much gratified by his willingness to share his knowledge. "Yes, yes, of course. I'm at your disposal."

"Wonderful," she said. "I will send around a note in a few days with some questions so you may know the topics I plan to discuss."

"I would like that," he said eagerly, "for it will allow me to order my thoughts."

She nodded and decided that if she had been genuine in her intention to write about a recent historical figure, she would likely produce a fairly accurate narrative. "An ideal arrangement, Mr. Jeffries. I cannot thank you enough. I would also be very grateful if you could give me the names of your lieutenants and where they may be found."

In a flash, the amiability was gone from his posture, and as he stiffened his shoulders, an expression of suspicion swept across his face. "Just what kind of biography of Mr. Pitt are you planning to write, Mr. Wright?"

Bea was shocked that her seemingly harmless request could elicit such a strong response and assured him her book would provide an honest portrayal of Mr. Pitt.

He acknowledged her claim with a tilt of his head. "Then I can see no justification for your request. There can be only one reason you would seek out other members of the guild—you have found me unsatisfactory to your purpose."

Although she could not understand the cause of his observation, she rushed to assure him of its inaccuracy. "You have been everything that is kind, helpful and forthright."

This compliment did nothing to assuage him.

"Exactly!" he cried as he pointed an accusing finger at her nose. "You were expecting a rougher man, a more pugnacious individual who would fit the image of the English Correspondence Guild as a violent organization committed to the overthrow of the English government. But I *am* kind, helpful and forthright, a man devoted to peace, and that will never do, so you wish to find other members who will support your assumptions. Mr. Wreston was the same way."

"No, no, I'm nothing like Wreston," she said with ardent sincerity. It was very vexing indeed to be called to account for another man's sins. Damn Mr. Pitt's biographer! "I have no established narrative in my head that I wish to support with the careful selection of substantiating facts. I assure you, my mind is completely open to every possibility."

"So you admit it!" he said with triumphant derision.

Taken aback by his exultation, she had no clue what she'd confessed. "Admit what?"

"That your opinion can be swayed. If, in talking with my lieutenants, you find their manner is different from mine, the tone and tenor of their arguments more passionate and seemingly more inclined to violence, you will alter your view of the guild accordingly. No, Mr. Wright, I cannot provide you the names and locations of my fellow members. I have learned the lessons of Mr. Wreston well. I will thank you to leave now."

But Bea could not leave, not yet, not when she was so close to discovering the names of the men who might have murdered her parents. All she had to do was convince him that she was nothing like her predecessor. As unkind as it was to sully the good name of a man she'd never met, she had little choice but to harshly criticize Mr. Wreston in an attempt to win over the shoemaker. "And I will thank you not to compare me with the hackneyed Mr. Wreston, a more slapdash writer I have yet to read. His command of the English language is questionable and many of his conclusions laughable. I'm not surprised he felt the need to malign the guild, as creating a violent and antagonistic organization was the only way he could make his dreary prose seem interesting. I will not have to resort to such methods because I'm much more skilled at the craft. You have no cause to worry."

"I'm convinced Mr. Wreston has a similar faith in his abilities," Jeffries said cynically. "Good day to you, sir."

Flatter him, Bea thought.

"No matter how rough your associates are—and I expect you are doing your friends a grave disservice—it does not matter because it's your words that have impressed me. Your treatises are so well written," she said, wishing she'd read at least a snippet of one so she could quote it now in tribute. "Your arguments are so well articulated. The roughness could never matter because the ideas are so beautiful."

Jeffries was unmoved. "I remain at your disposal, Mr. Wright, and will provide you with all the information you require. But I'm not revealing the names of the men who were my lieutenants. That decision is not up for negotiation. Now, I look forward to receiving your questions, which I will answer with all the specificity available to me. In the meantime, however, I must insist that you leave."

Bea wanted to stay and argue with him all afternoon, maligning Mr. Wreston and praising the guild, but she knew it was futile. Mr. Jeffries was resolute.

Sighing with frustration, she walked to the door. It was just as well, for she had to make herself presentable for tea with the dowager and knew taking a little extra time with her appearance would not go amiss.

Nevertheless, as she was crossing the threshold, she turned to the shoemaker and made one last attempt. "What if I promise not to submit the manuscript to my publisher without first getting your approval?"

It was, she thought, a shocking compromise of authorial integrity, but she was happy to make it in the advancement of her cause. Mr. Jeffries, perhaps not understanding how egregiously her generous offer lowered the standards of her profession, simply stared at her without responding. Under his withering gaze, she slowly backed out of the shop and watched as he closed the door in her face.

Bea growled with frustration as she realized she would have to return to the neighborhood the next day and start from the beginning. She'd found information about Mr. Jeffries easily enough, but she knew that had been a function of his position within the organization. As the founder, he had appeared in more stories than ordinary members. Now she would have to rely on luck, for it would take nothing but very great fortune for her to discover the name of his lieutenants in one of the newspapers.

Or any name, she thought as she climbed into a hack. All she needed was one bread crumb to follow.

As the carriage drove past Fleet Street, she sighed with regret. As exasperated as she was by the thought of sifting through dozens of broadsheets for information Jeffries could have effortlessly given her, she was eager to begin the search. If only Kesgrave had resisted his grandmother's efforts to look Bea over! The meeting between the two women would bear no fruit, for no amount of polite chatter could induce the dowager to welcome a plain-faced spinster warmly into the family. Kesgrave's optimistic assurances offered little comfort, for she felt certain the dowager was too clever to alienate the affections of her grandson by criticizing the match. No doubt she would smile at Beatrice too, all the while hurling mean-spirited little darts at her to make her displeasure known.

Bea tensed, as if already struck by one of the poisoned needles, and was sullenly annoyed at the dowager for holding her responsible for a situation that was in fact of her grace's own making: She'd had more than a decade to arrange an advantageous marriage for her grandson, and neither of them would be forced to feign excessively bright smiles over tea if she hadn't failed so spectacularly in the effort.

CHAPTER SIX

Knowing the case to be hopeless did little to weaken Beatrice's determination to make as impressive a showing as possible. 'Twas a salve to her pride, for her first meeting with the dowager had been disastrous, with Bea dressed in her maid's clothing and her color high as she spat angry invectives at the duke for foiling her plan to cajole vital information from a snuff dealer. He'd thought himself very clever, sending her to the wrong shop to catch her in the middle of an investigation that he considered to be in violation of their agreement. And then *he* had had the audacity to be angry with *her* for lying, as if he hadn't just perpetuated an elaborate fraud and wasted her entire morning.

Irate at her duplicity, he had brought her to his grandmother's house so that he could scold her with unrestrained passion in the privacy of her grace's elegantly appointed drawing room.

Naturally, Bea was uncowed by his fury, but the thought of greeting the dowager in Annie's ill-fitting frock caused her to shrink in terror.

The old lady's discerning eye missed nothing, and the first words she'd spoken to her were an exhortation to stand away from the window, for the sun's bright rays did little to flatter her complexion, which, at six and twenty, hardly retained the rosy blush of youth.

Now, as Bea sat down on the forest green settee at the direction of the dowager—a tall woman with narrow lips, rouged cheeks and blue eyes that had begun to fade to milkiness—she tried to find amusement in the fact that her complexion had never displayed the rosy blush of youth. Except in the summer months, when her cheeks turned red from too much exposure, her skin was pale, almost disconcertingly pallid. As her aunt was fond of saying, she was a wan creature and had always been.

Recalling Aunt Vera's lament threw into relief the futility of believing a gown could improve her appearance. The clothes might be alterable, but her visage was not.

Nevertheless, she felt a certain polish—a well-tailored fit, a tidy hairstyle—provided a compensatory gloss, and she returned the dowager's frank gaze with equanimity. Her sense of calm was aided by the awareness that the other woman's approval could not be won. If she'd believed it was only a matter of uttering the right set of words, she would have been awkward and stuttering as she grasped for the ideal combination. She knew this to be true because such behavior characterized her first six seasons and led directly to her current situation, for if she'd had any social graces she would have been married long ago to a well-regarded second son of a marginally respected family. She would have gone her entire life without shrinking under the withering gaze of the formidable Dowager Duchess of Kesgrave, whose regal bearing and rigidly straight shoulders emanated disapprobation.

It doesn't matter, Bea thought, stiffening her own shoulders as she kept her eyes level. Kesgrave was set in his course and would not be swayed by his relative's opinion, however severe. She would remain equally impervious to her judgment. If living with the Hyde-Clares for twenty years had taught her anything, it was how to accept harsh appraisals without showing dismay.

She would not allow the dowager to undermine her composure and resolved to maintain a mask of polite good humor. No matter how critical or cutting the dowager was, she would expose nothing of her true thoughts. She would be as impassive as a grand old oak standing in the forest.

And then, just as Bea was settling into the imperiousness of a tree, the dowager said the one thing certain to grind her invulnerability to dust.

"Why, that spray of freckles across your nose is charming."

Bea gaped. Her jaw dropped as if to the floor, and her bones felt as though they'd seeped from her body. A wild compunction to throw herself at the dowager's feet swept through her.

"People have been offering their condolences," her grace explained, seemingly unaware of the destruction her words had wrought, "as if Kesgrave were suffering from some dire complaint such as consumption rather than an unremarkable betrothal. They are particularly troubled by your looks. 'But she is so plain,' they keep saying. 'Her appearance is so drab.' On and on—'her hair is so dull,' 'her features are so ordinary.' I knew it was true, all of it, but I did not see how it mattered to a marriage, for a wife is not a bare wall one gets tired of looking at. In examining you now, however, I see a delightful smattering of freckles."

Beatrice heard every word the dowager spoke—drab, dull, ordinary, plain—but she was too staggered to digest them. As absurd as it was, as implausible as it was, as sadly revealing of the miserliness of her vanity as it was, she'd been waiting her whole life for someone to find her freckles delightful. She'd known, going into her first season, the vast limitations of her appearance and had fully expected the spray across her nose to provide a little redeeming whimsy, to give her face an endearing perkiness that would draw people to her.

Alas, it had not. It had taken her but a week to discover the vast limitations of the *ton,* which was quite incapable of looking beyond a whole to its various parts.

The dowager's compliment had such a devastating effect on Bea's composure that she didn't realize a reply was required of her for an entire minute. For a full sixty seconds—though, in truth, it could have been more, perhaps ninety, maybe as many as one hundred and twenty—she gawked at her grace in dumbfounded amazement, and it was only when a hint of impatience crossed the other woman's face that she recalled herself. Unable to think of something sensible to say, Bea knew herself to be on the verge of lapsing into a humiliating stammer.

Sputtering like the veriest pea widgeon.

Such a move would be fatal.

The dowager might be accepting of an uninspiring appearance, but she would be utterly intolerant of an insipid personality.

Say something, you nodcock!

With no clever thoughts in her head, Bea resorted to the truth. "Thank you, your grace. The compliment is deeply appreciated by me, and I must own that I did not come here today expecting such a charitable reception. I assumed you would be unhappy with the arrangement, as I'm not what you or anybody could have wanted for Kesgrave."

"You shouted," her grace said.

Bea, who had managed an intelligible comment by what felt like the skin of her teeth, wondered if perhaps the real problem was her hearing.

"I shouted?" she echoed.

"When Kesgrave brought you here to castigate you in private, you responded to his criticism with equal fervor and refused to melt in the heat of his anger," she explained. "I can think of no better basis for a marriage."

The shouting match had happened weeks ago, and yet Bea felt a slight flush creep up her cheeks as she recalled the vehemence of her response. It had not occurred to her that they could be overheard. "I'm sorry. I didn't realize my voice carried so far."

The dowager dismissed her comment with a brusque

wave of her hand. "Do not apologize. Damien is a domineering brute. He likes to have his own way, and if left to himself, he would rearrange the sun and the moon to suit his convenience, never mind the million or so other people whose preferences may differ. I have a very difficult time bending him to my will, as witnessed by that fool doctor he's saddled me with, and I have several decades to my advantage. You managed to not only defy his wishes by finishing your investigation but also secure his assistance in the endeavor. You are quite clever. Damien needs someone who is clever and will stand up to him, not a simpering miss who will drive him to an early grave by agreeing with his every thought. If I have to suffer a parcel of plain-faced great-grandchildren to see Damien properly settled with a woman who won't let him descend into full-blown tyranny, then I am happy to do so."

It was a heartening speech, to be sure, and Bea was elated to realize she had an ally in her efforts to keep Kesgrave's arrogance in check. It was too soon, of course, to mock his pedantry to his fond relative, but she felt the time would come quickly enough.

But it was also an unsettling one, for the dowager's knowledge of her quarrel with Kesgrave was far more complete than she had suspected. Bea could not believe her voice was so loud that the particulars of her argument had made it to the next room.

No, her grace had been listening at the door.

Lodging an accusation of eavesdropping against one's future grandmother by marriage was not an ideal way to begin the relationship, but she felt compelled to ask the dowager if she'd perhaps positioned herself next to the doorway.

Her grace made no move to deny it. "If my grandson wants to preserve the sanctity of his disagreements, then he should either restrict his vocal levels to a quiet roar or confine all heated discussions to his own drawing room. To expect other people to preserve his privacy for him is the height of presumption."

Bea could find no fault in her reasoning and assured her she would keep that in mind in the future even if the duke did not.

"I trust you will," her grace said, then leaned over to pull the cord for the bell. "We will invite Sutton in now to deliver the tea, and as soon as he's gone, you may tell me all about your investigation. Presumably, it had something to do with Lord Taunton, as I cannot believe you set yourself on fire without a purpose in mind. Was he the villain of the piece?"

Although Beatrice appreciated being given the benefit of the doubt, she was still annoyed that the on-dit continued to circulate. "He was indeed the villain, and he's the one who set himself on fire and I who extinguished the flames."

"Of course you did, my dear," her grace said with a placating smile. "Do tell me all about your heroics."

It was a request with which Bea found it impossible to comply because one simply could not paint oneself as a heroine, but she did explain what had actually happened on the terrace, leaving out the aspects that pertained to her and Kesgrave's relationship. Then, as the butler set out the tea, she provided an abbreviated account of her adventure, eliding all references to previous investigations and strongly implying that her interest in Mr. Wilson's untimely death was a unique event.

The dowager was not entirely persuaded of the truth of this, as she professed a profound confusion as to why a man of Mr. Skeffington's seemingly keen understanding would seek out a woman's assistance in identifying a killer rather than a professional who had been trained in the skill of detection.

"Or a Bow Street Runner?" she asked after suggesting that the situation would have been better served if a magistrate or a constable had been consulted.

Given that no reasonable reply could be provided, Bea merely repeated the same response about Skeffington not wanting to involve the authorities, which the dowager had the grace—eventually—to accept.

"I suppose clarity of mind cannot be relied upon when a man dies a violent and horrible death under your nose," she conceded. "And while I find your daring rather remarkable, it's not entirely surprising considering your mother's exploits."

Startled, Bea rattled the teacup against the saucer she was holding and gently placed both on the table as she stared at the dowager. "My mother's exploits?" she said, her voice hitching as she articulated the question.

"Oh, yes," the older woman said. "She loved a lark. How did Wem describe her all those years ago? Game for anything."

Bea could hardly breathe for her eagerness to learn more. "I didn't realize you knew my mother."

"Not well," she conceded, "mostly by sight. I can't imagine we had more than a few conversations about mundane things, as we did not move in the same circles. I recall once reaching for a glass of ratafia at a ball at the exact same moment as she and being struck by the beauty of her bracelet—gold chain with heart-shaped links and marquise-cut sapphires. 'Twas exquisite. She said it was a beloved heirloom from your father she couldn't bear to take off. As I'm sure you know, she was quite beautiful, very appealing in an open-hearted way. I suppose some might call her a flirt, but I think her warmth came from a more sincere place than a desire to collect dozens of admirers."

In fact, Bea knew none of these particulars about her mother. Misers at heart, her aunt and uncle had never been generous with details about her parents, and Lady Abercrombie, whose munificence could not be doubted, had not considered the information important. Bea had seen only one picture of her mother, a miniature whose dark colors concealed more than they revealed, making it impossible for a despondent young lady in her first season to discern a spray of freckles across the subject's nose.

Although she knew it was perfectly reasonable for her to be interested in her deceased mother, Bea strove to keep her tone mild, almost indifferent, as she asked the dowager for elaboration. "What did you mean by exploits?"

"I'm gossiping. Damien would disapprove," she said with such relish it was clear that his likely censure only made the activity more appealing. "Mind you, he would be right, for the source of my intelligence is Braxfield, a rogue if there ever was one."

Braxfield…Braxfield…

Bea's mind struggled to recall where she'd heard that name before. It was definitely recent, for the memory felt newly formed as if only that—

Of course! Mr. Jeffries had mention him just a few hours ago.

"You would do well to take anything he said with a grain of salt," the dowager advised, "but he was unusually vehement in his avowal that Pitt—William Pitt the younger, that is, the former prime minister—had recruited him to spy on the radicals who were stirring up so much trouble at the time. They wanted a revolution here as in France and would stop at nothing to get it."

Her grace shuddered dramatically at the recollection, as if a guillotine had nearly been erected in Oxford Street. Then she continued, "If Braxfield is to be believed, we owe the continued good health of our monarchy to him, for he moved among the radicals and reported their activities to Pitt at great personal risk to himself. Knowing how much he liked to preen for the ladies, I cannot believe his contribution was quite as fulsome as he described, but I don't doubt he performed some service for Pitt. Your parents were engaged in the same work. Obviously, Pitt would never enlist a female for such a dangerous assignment, but your mother wanted to be involved in the operation and your father could deny her nothing. Or so Braxfield said. I wouldn't be startled to learn Pitt *had* enlisted a female, for he was quite without scruples."

Bea knew, of course, that Pitt had nothing to do with Clara's involvement, for her mother's letter made it quite clear that attending English Correspondence Guild meetings had been her own idea. This Braxfield, therefore, wasn't an entirely unreliable source. His insistence that this assignment was hazardous, however, ran counter to what Jeffries had said.

Obviously, she could not assume the shoemaker had been completely honest with her. Despite his complaint that Wreston had manipulated the facts to support his established suppositions, he was clearly not immune to the practice himself. Otherwise, he would have provided her with the names of his lieutenants without fear or quarreling.

Ultimately, it did not matter if the guild had been a violent group on the verge of exploding and taking the whole of English society down with it, as Braxfield reported, or a peaceful society committed to effecting change though political organizing, as Jeffries insisted. She was interested only in how it treated her parents, whose marital accord, sensed by other members, made them unique. It was entirely possible that both things could be true: The guild was nonviolent and the guild violently murdered a pair of sodomites.

Bea revealed none of these thoughts, however, as she opened her eyes wide, as incredulous amazement seemed to be the only appropriate response to discovering that one's parents were spies. "I cannot believe my mother and father were so bold as to infiltrate the—"

Almost too late, Bea realized the dowager had not used the name of the organization, so neither could she. Stumbling only slightly, Bea quickly thought of a reasonable substitution and amended the statement to say "the radicals who threatened England."

The dowager, noting nothing amiss, nodded. "Oh, yes, quite audacious. Not quite as audacious as Viscount Braxfield, of course, but then nobody ever is in his retellings. What was his complaint about them?" She paused for a moment as she tried to recollect something the peer had said some twenty years ago. "I believe that they didn't subscribe as wholeheartedly to their mission as he. I seem to remember some squabbling over his methods, to which they objected—hardly a surprising development. Nobody is quite as pugnacious as Braxfield. Had a dreadful temper when he was young. He has mellowed with age, like a bottle of fine claret. It suits him. I wish I could recall more details, my dear, but my memory is distressingly hazy these days. I just remember thinking that it was perfectly in keeping with my opinion of Mrs. Hyde-Clare that she would throw in with radicals. Your father was a bit more of a mystery to me. They were both very well liked. You have nothing to be ashamed of in your family tree."

Bea, who had never thought for a moment that there might be, especially bearing in mind the self-effacement with which her aunt and uncle conducted their business, thanked the dowager for her generosity and wondered what other interesting snippets of information about her parents she might be able to wrest from her. Alas, her grace knew nothing else about the assignment with the English Correspondence Guild and could recall only the flimsiest of gossip such as Clara once wore an ostrich feather—to the Worcester ball, her grace was reasonably confident—that exceeded the Duchess of Devonshire's by a full two inches. Although the information brought Bea no closer to discovering what had happened to her parents all those years ago, she found herself engrossed in the details and grateful to the dowager for providing them.

The conversation turned, as inevitably it must, to Kesgrave's family tree and the many august branches to be found there. Bea had known from the duke's own high-handed manner that he was descended from generations of accomplished men, and it came as no surprise that he could trace his lineage back to the fourteenth century, when the first Matlock to earn a knighthood distinguished himself by helping to suppress the Peasant's Revolt of 1381. The dowager had barely progressed to the first duke, having lingered perhaps a little longer than necessary on the second Earl of Kesgrave, who was a patron of the philosopher Thomas Hobbs, when the duke himself arrived to escort Bea back to her house.

As she'd had no cause to anticipate his arrival, her heart fluttered with painful happiness the moment his handsome form crossed the drawing room's threshold.

Having ascertained the topic under discussion, he greeted his grandmother with a kiss on the cheek and observed that Beatrice looked well for a woman who had expired from boredom at least twenty minutes before. "Presumably, sometime during the colonization of the Bermudas by the first earl, for I can think of no other reason why she isn't protesting this gratuitous display of Matlock family history. Any time I attempt to expound on a topic with which I'm knowledgeable, I provoke only her disapproval."

"Do not be modest, your grace," Bea said, unable to suppress a grin, "you provoke my contempt as well. But you mustn't tease your grandmother. She has been a lovely host, and I'm grateful to know just how many pairs of shoulders you stand upon when you look down on us peasants from that very great height."

Charmed, the duke sat next to her on the settee and, unable to resist, embarrassed her further by kissing her hand under his grandmother's satisfied gaze. Then he began to berate the dowager for overexerting herself on a walk with his cousin Josephine the day before.

"Crossing the short distance from Hyde Park Corner to Kensington Gardens is hardly an overexertion, and if you find it to be so, then I suggest you consult with Dr. Stafford immediately, for it appears your own health is sadly lacking," she said with considerable asperity before offering her grandson a cup of tea.

They remained for another half hour, with the dowager resuming the narrative where she'd left it, at the many accomplishments of the second duke (Chief Justice of the King's Bench, Lord Steward of the Household,

Lord Lieutenant of Ireland), and Kesgrave interrupting to offer corrections (Lord President of the Council, Lord Privy Seal, Exchequer). To Bea's amusement, there were many such disagreements, and their recollections of their shared history digressed to such a wide degree, she began to wonder if the dowager was getting the information wrong just to goad her grandson.

Watching the exchange, Bea suspected a kindred spirit.

Kesgrave kept up the recitation in the carriage ride home, rushing to assure Beatrice that though his forebears sounded illustrious, many were quite degenerate and untrustworthy.

"I do not want you to develop a sense of inferiority," he explained, his eyes twinkling with humor, "just because you're not preceded by six Lords Privy Seal."

"According to your grandmother, neither are you," she said.

Bea was grateful for his chatter because she feared if the conversation was left to her, she would ask about Braxfield. Now that the dowager had presented his connection to her parents, she could not smother her excitement at having another source of information—and a contemporaneous one at that. She felt certain the viscount had worked alongside her parents, for her mother had mentioned a peer in her letters, a confrontational one whose determination to rile up the membership worried her father. If Braxfield was indeed that man, then he would be able to supply her with the names of the guild members that Jeffries had withheld. Her investigation was not without possibilities.

The most consuming question was how to approach Braxfield in the manner most likely to extract information. Would presenting herself as his fellow conspirators' daughter help her cause or hinder it? She rather feared it might be the latter, as the dowager's comments indicated that Braxfield's respect for her parents was lacking. She considered introducing herself as the late Hyde-Clares' solicitor but could not imagine what business remained to be discussed so many years after the fact. Additionally, she would not make a convincing older man, for every time she donned Russell's clothes, she seemed to lose a few years. Perhaps Mr. Pitt's biographer would have greater success? If her grace's estimation of his character was accurate, Braxfield seemed like the sort of man who would relish an opportunity to recount his daring deeds.

It was impossible to settle on the best tactic without knowing more about the viscount.

Perhaps Aunt Vera would have useful information. Although her relative abhorred gossip, as she considered it a great presumption to speculate about her betters, she had an unexpected talent for acquiring useful nuggets. Lady Abercrombie could also be a fruitful source.

Relieved to have decided the next steps of her investigation, Bea looked up from the door handle she'd been scrutinizing without seeing and realized Kesgrave was watching her intently.

When had he stopped talking?

Having no idea where the conversation had left off, she held her tongue and tried to squelch the wave of guilt that rose within her. In this, she failed and the remorse lodged itself in her stomach, causing it to roil queasily as if the carriage were lurching back and forth over an uneven road. She knew that by not mentioning her investigation, she was turning it into a larger issue than it actually was. Now she had a secret, and a small but discernable gulf opened between them as she sought to protect it.

Tell him everything, the voice inside her urged. Just say the words and be done with it.

In her head it seemed so simple: I'm investigating my parents' deaths and cannot stop until I discover the truth.

Kesgrave was not an unreasonable man, she reminded herself. Indeed, it was his surfeit of reason that had annoyed her at first, even before his pedantry and superiority. If she told him about her mission, he was certain to understand.

But even as she assured herself of this, she knew it was too simplistic. Kesgrave might be reasonable but love was not, and the nausea in her belly intensified as she contemplated the limits of her own self-determination. If the duke drew a line in the sand and demanded she comply, if he issued an ultimatum and said it was either the investigation or their future, she didn't know how *she* would respond. She'd like to think she would straighten her shoulders, thank him for the honor and gracefully bow out, for an ultimatum about one thing was really an ultimatum about everything.

But Bea knew the scene was far likelier to go in the other direction, with her succumbing to his authority and chiseling off a tiny sliver of her soul.

It was such a minor thing, to make a concession in the name of marital accord, and women did it every day. All relationships required compromise, and the intimacy of marriage commanded additional pliancy.

And yet giving in now on this particular matter felt deeply ominous, as if the great whittling of her deepest self began here and ended....

She did not know where it ended, which was, of course, the problem.

Surely, she was overreacting. Kesgrave was a good man and wouldn't wear her down to the bone with his demands. He would get no satisfaction from reducing her to a meager shard.

But how well did she really know him?

More to the point: How well did she really know herself?

For decades, she'd pulled herself into an ever tighter ball, making herself smaller and less significant in order to preserve her aunt and uncle's goodwill, and she felt naught but the slightest affection for them. How much worse would it be with Kesgrave, whom she loved with a desperation that almost terrified her?

She could not risk it.

Although the duke looked at her curiously, he did not

remark on her unusual silence and merely observed the mildness of the weather as he escorted her up the walk at Portman Square. Aunt Vera, whose immediate appearance in the entry hall indicated she'd been keeping watch for the carriage, invited Kesgrave to tea, but he could not spare the time, as his grandmother was waiting for him to return.

"She's eager to share her opinion of Miss Hyde-Clare," he explained.

Her aunt nodded in kind understanding. "How very difficult this must be for her. Please let her know she's in our thoughts."

The elegiac note in her aunt's tone amused Bea, who recalled the dowager's observation that many people had offered their condolences on her grandson's unfortunate engagement. "Do convey my sympathies as well," she said. "It is such an unfair burden for her to suffer under."

Although Vera had no idea she was being mocked, the look on her face indicated some awareness of her niece's insincerity, for she seemed confused by how Bea could at once profess sympathy for the elderly peeress's predicament while at the same time doing nothing to alleviate it.

"On the contrary," Kesgrave said, "she couldn't be more thrilled. She thinks Miss Hyde-Clare is charming and advised me to propose to her within hours of making her acquaintance. Indeed, she has assumed an intolerable air of triumph, as if the match were entirely of her own contrivance. I assure you, she considers me and Miss Hyde-Clare to be quite incidental to the accomplishment."

Even though the dowager had made her approval clear, Bea was still startled by the overwhelming force of the endorsement and looked at the duke to see if he'd made the statement only to tease her aunt.

"Do you doubt it?" he asked her softly.

To her surprise, she found she did not. If his grandmother truly believed that a willingness to quarrel was essential to the happiness of a marriage, then she would have indeed been won over the moment she heard Bea shouting at the duke.

Having professed himself impatient to return to his grandmother, Kesgrave seemed oddly reluctant to leave and looked at Bea with an uncertain expression. She was hardly astonished, for her reticence in the carriage had indeed been out of character.

Alas, she could not wave a magic wand and make the problem of her parents' murders disappear, and she found she did not want to do so. It was the first service she could perform for them. It was also the only service.

With a promise to call on her soon, Kesgrave left, and Aunt Vera, who had seemed content to linger in the doorway for hours, urged her niece to change for dinner at once, as Mrs. Ralston and her daughters, Amelia and Esther, would be arriving within the hour to join them for the meal.

"Mrs. Ralston?" Bea said, surprised, for her aunt most heartily disliked hosting. Nothing troubled her more than having to trouble herself for someone else. She much preferred being a guest, for which her graciousness did not require any capital expenditure.

"Yes," Vera said with a mournful sigh as she gently pushed her niece toward the stairs. The girl's betrothal, though only a few days old, had already begun to make demands on her, and she could find no way to evade the social obligations of being adjacent to a duchy. Her friend had pressed and pressed until Vera issued the invitation simply to change the subject. It worked, of course, and Mrs. Ralston, having attained her goal, obligingly observed that Lady Barbara's overbite seemed to be getting worse—a comment with which Vera had gratefully and enthusiastically agreed, although, in fact, she had never noticed that the girl's front teeth protruded to a particularly egregious degree.

Her aunt explained the ordeal with the persistent Mrs. Ralston in minute detail, as if determined to make Bea feel every moment of her suffering. When they arrived at the top of the staircase, Vera seemed unable to decide which activity was more necessary—complaining or changing—and only released her niece when her own maid observed the lateness of the hour.

"Good gracious!" she explained, with a disapproving glare at Bea, as if she had deliberately distracted her with a dozen niggling questions.

Bea's amusement at her aunt's predicament lasted only as long as it took for her to enter the drawing room and recall how tedious she found Mrs. Ralston and her two daughters. The elder was a society matron who considered knowledge to be currency and expended it in an effort to grow closer to power. She had recently regaled Prinny with tales of Brummell's increasing debt, predicting that the regent's *bête noire* would soon have to leave London to escape his creditors, and had proven so entertaining, she had earned an invitation to the pavilion in Brighton. It was in hopes of obtaining salacious details about Lady Skeffington's ignominious flight to the Continent that she'd originally sought a closer relationship with Mrs. Hyde-Clare, who, as a guest at Lakeview House, had had an unobstructed view of the shocking events. In this, the experienced gossip had grossly miscalculated, for Vera would never reveal facts that exposed her own family to vulgar chatter. Mrs. Ralston could have had no idea of this, of course, as word of Bea's pivotal role had not spread, and it was only when rumors of her bizarre confrontation with Taunton began to circulate that she started to wonder if the spinster's participation in the Skeffington affair was more involved than she'd supposed.

Her attempts, however, to discover the true details of the encounter with Taunton, for she clearly did not believe that bagatelle about the girl's dress catching fire, were thwarted by Bea's blank stares and her own daughters' determination to earn the drab spinster's good opinion. Unlike their mother, they were not the least bit interested in the acquisition of power through knowledge and simply wanted to be the intimates of influential people. Although the pair had scarcely noticed Bea during their two seasons, they professed themselves now to be long enamored of her unique temperament and alluded to a shared history that in no way existed.

"That was the Thurston rout, was it not?" Amelia said with a coquettish laugh, as if determined to beguile a suitor. She was a very pretty girl, with light-brown eyes, peach skin and arched brows, and had no doubt brought many men to heel. "Lady Marchand's glove tore when it got caught on Sir Clifford's signet ring, causing her to pull away swiftly, which knocked over the Chinese vase on the mantel, and we were all silent for a moment before Esther said, 'We're having a cracking good time.' And we all laughed, didn't we, Miss Hyde-Clare?"

Beatrice, who was fairly convinced she had never attended a rout at the Thurstons', nodded politely. To disavow their memories would only come across as churlish, and she saw no reason to discomfit her aunt in that way. It was not as if their false recollections would persuade her to call them friends. She understood their motives and didn't even blame them for working so hard to secure the goodwill of a future duchess. They were merely doing what they had been taught to do since the cradle. Perhaps if they had been a little more subtle in their attempts to manipulate her, she might have taken offense at their hypocrisy. But their blatancy only amused her.

As the evening extended into dinner and then tea in the drawing room while Uncle Horace had his cigar, the entertainment value of the Ralstons began to wane and Bea longed to excuse herself from the gathering. It had been hours since her interview with Jeffries, and she yearned to have a few moments in peace to review the evidence she had gathered. His understanding of her parents' relationship as illicit love between men continued to amaze her, and although she did not properly comprehend the depth of the shoemaker's horror at their immorality, she'd felt the force of his revulsion. It was somehow still fresh all these years later.

Had that repugnance been enough to incite his lieutenants to murder?

It was astounding to her that the thought of two men behaving immorally together in private was more offensive than one man—Viscount Braxfield—blatantly attempting to rouse the membership to riot.

And then she thought: Braxfield!

She had one of the kingdom's most accomplished gossips in her very own drawing room, and it had not occurred to her before this moment to ply her for information. Eager to get some answers, she lifted her head to address Mrs. Ralston and discovered five pairs of eyes staring at her.

Her aunt's were set at a particularly disapproving angle as she said, "Amelia was just asking where you were planning to go for your wedding trip."

Bea stared blankly, for not only was the subject of wedding trips currently the farthest thing from her mind, it had always been the farthest thing from her mind. Even when she was a giddy young miss fresh from the schoolroom and full of exciting dreams for her first season, she had never contemplated taking a wedding trip.

Her cousin Flora, who was sitting next to her on the settee, patted her hand gently and said, "They're still discussing ideas and haven't decided yet."

Although Amelia nodded in understanding, she failed to comprehend the response as the polite attempt at evasion it was. "Of course. There are so many places in the world for a duke to choose from. Tell me, what are the options under discussion? Are you considering Italy or Greece?"

Flora, who had thought her answer was quite definitive, had no ready reply to these follow-up queries and darted a look at Bea as she opened her mouth without speaking.

Impatient now that she had found a subject she wished

to discuss, Bea said dismissively that she was considering Italy *and* Greece. Then she turned to the girl's mother and asked her what she knew about Viscount Braxfield.

It was a non sequitur, to be sure, and while it caused Aunt Vera to stiffen her shoulders as if preparing for a blow, Mrs. Ralston said smoothly, "Ah, Braxfield. A scamp of a man if I've ever met one."

"What interest can you have in Braxfield?" Vera said with a nervous laugh, worried that the reference to a peer nobody in the house had ever mentioned before was further proof that her niece's mind had been corrupted by recent tragic and shocking events, such as the discovery of Mr. Otley's corpse in the library at Lakeview House or the death of her former secret lover, Mr. Davies.

Bea considered teasing her aunt with an oblique response but decided it would not help her goal so she told her the truth. "My soon-to-be-grandmother-by-marriage—that is, the Dowager Duchess of Kesgrave," she explained and paused to look all three guests in the eyes to underscore the august status of her future relations, "informed me during our visit that he was friends with my parents. I hadn't realized that and was hoping to learn a little something about him, as my parents did not have many friends. Unless Mrs. Ralston does not know anything. If that is so, please accept my apology, ma'am, for putting you on the spot."

The social matron tittered, as if being on the spot was quite her favorite place to be, and said, "What nonsense, my dear, for your parents were quite popular and had many friends. There was Lady Abercrombie, who adored your mother, and Mrs. Parmitigan. She hosted a literary salon that only the crème were invited to. I went several times. And Lady Celia. I believe she's Mrs. Porter now. Married beneath herself and her family never forgave her. That happened after your parents' passing, though. And then there were the admirers, for your mother had so many: Mr. Newson, who insisted on writing sonnets to her beauty even though he was a dreadful poet, and Sir Charles, who tried to jump a fence in Hyde Park because your mother was nearby and he hoped to impress her. He failed miserably and got a stern talking-to from the Duke of Tisdale, whose Arabian lost a shoe in the commotion," she recalled and paused to smile as if enjoying the gentleman's humiliation anew. "Richard was never quite as popular, but he was amiable and easygoing, with his own coterie of friends. And he had Wem, of course—the Earl of Wem, that is. Your father had known him his whole life, as Wem's estate marches to the east of yours. He loved both your parents and styled himself as something of your mother's protector. I don't recall their having a particular connection with Braxfield. He was never the type to waste his charms on happily married women, for he liked conquests and relished the irresistible feeling of success."

Although Bea wasn't interested in the viscount's romantic liaisons, she knew it was to her advantage to let the woman say too much rather than too little. Eventually, she would ramble in the right direction, and even if she didn't, the information would not go to waste. The more she knew, the better she could formulate a successful tactic. "Conquests?" she asked, inflecting her voice with a note of salacious interest.

"Oh, my, yes," Mrs. Ralston affirmed with relish. "Braxfield is quite the charmer when he sets his mind to it and is always gathering feathers in his cap—some literal, now that I think about it. Miss Embury-Dennis was persuaded to give him a plume from her bonnet right there in the middle of Bond Street. It was quite a shocking declaration, and as no engagement was announced it made quite the nine days' wonder. That was more than two dozen years ago now, but he has yet to change his way. He still delights in convincing ladies to part with something of significance to demonstrate their affection. That is why he takes especial pleasure in dallying with married ladies, for he loves to flaunt their allegiance in the face of their husbands.

I recall when my friend Delia was coaxed into giving him her fan at Mrs. Givenhall's rout. Her husband was irate."

Aunt Vera, whose face had turned first white and then red in embarrassment over her niece's interest in the viscount's affairs—for goodness' sake, what business was it of hers what that scoundrel had done years ago?—asked if the Ralstons were going to Lord Stirling's ball on Friday. "Lemon ices will be served," she added, as if this were a treat unparalleled in the modern world. "And…um, gooseberry pudding."

Bea bit her lip to keep from smiling at her aunt's brazen attempt to change the subject to something wholly unrelated. "That is good news indeed, for I know you are very fond of gooseberry pudding," she said kindly, before returning to the topic at hand. "What about his political leanings? Did Braxfield take up his seat in Parliament?"

"Not until 1809," Mrs. Ralston said with what Bea considered to be alarming specificity. "I remember because it was after the Battle of Grijó, during the Peninsular War. His sister's husband was killed during the fighting and he wanted to make sure the army was properly outfitted. Nuneaton took up his seat the same year, too."

Bea was startled to hear the name of the viscount who had been a guest with them at Lakeview House and had became a confidante of sorts to her and wondered how he'd entered the picture. "Nuneaton?"

"The son of his brother-in-law, the one who was killed in Portugal," Mrs. Ralston explained with an air of satisfaction. "You did not realize the connection?"

Slowly, she shook her head. "No, I did not realize Nuneaton was Braxfield's nephew. Are they close?"

"Reasonably," Mrs. Ralston said. "I saw them at the theater together only a few weeks ago."

As far as Bea was concerned, this was the best possible news, for she felt quite confident that the viscount could be persuaded to make the introduction. "He resides in London, then?"

"Trifle!" her aunt called out.

Lady Ralston, who had been about to answer, looked at her hostess as if she'd belched into her tea and asked if she was all right. "Can I get you something? Perhaps some wine to aid in your digestion?"

"The Stirling ball will also have trifle," Vera said, her color rising.

"I did not realize you were so enamored of dessert," Mrs. Ralston said, a hint of calculation entering her eyes as her hostess's behavior crossed an unseen line into interesting.

She was recording the story for later, Bea thought.

"Oh, yes, indeed. I'm very fond of sweets. Cakes, puddings, pies. I understand Lord Stirling's ball will have them all," Aunt Vera said, pulling the velvet cord to call the servants. "It will be a very lavish affair, and we should all get as much rest as possible to ensure our fullest enjoyment."

As practical as this statement was, it caused several pairs of eyebrows to dart northward in confusion.

"But the ball is five days away," Esther said.

"How very lucky we are to have so much time to rest," her hostess said with alacrity. "Ah, there is Dawson. Prompt as always, Dawson."

Flora darted a troubled glance at her cousin and then leaped to her feet to assist her mother in seeing their baffled guests off. Bea watched in amazement as Aunt Vera helped Amelia slip on her pelisse, opened the front door and, perhaps most remarkable of all, insisted Mrs. Ralston and her daughters come back for dinner again soon.

"It was such a treat to have you here," she called down the path before closing the door with a thud. "Now I suggest you young ladies get some sleep yourself. You both look exhausted."

Uncle Horace, who was expecting to find a bevvy of females chirping away in his drawing room, was happy to encounter his family in an otherwise empty hallway.

"Right, then, I'm off to my club," he said and sauntered to the door.

Vera yawned widely and announced she was going to read quietly in her room, which was an obvious plumper, for she was almost doggedly illiterate. But she ran up the staircase as if the most consuming tale awaited in her bedchamber, and her daughter and niece were left to marvel over her strange behavior for the next hour.

"I fear it's my fault," Bea said when no other explanation could be found. "She is so worried about what she perceives to be my mental imbalance, her own stability has begun to fray. I can't imagine what she thought I was about to say, but it was clearly something outrageous."

"Was it?" Flora asked.

Bea reviewed the conversation with Mrs. Ralston, with its trivialities about Braxfield's romantic diversions and tales of fine plumage, and decided it had been quite helpful indeed. All she'd really needed to know was that he stood as uncle to Nuneaton. As she'd suspected, letting the gossip speak freely provided her with the opportunity to stumble across the relevant information. For that, Bea was grateful and had intended to do nothing more than express her appreciation sincerely.

"No," she said now in response to her cousin's question. "My reply was to have been the height of mundanity."

CHAPTER SEVEN

Bea was not a fool. She knew the reason sending a missive to arrange a meeting with Nuneaton felt wrong was because it *was* wrong. 'Twas not only the impropriety of convening a secret assignation with the gentleman to whom she had no connection but also the fact that this gentleman in particular had aroused Kesgrave's jealousy before. She had not realized it at the time, of course, for she had no cause to suspect the duke felt anything but scorn and exasperation for her. But now, in retrospect, she knew his angry looks and sullen behavior were the result of his concern that there was something more than friendship between her and the viscount.

She wanted to laugh at the ridiculousness, for anyone who saw Nuneaton, a dandy of such exquisite languor he could barely raise his own eyebrow in contempt of his fellows' poor sartorial choices, would know he could never develop a tendre for someone with her limited advantages. At the same time, she could not entirely dismiss his interest, for he did seem genuinely amused and impressed by her exploits. There had been a moment in the field behind Lakeview House, after she'd escaped from a shed plank by plank, when he had stared at her with deep contemplation and she felt certain he had seen her clearly in a way few ever had.

Since then, he had assisted in her investigations, although not exactly by choice. The precise nature of his participation had mostly been withheld from him.

She considered how much to reveal now as she composed her letter asking for an introduction to his uncle. As the request seemingly came out of nowhere, she knew her cause would be furthered by an explanation. And yet she could not bring herself to give him details because sharing the particulars of a surreptitious plan would feel too much like scheming and she didn't want to scheme with anyone but the duke.

Oddly, guilt wasn't the crushing emotion she felt while affixing her signature to the missive but loneliness. She'd seen Kesgrave the day before and the day before that, and yet it felt as though weeks had passed since she'd last laid eyes on him. Harboring a secret had opened up a gully between them, as wide and vast as the one that had separated them before, and she could hardly comprehend its existence. How absurd it would seem to the Beatrice Hyde-Clare of just three nights ago, who'd proposed to a duke whilst sitting on the chest of a marquess. Then, the bond between them had felt unflinching and resolute, as if sheathed in iron armor like the hull of a ship.

Kesgrave felt the distance too. His pensive looks in the carriage yesterday and in the hallway during the conversation with her aunt revealed an awareness that all was not well. Eventually, he would ask her what was the matter, for he was nothing if not forthright, and she could not fathom how to respond. Inventing a story was intolerable, for lies were the thing she told suspects in her investigations and her aunt and uncle. Without question, the duke deserved better.

By the time she'd handed the envelope to Thomas to ensure its swift delivery, Bea was feeling wholly wretched and she recalled the moment in Lady Abercrombie's drawing room when the countess had tried to put her off with a fiction about a missing locket.

But no, she had to be clever and figure out the truth for herself.

Nuneaton's reply came with reassuring swiftness and he offered to escort her to Lord Pudsey's salon that very evening, which his uncle would be attending to discuss political matters with likeminded associates.

"As I am already accompanying my sister, who shares my uncle's argumentative bent, your presence will be most welcome," he explained in his note.

Whether or not the reference to a chaperone was intended to put her mind at ease, she was grateful to know the outing would conform with propriety in every way.

Circumspection, however, did not guarantee her aunt's approval, and the poor woman tried to dissuade her from attending up until the moment Bea crossed the threshold to leave the house.

"Hyde-Clares do not engage in public debate," she explained, wringing her hands over the prospect of her niece expressing her thoughts in a forthright manner as if they deserved to be heard. "We give our opinions only in response to direct queries. And that is only after every attempt to change the topic to the weather is thwarted."

Flora, who did not share her mother's prejudices against spirited discourse, expressed concern at her joining the viscount for the evening.

"I trust you know what you are about," her cousin had said firmly. But she could not keep the doubt from furling her brow, and Bea felt her uncertainty with every word.

Although Bea had assured her there was no need to show such concern, she felt her own anxiety wind through her as she greeted Mrs. Palmer, a tall woman with wide green eyes and sharp cheekbones. As energetic as her brother was languid, she began by complimenting Bea on her engagement to Kesgrave and immediately pivoted to the matter of the income tax, which, to her grave dissatisfaction, had been repealed only a few days before.

"Beetle-headed shortsightedness, I say! Only a nodcock would believe just because the war is over, our need for funds is too. What about the debt we acquired to pay for our tiff with Napoleon? All those warships! All those muskets! All those soldiers requiring pensions! Where will that money come from? Not from our stores of gold in the national treasury, for the coffers are already depleted. It's the same thing every time. Do you not recall, Miss Hyde-Clare, that they repealed the tax in 1802, after the treaty in Amiens, only to reinstate it a year later? Addington was a fool. Repealing and reinstating as if a tax were a horse you rode in the meadow, fetching it from the stable and returning it when you are done. I tell you, people would not notice it so much if you just stopped fiddling with it. It's infuriating, I say! Simply maddening beyond belief to have to stand by speechlessly while such decisions are made."

"Surely, not speechlessly," Nuneaton teased as the carriage pulled to a stop.

Conceding the truth of the statement, his sister amended it to "powerlessly" and Bea decided she liked her very much.

"I do indeed recall that the prime minister restored the tax almost immediately and agree that it's better to keep it in place to protect against unexpected expenses, which all governments accrue, for all it takes is one bad growing season to undermine the security of a nation," Bea said graciously. "But I understand the desire for relief and wonder if it would not have been better to simply return the rate to five percent, as in Addington's original proposal."

Mrs. Palmer stared aghast at Bea. "By all that is holy, an educated female! What on earth are you doing associating with my woolly crown of a brother? No matter," she said, linking her arm through Bea's as they strolled up the path to Pudsey's town house. "You are in safe hands now and will not have to hear another word about Schweitzer."

"Good God, Katie, you do me a gross disservice," Nuneaton cried, genuinely appalled by the charge. "To imply that I would visit a Cork Street tailor and one with a military bent, as well. I am no Brummell to content myself with plain fabrics and severe cuts. Bah!" He shuddered with seemingly sincere horror, though Bea felt certain she detected a hint of mockery in his eyes. "I give my custom to Weston, who appreciates the value of a pleat with an almost religious fervor."

Mrs. Palmer shook her head sadly and apologized to Bea for failing her so quickly. "Here I am, promising to save you from my brother's peculiar passions, and instead I subject you to yet more lectures on tailors."

"Yet more?" Nuneaton said with a cocked eyebrow. "How many lectures on tailors do you suppose I give weekly?"

His sister hazarded several dozens, and Nuneaton darted a pained look at Bea before saying, "I invited you in hopes that your presence would lessen the abuse I suffer from my older sister, not double it."

Bea laughed. "Now I must apologize for failing you."

"Nonsense," Mrs. Palmer said, "he failed himself by having unreasonable expectations. Now, shall we go in? As you may have perceived from our carriage ride, I'm most impatient to discuss my dissatisfaction over the repeal of the income tax with those who supported it. Do stick close to me, Miss Hyde-Clare, and I will ensure you do not miss out on any of the fun."

"Fun," her brother muttered under his breath as the front door opened and the butler admitted them.

Although the salon was not as well attended as the last rout Bea had gone to, it was more crowded than she'd expected, with dozens of people arrayed around the drawing room, which was appointed in shades of green and gold. True to her word, Mrs. Palmer sought out the men she considered most responsible for the tax's repeal, starting with their host, who listened to her complaint with a bland smile on his face, as if accustomed to these reprimands.

"You flatter me as always, Mrs. Palmer," he said evenly when she paused to gather her breath, "with your belief that I hold the fate of our country in the palm of my little hand."

"And as always, I'm not fooled by your display of humility, for I know it is not supported by fact," she responded coolly before resuming her attack.

Lord Pudsey's expression did not change during the assault, but as soon as it was clear his guest was finished, he thanked Bea for attending ("Always a pleasure to welcome a fresh face to our little gathering") and quickly excused himself.

Mrs. Palmer let out a gratified sigh and said, "On to our next victim."

Although Bea did not think the use of *our* was in any way accurate, she was delighted to be considered an ally and happily followed her across the room to Lord Tierney. As she did, she passed Nuneaton, whose inquisitive look conveyed concern for her circumstance, and she assured him with a smile that she was content to remain in his sister's care.

Lord Tierney's dismissive attitude was very similar to Lord Pudsey's, and it matched the tone of Lord Brockstone, with whom they spoke next, and Bea bristled at the condescension. It became clear that the men were unable to take an opinion expressed by a woman seriously when she heard a peer in a jonquil waistcoat make the same argument about replenishing the nation's treasury and his listeners nodded as if he had made a thoughtful but misguided point. Then they proceeded to debate the matter, a courtesy none had paid to Mrs. Palmer.

No wonder she protested so vociferously. It was the only power she had.

Bea began to join her in the tirade just to increase the amount of time their victim—and, yes, *their* was an accurate term now—had to suffer in polite silence. That she enjoyed adding to their annoyance did not come as a surprise, for she had discovered she harbored a perverse nature when she started to take pleasure in pricking Kesgrave's vanity.

"You are doing very well, my dear," her new friend observed as Mr. Darber scurried away in search of a glass of port. "I would suggest one small modification, if you will. Repeat your point about lowering the tax to only five percent two additional times. Members of the House of Lords consider themselves men of action and abhor the notion of moderation. They're extremists at heart, though they are hardly able to articulate that fact about themselves. But whatever their delusions about themselves, they are who they are and hate to be reminded of what they aren't."

Bea adored her philosophizing and, desiring to hear more, asked why she should repeat it twice more.

"In my experience, three is the number of times a man can hear an argument before being compelled to refute it," she explained. "I learned this from my husband, who is particularly adept at ignoring my opinions. I'd still be living in a dark town house in Little Titchfield Street if I hadn't discovered the benefits of repeating myself three times. You see, you cannot win an argument if your opponent refuses to engage in one with you. Now we are in Wimpole Street next to Lord Harpenden, who is, for the record, an exception to the rule of three repetitions. With Harpenden, you have to repeat your point five times before getting a rise out of him, but once you do, he's comically easy to win over. Although he considers himself quite an impressive thinker, his brain is pleasingly malleable. Once you've dismantled his argument, there's really nothing left of him but his powdered wig and the stench of snuff. Ah, here's my uncle Braxfield."

To say that Bea froze upon hearing his name would be to overstate her reaction, but she certainly started at discovering her quarry was so near.

"Uncle, darling, do let me have the pleasure of

introducing my dear friend Miss Hyde-Clare. We met little above an hour ago, but she has all the right opinions, so I'm determined to adopt her," she said in greeting.

Given what she had heard of his lordship's romantic conquests from Mrs. Ralston and his pugnacity from Mr. Jeffries, Bea expected him to cut a dashing figure, with a handsome visage and a powerful build. Instead, she was greeted with a figure not much larger than she, with a narrow chin, a slight nose and ears that seemed to meet his head at an almost perfect corner.

When he spoke, however, his voice was smooth and assured, with an appealing huskiness. "Then it's my pleasure as well," he assured his niece before turning his green gaze to Bea. "It's rare to meet someone who has *all* the right opinions, Miss Hyde-Clare, and I am enchanted by the novelty. I'm also impressed with anyone who can earn my niece's approval, for she withholds it more than she bestows it. It has been more than three decades for me, but I'm still holding out hope that one day I may pass muster."

His eyes were as warm as his tone, and Bea could now see the charming gentleman Mrs. Ralston described, the one who secured hearts and tokens. "As much as I value Mrs. Palmer's esteem, I fear she simply hasn't discovered yet which of my opinions are wrong."

"And she's modest," Braxfield said with approval. "You must adopt her posthaste before her clear thinking is corrupted by old reprobates like me."

"My uncle believes quite vehemently in the repeal of the income tax," Mrs. Palmer explained. "He also supported the Importation Act because it benefits landowners such as himself at the expense of the poor. Is it any wonder, then, that he has failed to earn my approval?"

Braxfield shook his head and laughed, as if genuinely amused by her antics. "My niece, the Whig."

Mrs. Palmer protested the designation. "I refuse to align myself with any particular group, for the moment I do so it inevitably promotes a policy or position with which I stridently disagree. My uncle does not suffer from this problem and will join any group that will have him. Would you believe he was once a member of the English Correspondence Guild? And *he* calls *me* a Whig."

At the mention of the society, at the reference to the *precise* reason she was there, at Lord Pudsey's salon, Bea's heart stopped and she thought she heard a buzzing in her ear.

Surely, it was a ruse or a trap or part of some dastardly scheme to...to...

There, Bea's imagination collided with a brick wall because she couldn't think of a single thing Mrs. Palmer would stand to gain from tricking her into revealing what she knew about the English Correspondence Guild.

"It was a radical organization that sought the franchisement of beggars and thieves," Braxfield said to Bea.

"Which you joined," his niece added with a mischievous grin.

"Which I infiltrated," he clarified almost on a sigh, as if tired of having to make the distinction.

Listening to them banter, Bea realized that he had in fact said this very thing many times before. His stint in the guild had clearly passed into family lore and provided his niece with a most cherished topic for teasing.

"Ah, yes, that's what he likes to tell us—that he joined the radicals for God and country," Mrs. Palmer said before asserting in a teasing tone. "He had no sympathy for their cause."

"I *had* no sympathy for their cause," he insisted. "I *did* join for God and country. Everything I learned, I reported to the Crown at my own peril."

Even as the truth sunk in, Bea still could not trust her good fortune, for it seemed to be in excess of what a human being could reasonably expect. Not only had the topic been raised in the most natural way possible, it had been done without any assistance from her. Nothing about the exchange suggested the coolheaded implementation of a scheme.

Nuneaton wasn't even in the room.

Surely, Kesgrave would have no cause to object.

"My uncle likes to portray his time with the guild as daring and full of peril, but it was actually quite dull," Mrs. Palmer explained to Bea, her eyes twinkling with humor. "He tried his hardest to rile them to rebellion, but they preferred the pen to the sword."

Lord Braxfield smiled without offense. "Alas, there she speaks the truth. Every time I thought I'd stirred the members to rise up like proper insurrectionists, they'd write another demmed political treatise. As a man of action who is ready to defend his beliefs with his fists if necessary, I was driven to distraction by their passivity. Katie laughs, but they were still dangerous men for all that. Their ideas could have brought our country to its knees as they had France. I consider the work I did important and know it was instrumental in drafting the legislation that made reform societies illegal."

Mrs. Palmer shook her head sadly. "'Tis our family's secret shame."

"What shame?" her uncle asked. "I proclaim it proudly."

"Yes," she said, "and *that* is the shame."

As this censure, too, appeared familiar to the viscount, Bea decided the moment was not a sensitive one and raised the issue of her parents. "I wonder, my lord, if you knew my parents, Clara and Richard Hyde-Clare. They also joined the English Correspondence Guild at the behest of the government. They did it at the request of Mr. Pitt."

Far from being surprised by this extraordinary coincidence, Mrs. Palmer considered it an affirmation of her instincts. "La, I must adopt her at once!"

"Richard and Clara? Yes, of course," he said thoughtfully after a brief moment of consideration. "Yes, I knew them. Mr. Barlow and Mr. Piper—if I'm remembering their aliases correctly. Your mother was one of the most beautiful women I have ever seen. So you are their daughter. I wonder how I did not make the connection myself."

If he remembered her mother as an Incomparable, then Bea thought it was hardly surprising the connection eluded him. "It is a pleasure to meet someone who knew my parents. They died while I was barely out of leading strings, so I know little about them. Lady Abercrombie very kindly gave me my mother's letters, which is how I know she and my father spied on the organization."

"I fear the word *spy* rather misstates the case, my dear," he said with amusement. "Although Pitt sent your father in to collect damning information about the guild, he was swayed by their rhetoric. Your mother too, though God knows what he was thinking, allowing her to consort with those ruffians. They both became believers, subscribing to the concept of universal suffrage as if giving uneducated farmers and bootmakers a say in the government would not destroy the entire apparatus. Richard and Clara Hyde-Clare." He shook his head, recalling them. "Charmingly naïve they were. I liked them both, especially your mother. She was a rare one. Beautiful and spirited with a mind of her own. You don't come across that combination often."

Although Lady Abercrombie had told her about her mother and Clara's own letters had provided some insight into how she thought, Bea still knew very little about her parents and it lightened her heart to hear him echo the countess's lovely description of her mother. "You were members at the same time as they?"

"I was, yes. Pitt was not satisfied with the information your father provided, for he was insistent the group was no threat. Obviously, that could not be true, so I was asked to step in to get a proper perspective. I could see at once what had happened. That your mother was won over, I could understand because she had a sympathetic female mind," he said, glancing at his niece the Whig who wasn't a Whig. "But there was no excuse for Richard. He should have known better, and we quarreled about it often. I am a fair man and can concede that the founder himself was a rational creature whose intelligence I admired. His casting a vote would not have undermined the kingdom. But the others…"

He trailed off, his inability to even articulate their many shortcomings a condemnation in itself.

But Bea could not let the abbreviated thought stand because it was precisely to gather the names of the others that she had arranged the meeting.

"You mean Mr. Jeffries, I suppose," she said consideringly. "My mother mentioned him in her letters as a worthy individual whom she respected. But his lieutenants, the men he relied upon most—their names escape me at the moment—she did not have such kind words for."

"Berks and Thorpe," the viscount supplied accommodatingly.

"Yes, of course," she nodded as if she'd heard them before. "My mother described them as rough men."

"Rough men?" he repeated, tilting his head to the side as he rubbed his pointed chin. "A mild description, perhaps, for I would call them brutes, but nonetheless accurate."

Knowing their surnames would certainly help her locate them, but more information would facilitate the task. "Is it any surprise, given their occupations?"

It was a leading question, to be sure, but Bea assumed either direction—affirmation or disavowal—would provide an answer.

Once again, Braxfield obliged. "You are right, of course. Clockmakers and weavers and all tradesmen are cut from the same rough cloth. They should be grateful that men such as I care enough to look out for their welfare."

"By raising the price of grain," his niece said.

"By abolishing the income tax," Braxfield asserted before calling to a younger man who was briskly crossing the room to the refreshment table. "Villiers, I don't believe you've had the pleasure of being scolded by my darling niece yet, for I've been selfishly monopolizing her attention, which is beyond everything rude, especially as I will be seeing her again on Thursday for the theater. There's a good chap. Now, I strongly advise you not to make that petrified face, for she can be quite a bully if she senses fear. I should think you'd remember that from last time."

"You are running away from me," Mrs. Palmer observed with unrestrained glee.

He made no attempt to deny it. "Always, my dear, and whenever I can. It was an exquisite pleasure, Miss Hyde-Clare, to meet the daughter of Richard and Clara. Villiers, my condolences on your misfortune."

Although Bea would have liked to talk to him more about the English Correspondence Guild, she could not object to his departure. It was extremely doubtful he would be able to tell her anything more about Berks and Thorpe, such as what had become of them or their current location.

She had gotten precisely the information she had come there to get and should be satisfied.

Ah, but he had dropped such tantalizing tidbits about her parents' involvement in the group, and she wanted to hear more. It was gratifying, to be sure, to know they had agreed with the guild's principles, for they seemed to Beatrice to be reasonable. If parliamentary decisions were to have a bearing on every aspect of every man's life, then every man should have a say in who got to make those decisions.

Indeed, it struck her as a rather modest goal, and if she were to helm a radical society, her demands would be much greater, such as providing basic provisions for the poor and making it against the law to use small children to clean chimneys.

While Bea outlined the agenda for her fictional organization, Mrs. Palmer ascertained Mr. Villiers's stance on the matter of income taxation and took him to task for having the wrong one. Although almost the same age as his tormentor, he appeared to grow younger and younger the longer she talked, and it was only when Nuneaton came over to lead them to the buffet table that she ceased her harangue.

"My dear sir, you appear famished," Mrs. Palmer said

to her victim, who, looking more weary than hungry, could not help but flinch when she linked her arm through his. "Let us get you sustenance so you may continue with your spirited defense of a wrongheaded position."

"Knowing Katie, I cannot believe *continue* is the correct word," Nuneaton said in amusement, "for she would never have let him begin."

"She is a marvel," Bea said with sincere admiration.

"Yes, that is certainly one way to describe my sister. I see you succeeded in your goal to have a word with my uncle. I trust it was all that you required?" he said, his tone rising at the end to make it a question.

"I did, yes," she said simply. "Thank you."

"As closemouthed as ever, I see," he said, not altogether disapprovingly. "Very well, you may keep your secrets, for I am far too grateful to plague you for information. This is by far the most pleasant political salon I've been coerced into attending, and if I weren't worried about Kesgrave's strongly worded objection, I would insist you accompany me to every one."

Guilt twisted inside her at this statement—and it was not merely the mention of the duke that reignited her remorse. It was the way it laid bare the truth and deprived her of the comfortable fiction she had told herself. She had come there in his company, not his sister's.

It was still a scheme.

She absorbed the sensation, wondering how it could feel so much like a betrayal when she had spoken but a few words to the viscount all evening, and asked by what method his attendance was coerced.

"To answer that question," he said, "I must start by explaining a couple of things. One, my brother-in-law loathes politics. Two, he cheats at cards."

"That is quite a serious allegation," she said, understanding at once that he'd lost a bet in what he believed was an unfair contest. "Men's reputations have been destroyed by far less."

"Indeed. But I know you will not bandy it about. You will note, I hope, the level of trust I'm displaying," he said, casting her an aggrieved look out of the corner of his eye. "I don't doubt for a moment that you will refrain from bandying about my brother-in-law's perfidy."

Bea laughed. "Too grateful to plague me, are you?"

"I am merely following the dictates of the Bible," he explained.

"The Bible, my lord?" she asked.

"Do unto others. Now can I interest you in something to eat? The options here are considerably more appealing than the meats boiled to gray perfection on offer at the last sideboard we examined together," he said in reference to the Red Corner House, a gambling establishment to which he had escorted her during her last investigation.

Kesgrave, suspecting she would visit the hell in open defiance of his prohibition not to, had appeared just as she was laughing at one of Nuneaton's sallies.

The duke had that way about him—the disconcerting habit of showing up where one least expected him.

Bea almost believed it would happen now and glanced around the room, as if to meet his insufferably satisfied gaze.

Of course she did not and yet she felt an inexplicable stab of disappointment at this proof of his lack of omniscience. How easily the matter would be resolved if Kesgrave simply inserted himself now as he had in the past. Then the decision would be made for her.

'Twas the coward's path, she knew.

Resolutely, she turned her thoughts to other things, acquiescing to Nuneaton's suggestion that she try the ham and explaining to Villiers the advantages of dropping the tax to five percent at Mrs. Palmer's prompting.

"See?" the woman said cajolingly. "It doesn't have to be all or nothing. We could test the benefits of moderation before eliminating the tax entirely. Think of the coffers, sir, languishing in their emptiness. It makes me despondent.

Do you not find it equally despairing, Miss Hyde-Clare?"

Bea avoided the viscount's amused gaze as she testified to the depth of her despair. Then she added with excessive lachrymosity for the benefit of her new friend, "That poor last farthing, languishing alone at the bottom."

Mrs. Palmer clapped, quite ruining the effect.

In the carriage ride home, she insisted that Beatrice join her for tea sometime in the coming week. "I'm sure you're run off your feet with betrothal commitments, but if you had enough time to come berate politicians with me this evening, I'm sure you have enough time for tea. I will send around a note."

Nuneaton made a valiant effort to intercede on her behalf, but his sister would not be dissuaded, and Bea, who had few friends, could not imagine being so busy as to be unable to manage a pot of tea in Wimpole Street.

"When my sister bores you to flinders with politics, you will recall, I hope, that I tried to save you," his lordship said as he escorted her to the door.

"What I recall is she said the same thing about you and your tailor," Bea observed, smiling.

He conceded the truth with a bow and bid her good night as soon as Dawson opened the door. Bea entered the house, pleased to discover her family was still out for the evening. Grateful to be spared the inquisition, she retired to her room and changed into her nightclothes. As her mind was still humming with Braxfield's revelations and her own guilt, she picked up the history of Renaissance painting she had started the night before, read a few dozen pages until she was too tired to think and promptly fell asleep.

CHAPTER EIGHT

By the time Bea joined her family at the breakfast table the next morning, she was so consumed by the challenge of finding Misters Berks and Thorpe that the curious way she had gotten their names had quite slipped her mind.

Her first thought, naturally, had been to return to the Addison to scour the newspapers for references to the men. She still imagined the search would be long and tedious, but having two names gave her something specific to look for and she was convinced that would make the task somewhat easier.

But having their names and professions did not mean she could easily find their directions. Any newspaper reference she managed to locate would probably cite the guild's headquarters rather than their particular shops. And if the article was so obliging as to provide specifics, it was unlikely the men still resided at those addresses. Mr. Jeffries had been a lucky stroke, and she could not depend on it happening again.

She had little cause to be optimistic.

Furthermore, slipping out of the house unnoticed this morning would not be as easy as it had been two days ago, for her aunt would not blithely allow her to go shopping with Lady Abercrombie again. The countess's modiste was in the wrong part of town, situated in the heart of Mayfair, in Bond Street next to Mrs. Duval, which was far too fashionable for the Hyde-Clares, who preferred Miss Scribe's modest shop. The Amwell Street establishment was filled with moderately appealing dresses that kept one's desire for pretty things easily in check.

No, there had to be a better, more reliable method for finding the men. They were tradesmen, were they not, and as such were members of a specific guild. Mr. Berks, for example, should belong to the clockmakers guild. Did the guild advertise its wares? Did it publish a list and distribute it to the public?

"Tell us, my dear, how is the state of the country?" Aunt Vera asked as her niece sat down. "Are we on the verge of a peasant uprising or are the reports of unrest in Middlewich greatly exaggerated?"

Bea looked at her relative in confusion.

"Middleham," Uncle Horace said from behind the newspaper he was reading, correcting his wife's understanding of current events. "Middlewich is in Cheshire."

"Then where is Middleham?" his wife asked.

"Yorkshire," he said.

"Is that a distinction really worth making?" Flora wondered. "They're both frightfully north."

"Middleham is where Henry the Third was raised," Russell explained patiently.

"Richard the Third," Uncle Horace said, his voice rippling with irritation as his eyes remained focused on newsprint. "Cheshire is south of the Lake District."

"Then where was Henry the Third raised?" Russell asked.

"Up north," said Flora.

"Hampshire," her father said.

"Yes, that is what I said," Flora explained.

Unable to bear his children's ignorance of historical and geographic matters, Uncle Horace struck the table with his newspaper and left it lying next to his plate as he bounded out of the room.

"Now see what you did," Vera said heatedly to her niece.

Bea, whose bewilderment had grown with each inaccurate assertion, looked around to make sure her aunt wasn't addressing someone standing silently behind her.

"Well you look blameless! But I'm not fooled. Did you or did you not go to Lord Pudsey's salon last evening to discuss politics?" Aunt Vera asked angrily.

Her niece resisted the absurd impulse to hang her head in shame. "I did."

Aunt Vera nodded. "After you finish your breakfast, you will apologize to your uncle and assure him his daughter knows very well Hampshire is in the east, near Norwich."

"It's on the southern coast, near Portsmouth," Bea said.

Aunt Vera colored slightly and muttered, "Rude girl."

To appease her, Bea agreed to seek out her uncle as soon as the meal had concluded. Then she calmly thanked Thomas for filling her teacup and accepted a plate of eggs and a roll. As she buttered the bread, she returned to the puzzling matter of locating Berks and Thorpe. If pamphlets of tradesmen did exist, then presumably they were distributed to people who were in need of their skills.

Had just such a publication been delivered to her house?

"Do not think I haven't noticed how you cleverly evaded answering my question," Aunt Vera said.

Once again, Bea turned to her aunt with bewildered eyes.

"Lord Pudsey's salon?" Vera said impatiently. "How was it?"

"Ah, yes," Bea said with what she hoped was a conciliatory smile. "It was quite enjoyable, thank you."

"Sounds dreadfully dull to me," Russell said. "A bunch of starched politicians engaging in high-minded debate."

"Did you engage in high-minded debate with starched politicians?" Flora asked, a little in awe of the prospect.

Bea recalled Mrs. Palmer's unwieldy method of browbeating her fellow guests. "It was more like heavy-handed persuasion."

"And Nuneaton?" Flora said. "Was his persuasion heavy-handed as well?"

"Nuneaton?" Aunt Vera said sharply. "You went with Nuneaton?"

"And his sister," Bea replied promptly. "A remarkable woman who taught me the finer points of political discourse."

Her aunt put little stock in the presence of a female sibling. "I do hope you're not planning to throw over a duke for a viscount, for there is no advantage to be gained from the demotion. If you were willing to settle for a baronet, I would support it, for that would be a vast improvement."

Bea resisted the urge to smile.

"Speaking of Kesgrave," Flora said, "I need a new gown for the Stirling ball on Friday."

"What does Kesgrave have to do with your wardrobe?" her brother asked, his tone rising in suspicion.

"Now that I am going to be cousin-in-law to a duke, my dresses must rise to the level of my new status," she explained. "Is that not correct, Mama?"

Aunt Vera spared a seething look at her niece before half-heartedly agreeing with Flora. "But that doesn't necessarily mean an entire closetful of new clothes. We can purchase a few judicious pieces to elevate your look in general."

As practical as this cautious plan was, Russell was incensed by what he considered to be his sister's windfall. "If she needs new dresses because she will be cousin-in-law to a duke, then surely my requirements must increase as well. I must have lessons with Gentleman Jackson, as a knowledge of the pugilist arts is de rigueur for men of my new station. Only a few weeks ago you said I may take them, Mama, and then promptly withheld the funds."

Now Vera glared at Bea, who tried to appear contrite by staring down at her plate. For a moment the room was so silent, you could hear the clock ticking and Bea looked up sharply.

"Who repairs our clocks?" she asked.

Vera swung her head around as if some part of her

niece's brain had suddenly become dislodged. Had she really just asked about the clocks?

Unaware of her mother's surprise, Flora asked what she meant by *judicious pieces,* for the term was quite open to interpretation. "Do you mean just a new handkerchief or something wonderful and sparkly like diamond earrings?"

Bea, convinced she had stumbled upon the perfect avenue of investigation, elaborated by asking if the family had a particular clockmaker to fix the devices when they fell into disrepair. "That is, we don't hire a different one each time, do we?"

If the Hyde-Clares gave their custom to a particular clockmaker, then she could enlist him in her efforts to discover the whereabouts of Mr. Berks. She felt certain the community of London clockmakers could not be very large and that the members all knew one another. Without question, it was a smaller group than weavers, for cloth was a necessity and far more common.

"Why in the world…"

But unable to finish the thought, Vera merely shook her head.

Bea, realizing her aunt would be of no help, resolved to put the question to her uncle when she sought him out with her apology, tilted her head down again and picked up her fork to eat her eggs.

"I say, if Flora is to get a pair of diamond earrings, then I must insist on a new mount," Russell announced forcefully. "Fair is fair, after all."

Alas, Flora considered such a proposal to be patently unjust, as the extravagance of a new horse far exceeded the luxury of diamond studs, and immediately began to design a piece of jewelry of equal worth. "If Russell gets a new horse, then I want a bracelet with…diamonds and…and rubies and emeralds and sapphires."

At the mention of sapphires, all the muscles left Bea's body and her fork clattered to her plate.

Aunt Vera shrieked at the clanging sound and cried,

"Good God, Beatrice, have you not tried my nerves enough this morning!"

But her niece did not hear her, for she was no longer at the breakfast table with her family but several blocks away in a drawing room in Clarges Street. The dowager had said something about a bracelet with sapphires. What was it?

She closed her eyes and pictured the scene: the velvet curtains, the forest green settee, the beautifully carved table where Sutton had laid the tea. They were talking about her mother, whom the dowager said she had known, though not well, and she mentioned a bracelet.

Her mother's sapphire bracelet!

Yes, that was right.

She recalled the dowager's exact words: *She said it was a beloved heirloom from your father she couldn't bear to take off.*

Bea had no beloved heirloom from her mother. Indeed, she had nothing from either parent, and the only item she had managed to secure for herself as a small child—a lone, threadbare glove that still smelled of her mother—had been ruthlessly discarded by her aunt, who called it a worthless rag. Everything else, she'd been told, had been sold off to pay for her upkeep.

But even her uncle, with his small-minded bitterness and frugality, would not sell a family heirloom. He would preserve its dignity by giving it to his wife. Aunt Vera had her mother's beloved bracelet.

"I say, my dear, it's most dreadfully rude of you to close your eyes when I am speaking to you," Aunt Vera complained sharply.

Bea's eyes popped open, and she sent her aunt such a scathing look the other woman shrunk back in her chair. Making no effort to explain her behavior or excuse herself from the table, she rose to her feet and left the room.

Undaunted now that her niece no longer faced her, Aunt Vera called after her departing back, "Do make sure to remind your uncle he's meeting with the steward at once."

Sparing no thought for her uncle, Bea climbed the

stairs and entered her aunt's bedchamber, a room as aggressively self-effacing as its inhabitant, with well-worn fabrics everywhere and curtains such a dull-colored gray, they seemed to disappear before your eyes. Although every other room in the house had been redone at least once, including Bea's, Aunt Vera insisted she wasn't worthy of the expense.

"Why should I care what it looks like?" she often said. "My eyes are closed whilst I sleep."

The sitting room, where she spent many hours with her eyes open, was in equally poor repair. The divan was recently of the servants' quarters, which had been granted the luxury of the drawing room's old settee when Uncle Horace bought a new one because he could no longer find a comfortable spot on the lumpy cushion. The other pieces also showed their wear, and Bea was able to open the iron chest with little effort, for the wood was so rotted it offered no protection against thieves.

Inside, she found her aunt's favorite necklace, a few rings she sometimes wore, a gold bracelet with a broken latch, some brooches, several pairs of earrings and a tiara.

No sapphire bracelet.

Disgusted, Bea left the jewelry in a disorganized pile and moved on to the clothespress. She had little interest in disguising her efforts and rummaged through her aunt's things with an impatient roughness that left a mess behind.

Thirty minutes later, she was forced to concede the bracelet was not in Aunt Vera's bedchamber.

Her blood still pounding with outrage, she considered where else it could be. In her uncle's rooms, among his papers and waistcoats?

She closed her eyes and tried to picture her uncle hiding a valuable family heirloom but could not make the image appear. Miserliness of that ilk more closely aligned with her aunt's modus operandi, for she had been as parsimonious in her affection as she had in details about Bea's parents.

There had been a very great rift between the brothers, she knew, and Vera had eagerly taken up the resentment like any dutiful wife, but that antipathy did not justify their treatment of her. Indeed, it should have died with the parents and not been visited upon the daughter.

How different her life would have been if Aunt Vera had only let her hold on to that keepsake of her mother's, as ragged and stained and worn as the glove had been. If she'd had just that much generosity in her heart.

Determinedly, Bea forwent searching Uncle Horace's possessions in favor of ransacking the linen storage room, whose organization her aunt oversaw with the precision of a general.

What was she trying to hide with her careful management?

A dozen minutes later, after the room's contents had been strewn on the floor, she was forced to concede that Aunt Vera had concealed nothing save the good linens, which she refused to use lest they become the bad linens.

Although her inability to find the bracelet indicated that it was not in the house, she reminded herself that a lack of evidence was not proof and marched upstairs to the attic just as one of the maids reached the landing of the third floor.

Noting Bea's direction, she called, "Can I help ye, miss?"

Bea did not bother to respond as she climbed to the attic, which housed the maids' quarters and a small room that her aunt used for storing old embroidery samplers and things she could not bear to throw away, such as a particularly ugly tea set her mother-in-law had given her during her first year of marriage.

She knew this because she and Flora had once sneaked into the room during a game of hide-and-seek, and poor Russell, unable to find them, began to cry uncontrollably because he assumed fairies had stolen them away. A few minutes later, Aunt Vera had come upon them, irate at their invading the privacy of the servants and insistent that they come down immediately. Before she had arrived, they had opened the first chest and laid out a pretend tea party.

Bea recalled the scene now as she entered the dark room and remembered how sweet Flora had been when she was only four or five, following her big cousin around and seeking her attention.

It was a period that had not lasted very long.

As thin as the light was in the narrow space, Bea could see the contents clearly: two large chests pressed against the long walls, a pair of smaller chests on top of each. She tried to recall which one had stored the tea set and samplers, but it was an impossible endeavor after so many years.

She started with the stack of chests on the right side, searching through the top one, which contained dozens of old books. Ledgers going back decades, she realized. She closed it and moved it to the center of the floor. Then she opened the next chest.

Ah, there was the tea set.

And it was just as awful as she remembered it, with oversize purple plums and disconcertingly fat green grapes hanging from thin, bare branches.

Laughing softly, she confirmed that it contained only the tea set and embroidered samplers. Then she placed it on the floor beside the other chest.

Now the large one, she thought, raising the lid, which was unexpectedly heavy, and immediately spotted something of interest: a handkerchief with a monogram. It was too dark to see in the dusky light, so she held it up to the narrow window and deciphered the intricate design: CDHC.

Beatrice's breath hitched as she realized it was her mother's and, suddenly feeling shaky, she sat down on one of the other chests. With grateful fingers she clutched the delicate silk square and raised it to her nose, foolishly hoping it still smelled like her mother—as if she had any idea what her mother smelled like.

Inevitably, it smelled like a musky attic, but nevertheless she thought it was the most beautiful scent in the world.

Calmly, almost peacefully, she looked through the contents of the chest, finding other possessions of her parents': an assortment of her father's snuffboxes, her mother's hair ornaments, a book of poems by Donne transcribed with "love everlasting" to her mother from her father, pristine gloves, more handkerchiefs, a riding crop, a red dress trimmed in lavishly embroidered lace, a partially torn hat with a wide crown and, at the very bottom, several dozen sheets of paper tied together with a silk ribbon.

It appeared to be a manuscript, and very carefully, Bea lifted it out of the chest. She read the title, "A Case for Equality Between the Sexes: Being an Elaboration on and Examination of Mary Wollstonecraft's *A Vindication of the Rights of Women*."

The handwriting, Bea thought as she raised the top sheet in the weak sunlight. It looked like her mother's.

Was it possible?

Could her mother have actually written an academic treatise calling for the elevation of female rights?

An unbearable excitement overcame her as she began to read the introduction, which took as its starting point Wollstonecraft's work and announced clearly and plainly how it would address the other authoress's points.

Her mother began by identifying three central reforms *Vindication* advocated for: the right of women to receive a useful education on practical matters that transcended domestic concerns; the ability of women to earn their own livings so they could support themselves; the establishment of government-supported education for all children in which girls would learn alongside boys.

Clara lauded these goals very highly, then proceeded to dismantle the arguments by which Wollstonecraft substantiated her demands, dismissing her justifications as "sugar to make a bitter fruit palatable."

"Herein," her mother promised, "you will find nothing to sweeten the case for female equality. Whereas Wollstonecraft sheathes her argument for female education in the comforting smock of motherhood to ensure the proper instruction of the young, I argue for the value of education for its own sake, for the purity of knowledge gained. Ultimately, Wollstonecraft validates the opening of the female mind by explaining its value to society: An educated woman is a virtuous woman. I will make no such promise, however it endears me to my readership and allows me to escape censure. I will promise only this: An educated woman is an educated woman."

Breathlessly, Bea turned the page, her eyes flying across the sheet as Clara joined Wollstonecraft in excoriating Rousseau, whose belief that women existed only to please and accommodate men she herself had found to be particularly infuriating. Indeed, she had been unable to read *Emile* without throwing the book across the room any number of times in disgust.

Now she imagined her mother doing the same thing, and tears began to slide down her cheeks. Terrified the drops might smudge the writing, she tilted her head up and found herself looking directly into the snow-white face of her aunt.

It was shocking to see, how tightly her skin seemed to pull against her skull, like a bed linen stretched to its limits, and Bea wondered if the woman was about to faint.

As if she shared the concern, Aunt Vera clutched the doorway, and as she sunk slowly to the floor, her skirt settled around her legs in an undignified heap.

"I knew this day would come," she said softly, no hint of anger in her tone or disapproval. Only resignation. "I allowed myself to think it otherwise, but you were always too clever for your own good. I knew it that very first day they brought you here. You said something about your uncle—I cannot recall what precisely, just that it had to do with the color of his stockings, and it was precociously insightful—and I knew in that moment this day would come."

Although Bea thought Aunt Vera's demeanor was overwrought for the situation, for all that had happened was she discovered that her mother was a radical thinker who fearlessly expressed her ideas, a sudden chill swept through her and her hand began to shake.

Defensively, she said, "It's only a manuscript."

"Yes," her aunt agreed, "but no."

The cold spread to Bea's shoulders, and she wrapped her arms around herself, her mother's treatise clutched tightly against her breast. "I don't know what that means."

Aunt Vera shifted her positions so that she was leaning against the wall, her legs drawn to her chest, as if seeking warmth as well. "That manuscript. It's not just what your mother wrote, it's what she believed."

Bea resisted the urge to make a snide remark, for one hardly wrote a treatise in support of ideas to which one didn't subscribe. Instead, she nodded.

"I do not know how far you got in the manuscript but there is a section in which she describes a concept she called equality of love," her aunt said. "In it, she addresses the difference in society's expectations for female virtue versus male virtue. I am to understand this topic is discussed in Wollstonecraft's book as well. Where the original calls for men to adhere to the same standard as women, your mother…" She paused, breaking eye contact with her niece for the first time since sliding to the floor, and stared down at her hands, which were tightly grasped. "Your mother calls for women to adhere to the same standard as men. She believed they may be…free…with their bodies and suffer no moral consequences."

Bea nodded again, as this information did not sound particularly evil to her. It was not how she would advise anyone to behave, but it wasn't very different from how Lady Abercrombie conducted her affairs and she was not wicked or shunned by society.

There's more, she realized as the cold settled in her stomach.

"I explain this only as a way to provide context for what happened next," her aunt said.

Nothing in Bea's life had ever sounded as ominous as the phrase *what happened next,* and her entire body began to shiver in earnest. She made no attempt to stop it.

"Your mother, practicing her beliefs, had an affair," Aunt Vera said.

Even as the tears clogged her throat, Bea's mind remained clear. "How do you know that?" she asked calmly, her voice displaying none of the defensive bent of earlier. Now she was merely gathering information in support of a conclusion.

"The Earl of Wem," she said simply. "He told me. After they…after they had passed, he came to see us. He was your father's oldest and dearest friend. He grew up in the same county, went to school with Richard, even introduced him to Clara. He was heartsick over the whole thing. Naturally, he had no choice but to tell your father everything he knew—honor demanded it. And then…when they were gone…he came to pay his respects to your uncle and the whole sordid story came pouring out. He did not want to tell us but seemed incapable of keeping it to himself. I did not believe it at first. We did not have much contact with your parents, but even from a distance I could see the affection between them. But, you see, Wem had confirmed it himself with…the gentleman. Even so I still had my doubts. Then I found the manuscript among her things and knew it all to be true. That was the missing piece that explained…that explained…"

Her voice cracked, and she could no longer speak. Tears, fat and slow, began to trickle down her face as her skin turned red.

It must be truly horrible, Bea thought, if it could reduce her iron-hearted aunt to uncontrollable sobbing. "Explained what?"

The room was silent for several moments as Vera struggled to restrain her emotions. "She was pregnant with another man's child. You must remember that. Promise me you'll remember that."

Bea's head began to pound, as she realized it was to be something far worse than she could ever imagine if her illegitimate half-sibling was to be a mitigating factor.

"Promise me," Aunt Vera demanded fiercely.

"I will," she said hoarsely.

Vera nodded. "It was a blow, such a devastating blow, to Richard, who loved your mother with a passion I'd never seen. It must have been a blow beyond reckoning because his mind snapped."

Bea flinched as she said *snapped,* as if startled by a clap of thunder.

"He would never have done it if not for the baby, I'm sure of it," her aunt said. "It's just that he loved her so much. Please believe that. He never, never would have done it."

Bea could bear it no more and screeched, "*Done what?*"

But she knew the answer before her aunt said the words. It was all there in the context, between the lines, on her face.

"Kill her."

Her body stopped shaking, and Bea felt a preternatural calm overtake her as she repeated the sentence, "My father killed my mother," over and over in her head. But it wasn't just the words. What a reprieve it would be if it was merely those words, as incomprehensible as they were, darting around in her head. No, it was much worse, for there were images too—of her mother's frantic face as she struggled desperately to bring him back to his senses.

How terrified she must have been to find herself about to die at the hands of the man she loved.

His mind snapped.

"The constable ruled it an accident, but he was a fool," her aunt said scornfully. "Anyone with eyes could see the boat had been tampered with. There was a very great crack in the center that could have been made only with an ax, I don't care how stormy the weather was."

Bea, who had moments ago thought the story could not grow worse, stared at her aunt in confusion, as if unable to understand what she was saying. A great crack? An ax?

Quietly, thoughtfully, frantically, she said, "My father killed them both? He killed my mother and himself?"

Aunt Vera nodded. "There is no other way to explain why they were on the river in a damaged boat during a vicious storm. Your father wanted them to die together. I know I haven't always done right by you, Beatrice. I know I've been harsh and disapproving, but I was so terrified you would turn out like her. Or him. Both of them came to such a tragic end. I don't know how it happened. I can't imagine what came over him, some madness surely, and he lost his ability to think. He became this creature that just acted…so horrifically. They were both such strong-minded people, so independent and unafraid, and I could see that in you, even as a small child. I'm sorry. I'm so, so sorry, but I did my best to stamp it out. I thought I had until—" But she shook her head, unable to deal now with the rebellion sparked by her experience in the library of Lakeview Hall. "You have every reason to hate me, and I would not begrudge it if you do. But I did the best I could. I did the best I could."

Tears swamped her again, and this time she did not try to fight them, yielding instead to her misery.

Bea heard her confession but could not give it any significance now, at this moment, when she'd discovered the truth about her parents.

My father killed my mother and himself.

Her brain, wallowing in the wretched muck of the past, seemed determined to remain there. She closed her eyes to block it out, but that only made the image sharper. All she saw was rain and fear.

She had to think of something else.

Frenziedly, she scanned her mind for another thought, another issue, another focus, something, anything, but the pictures in her head persisted: the little boat in the driving rain, her mother's terrified screams, her demented father someplace beyond reason chopping a hole into the little boat with an ax.

A challenge, she thought desperately. Something that required rationality and deduction.

What…what…what…

Her mother's lover!

Yes, yes, yes.

Aunt Vera had not revealed his identity.

Who could it be?

There were so many possibilities, she thought in horror, recalling both the dowager's comment about her mother being a flirt and Mrs. Ralston's mention of her many admirers.

The notorious London gossip had listed names, hadn't she?

Yes, Bea thought, Mrs. Ralston had referenced two gentlemen in particular, but for the life of her she couldn't recall either one. Her brain, ordinarily so quick to produce the details of prior conversations, felt sluggish and unwieldy and not entirely under her control. She could picture the scene—the drawing room, the tea tray, Flora next to her on the settee—but couldn't remember a single word that was said during the exchange.

How incredibly frustrating to be able to visualize her aunt's oddly agitated expression as she tried to steer the conversation to Lord Stirling's ball but not—

Bea's heart stuttered in her chest as she suddenly understood her aunt's strange behavior. Lemon ices, gooseberry pudding, trifle—the poor woman had employed every dessert she could think of to move the subject away from Clara's lover.

It fit, she thought, recalling Braxfield's tone as he commented on her mother's beauty. There had been a possessive quality to his admiration. And the missing bracelet. It wasn't here with her parents' effects, and Mrs. Ralston had said the viscount enjoyed collecting cherished tokens.

That her mother could be such a besotted fool as to give a beloved family heirloom to a coldhearted rake broke what was left of her composure, and she dissolved into a flood of tears.

"Oh, my dear, my sweet baby girl, come here," Aunt Vera said, her voice but a whisper of its usual force. "Come here."

Perhaps if Vera hadn't held out her arms, as if as desperate to receive kindness as to give it, Bea might have resisted. But it had been a long twenty years of loneliness and nothing seemed to make sense anymore, so she succumbed to the promise of comfort, and there, on the floor of the attic, in the narrow dingy room next to the maids' quarters, she threw herself into her aunt's embrace, and the woman hugged her tightly, as if trying to hold her soul together.

And Bea cried and cried and cried.

CHAPTER NINE

As exhausted as Bea was, she made no attempt to sleep, for she knew it would be useless. Every time she closed her eyes, she saw the scene: the driving rain, her mother's terrified face, the ax in her father's grip as it chopped through the wood of the little boat, both of them unable to understand how it had come to this furious moment on the river.

No, Bea thought, knowing it had been different for her parents, who had at least been present for all the inciting events, even if their actions had consequences they could never have foreseen. I'm the one who can't understand.

It was hardly surprising, of course. What child *would* be able to grasp the enormity of her father's destructive rage and the profound impact it had had on her life? That he would rather orphan his own child than allow an illegitimate one to enter the world would haunt her until the day she died.

Uncle Horace, who had sat with his brother's decisions for twenty years, was still unable to make sense of them, and Bea found his bewilderment oddly comforting.

"I did not know how to handle my grief over Richard's ignominious end," he said, his eyes meeting hers, steady and sharp, over the cluttered desk in his study, "and I treated you badly because you were a reminder of both the unfathomable evil of his behavior and my own anguish. I could not bear to look upon you." Now his eyes dropped to the inkwell next to the blotter. "I had such happy memories of my older brother as a child, always game for adventure and willing to take me along with him. When he became a member of the English Correspondence Guild, which is something I discovered on my own, for he did not have the decency to tell me about it, he went somewhere I could not go, could never go, and I felt betrayed at being left behind. I am convinced his actions were influenced by the low order of people with whom he chose to associate. Ah, but that is neither here nor there. I hope you can understand and forgive me."

Bea wanted to rage at him for the miseries of her childhood. Oh, how she wanted to rage. But she was not cruel and could not blame someone for behaving horribly in a horrible situation.

"He did not join of his own volition, you know," she said, recalling from her mother's letter that she and Richard had deliberately withheld that information. She wondered if knowing that his brother had been fulfilling an assignment for the Crown would give her uncle some peace.

Uncle Horace began to nod as if he did indeed know, then looked at her sharply. "What?"

"Mr. Pitt enlisted his services to keep an eye on the society and provide reports on its plans," she explained. "The prime minister feared the group was fueling an insurrection on par with the revolution in France, and my father agreed to help."

He sighed loudly, the long puff of air releasing slowly. "Richard said nothing of this. When I confronted him, he said nothing."

"I imagine he was under orders from Pitt not to," Bea said. "But you were not entirely wrong in your assumption. My father *was* sympathetic to their cause, as he found their arguments persuasive and their means peaceful. But he did not choose to leave you behind. I think that's important for you to know."

Uncle Horace considered her silently for a moment,

his fingers fiddling with a file on his desk, as if needing to do something to ease his discomfort. "I don't know how you can be so kind to me after all I have admitted. You are the best of your father, and through you some part of him has remained good and decent. I will hold on to that during difficult times and hope you can too."

Beatrice, who'd believed she had simply been wrung dry of tears during the episode in the attic, felt her throat clog up again. She nodded and rose to leave.

Her uncle stood up to escort her to the door. "Your aunt and I, of course, will leave it to you to decide how much of this to tell Kesgrave. Ordinarily, I would advise you to sweep this wretchedness under the rug, for it is most unseemly to have a murderous father and an adulterous mother who died at his hands, but I suggest you tell him everything. I cannot understand what the duke sees in you. You have none of the attributes a man of his station looks for in a wife, and your aunt and I have been quite puzzled by it for days," he explained with the offhanded callousness she knew so well from her childhood. "I don't say that to be hurtful. I say it because it indicates to me that the bond you have with him is sincere. As it escapes my comprehension—as well as the *ton*'s—I can only assume it is deep and abiding. It will not sunder with this information."

Moved by his observation, which demonstrated, despite his claims, a rather keen understanding of the situation, she earnestly thanked him for the advice.

Uncle Horace nodded, reaching out one arm to open the door and snaking the other around her back to give her a hug that was less than an embrace and more than anything else he'd given her before.

After the interview with her uncle, she had gone upstairs to check on the condition of the linen storage room, which, despite the efforts of the upstairs maid, was still in wild disarray. Without saying anything, Bea picked up a bedsheet and began to fold, which mortified Susie, who immediately protested.

"No, miss, no," she said. "It's no bother."

Bea nodded as if she understood but continued to fold as if the maid hadn't spoken, for she needed to do something with her hands.

Aunt Vera, observing her labor, gasped in horror but passed without comment.

Once the linen closet was restored to order, Bea sought out Flora and offered to help her select a gown for the Stirling ball. "I'm not as skilled as your mother with a needle, but I'm not entirely lost to usefulness. Perhaps there's some minor alteration we can make to spruce one up a bit."

"I very much doubt that," Flora said, "but as there are many strange things going on in this house today, of which nobody will tell me anything, not even Susie, who loves to gossip, I will allow you to try. I cannot say why, but I feel as though I am doing you the favor rather than the other way around."

"You are," Bea said as she followed her cousin to her bedchamber to examine her wardrobe, "and I appreciate your generosity."

Together, they settled on adding a lace edge to the bodice of a jonquil gown.

Throughout the day, Bea bounced from one activity to another, determined to keep herself occupied, and all the while the picture was there, in the back of her head: driving rain, terrified face, horrifying ax. For hours she had managed to keep it at bay, but now that she was alone in her room and the house was asleep, it was front and center, tormenting her.

I must do something, she thought desperately, lighting the candle next to her bed and picking up the book she had recently put down. All attempts to focus on a chapter detailing Michelangelo's fresco technique had proven fruitless only a half hour ago, but surely staring hopelessly at a page of text was better than staring hopelessly at the ceiling. At least with the former there was a chance of being engaged.

But it was no use. The images played in her head relentlessly, and being unable to read the book made her fear she would never be able to read a book again. Her nerves clattered to an unbearable degree.

Something had to be done, she thought, climbing out of bed to pace the room. Trying to evade the thoughts, to drown them out with constant activity, had accomplished nothing. It was a failed method, and she was far too clever to persist in any system that had already proved worthless.

She needed a new approach, one that was as different from the previous one as possible.

Confrontation, she thought.

As avoiding the truth had failed in every way, she would do the opposite by looking straight at it. She would investigate the events and uncover the details. Perhaps the more she knew, the less she would think about it.

It made a lot of sense, she realized, for it was her story as much as it was her parents'. She had spent several days deciphering the final movements of the Earl of Fazeley, a man she'd never met. Surely, she owed herself the same courtesy she'd extended to a random stranger who merely happened to die at her feet in the entranceway of a newspaper office on the Strand?

She would start by interviewing the Earl of Wem and discovering the evidence upon which he'd based his assertions about her mother's affair. The point of the examination was not to disassemble his story as if to look for inconsistencies and half-truths. No, it was merely to assure herself that her mother's judge had been properly discerning in reaching his conclusions.

It would be a lie, of course, to deny that she harbored a tiny sliver of hope that Wem was in fact mistaken. It was possible, was it not, for Clara and Richard had been so affectionate with each other even while dressed as Misters Piper and Barlow that the founder of the English Correspondence Guild had concluded they were a pair of sodomites. Surely, demonstrative behavior of that ilk indicated a sincerity of feeling.

Ah, but then there were the apricots.

'Twas naught but a harmless lie to tell your husband that the apricot ice cream you served on his birthday was really made from foie gras.

Indeed, she could not think of a mistruth less consequential.

And yet it indicated a willingness to mislead, did it not, a penchant for tweaking the truth to suit one's desires.

Going back and forth in her head, looking for evidence to support her argument and then immediately refuting it, would accomplish nothing, and Bea resolved to deal only with facts going forward. To do that she would have to gain the earl's confidence. The direct approach would hardly work, for Wem would not openly discuss a mother's adulterous affair with her daughter. Furthermore, as her father's oldest friend, he'd be within his rights to box her ears for even asking.

She needed a pretense and considered the disguises that had stood her in good stead: biographer, steward, solicitor.

The first one, she thought, was a little too specific, and the second one seemed to require some sort of prior business with the earl. Solicitor, however, was reasonably broad and could apply to a variety of situations.

Now, what pretext could she invent to justify the presence of a solicitor who asked indiscreet questions about a husband and wife who had died twenty years before? Naturally, the answer would have to relate to some current event.

No, Bea thought, shaking her head. It has to relate to me.

The only current event in her life was her betrothal to the Duke of Kesgrave, and she wondered what about that arrangement could excuse impertinent queries. Then, smiling for the first time in hours, she realized the more constructive question to answer would be the inverse, for everything about her engagement had invited impertinent queries, from her own aunt and uncle to the members of the *ton,* who kept extending their condolences to the dowager.

And then she thought: the dowager!

Quickly, a plan began to formulate in her mind, a particularly devious scheme that would not reflect well on her grace.

Could she do it?

Bea decided she really didn't have a choice because there was no better way to gain access to Wem's recollections than posing as a solicitor who had been hired by her grace to discover unsavory information about her grandson's betrothed.

Her conscience twinged at the disservice to the dowager, who would have been within her rights to disapprove of her sternly and had instead welcomed her warmly.

I will make amends, she promised, unable to abandon the perfect deception just because it exposed a kind elderly woman to Wem's harsh judgment. Given the direness of the circumstance, she felt positive the other woman would understand.

Kesgrave too, she thought, then she shook her head as if to clear him from her mind. It hurt too much to think of him now, for as much as she believed Uncle Horace's assessment of their bond was accurate, a tiny part of her doubted its strength. In agreeing to marry her, he had already compromised so much of what a gentleman looked for in a duchess: beauty, property, elegance, wealth, status. The only thing she brought to the union that society considered of value was an impeccable if unimpressive lineage, and now that was gone too. Her father killed her mother and himself. That was her past. That was what she came from. It was all so sordid.

It made her feel sordid too.

She shook her head again and focused on the accoutrement she required to make her disguise believable. She would take her leather case, which was still stuffed with old receipts and the pages of a book whose binding had torn from the last time she'd posed as a solicitor, and make calling cards announcing her profession.

Bea sat down at her escritoire to write them immediately but as soon as she was off her feet, she realized how weary she was and climbed back into bed. Laying her head against the pillow, she closed her eyes, pictured a calling card from a solicitor and fell asleep composing the words she would use.

Naturally, she was unable to recall in the morning the exact phrasing she had settled on before her slumber, but it was a minor thing and within a half hour she had a tidy stack of calling cards. She slid them into her leather case and dressed in her cousin Russell's clothes.

Slipping out of the house was easier than usual because nobody expected her to emerge from her room. A concerned Aunt Vera had delivered a breakfast tray overladen with options and assured her the family understood her need for seclusion. It was rather the other way round, Bea thought wryly, but she did not judge her aunt for wanting her tucked safely out of sight while she came to terms with the horror and her grief. It was difficult on all of them, and her relatives had already shown their limited capacity for handling tragedy with grace.

At the Earl of Wem's Mayfair address, she presented her card to the butler and explained that her business was of a most confidential nature.

"I would reveal all to you, my good man, if such candor did not violate my contract with the very, very, *very* esteemed personage who hired my services," she announced with what she hoped was overweening pomposity. To heighten the effect, she'd lowered her voice an additional octave, which created an uncomfortably ticklish sensation in the back of her throat, and she struggled not to let out a girlish cough. "I do hope you will allow me to enter out of respect for my employer, whose importance cannot be overstated. If you remain doubtful, I have been given leave to assure you I make this request at the behest of someone only slightly less important than a grand duchess. I will wait now as you consider my application."

The butler's sneer that first greeted Bea indicated a well-developed ability to puncture the hopes of impertinent upstarts seeking entry. But by the time she had uttered the third *very,* a flourish that signified true presumption, his expression had softened to curiosity.

"You may stand in the doorway while I discover if milord is at home," the butler said.

Grateful that he had made it so easy, she bowed.

The man returned a few minutes later to announce the earl waited for her in the library. As he led the way, she had just enough time to observe a carved balustrade edging an elegant staircase before being shown into a room of a vivid deep blue offset with light-colored bookcases and a white fireplace. The Earl of Wem was drinking coffee in a leather armchair with a table at his elbow and greeted her with a nod. Then he asked how he may be of service.

Bea was taken aback by his bearing. As he had been the bearer of devastating news, she'd expected to find someone with a monstrous disposition and appearance to match. The fact that he remained unmarried at the age of fifty seemed to corroborate this assumption. But Wem had a pleasant aspect, with a mild and welcoming manner, and he possessed an attractive face. A high forehead topped brown eyes rimmed by dark lashes and well-shaped lips. His hair, still an appealing shade of brown though peppered liberally with gray, was short and brushed forward à la Caesar.

"Thank you, my lord, for agreeing to see me. I would have sent a note ahead to arrange a meeting, but I fear time is of the essence," she announced in her low-pitched voice.

Wem showed no resentment at having his morning routine interrupted. "Sometimes that is unavoidable. Do take a seat and tell me what this is about."

Bea sat down on a bergère swathed in blue silk the same deep color as the walls. "Before I get to the substance of my visit, I must first explain that I'm here on a mission of the most confidential nature. I would request, my lord, that you agree to honor that before I begin," she said, hoping to preserve the dowager's dignity. "Naturally, I am in no position to demand it and will only trust in your decency to give it."

The earl waved away her concern. "Yes, yes, of course I give it. I have been a party to quite a few confidential dealings and understand the need for it."

"You are very gracious, my lord," Bea said with sincerity, realizing that this man, her father's oldest friend, was a true gentleman. It should have been a reassuring thought, and yet it only made her sad. His decency could not save her parents. "I am here on behalf of the Dowager Duchess of Kesgrave. As you know, her grandson recently engaged himself to a young woman who is not...let us say...up to the standards she has set for her family."

That Wem agreed immediately with this view altered her opinion of him slightly, for she could not believe it was entirely decent to visit the sins of the parents onto the child.

"I believe she was hoping for a more brilliant match in the form of Lady Victoria," he observed sympathetically. "It does happen that one's children and grandchildren sometimes let us down. But I don't think the duke has made an entirely bad bargain. A girl of her looks and prospects will be too grateful to cause trouble."

Bea wasn't offended by the sentiment itself, for she knew it was shared by the entirety of the *ton,* but rather by the fact that her father's oldest friend harbored it. She was the daughter of Richard Hyde-Clare, a man who died tragically in a boating accident for all he knew, and Wem should think more kindly of her if for no other reason than out of respect for his deceased friend.

She revealed none of these thoughts as she continued in her purpose. "I trust you will also understand when I say that the dowager has not quite given up on her hopes. And that is why I am here. My firm's records indicate that you knew the parents and were in fact quite close to them."

He nodded abruptly as a spark of pain seemed to dart across his face, and Bea felt herself warming to him again.

"Yes, I did know them," he said. "I knew them quite well."

"Ah, very good," Bea said, striving for a tone that suggested reluctance while stalwartly moving forward with an assignment. "There have been...let us say...concerns about the mother and her...hrm...decency. Our research leads us to wonder if you might have some information that sheds light on the topic."

"I do, yes," he said firmly before adding with a piercing bitterness that seemed out of place in the warmth of the blue room, "She was a harlot."

If Bea hadn't been sitting down, she would have toppled to the floor at the brutality of the statement. As it was, she opened her mouth to issue a stinging retort before she remembered she could not have a position on the matter and certainly not an offended one.

She slammed her mouth closed.

"I'm sorry," Wem said kindly, lifting the coffee cup to his lips, and for a moment Bea could believe he was apologizing to Clara's daughter. Then he added with measured calm, "I didn't mean to shock you, but, really, you should be beyond such things. You are very young, I will grant you, but a man of your profession has surely been exposed to the tawdriness of the world. I could have stepped lightly around the subject for several minutes, implying an indecency but never quite stating it, but that would be wasting my time, of which I am most possessive, as well as yours. As much as it pains me to say it, the woman in question was quite promiscuous with her favors and could not be relied upon to remain faithful to any man. Is that not what you came here to discover?"

God, no, Bea thought, panic rising in her breast as she realized how much worse it could all be. One lover, Braxfield, had been devastating enough, and now she was confronted with a seeming horde. A new horror struck her as she wondered if her mother even knew who the father of her unborn baby was.

The earl took another sip of his coffee as he waited patiently for her reply.

Calmly, Bea straightened her shoulders as her heart raced out of control and said, "Yes, my lord. That is exactly what I came here to discover. I know your time is valuable, but I hope you will provide me with a few more minutes to ask follow-up questions. Given all that is at stake, I would like to ensure my report is as comprehensive as possible."

Wem dipped his head graciously. "Yes, of course. Do proceed."

"Thank you, my lord," Bea said, struggling to order her thoughts. Although the magnitude of the charge had changed, the substance had not. The questions she'd come there to ask, therefore, were the same. "Now, to be clear, I've spoken to several people and there have been indications that Mrs. Hyde-Clare may have engaged in an adulterous relationship with Viscount Braxfield. Do you know anything about that relationship?"

"I do, yes, quite a bit," his lordship said.

"Would you object to addressing a few of the particulars?" she asked.

The earl's lips curved into a smile. "I wonder at your firm's sending a boy to do what is clearly a man's job. I have no objection to addressing the particulars."

"When did you first become aware of the improper relationship between Mrs. Hyde-Clare and Viscount Braxfield?" she asked.

"Several months before her death," he said. "I saw her climbing out of Braxfield's coach in front of her home, and the goodbye she gave him in parting was far too warm for a passing acquaintance. Before that moment, I had not been aware that they even knew each other. After that, I saw them in back alleys together quite frequently, often leaving disreputable establishments that could be used for only one thing—and with she in disguise, dressed as a man. Naturally, I was reluctant to condemn the wife of a dear friend, so before coming to any conclusions, I confronted Braxfield. He confirmed it. At that point, I had no choice but to tell Richard what I had discovered, for we were peers as well as friends, and the gentlemen's compact requires honesty. He accepted the news with calm stoicism, but I've always wondered if the truth was weighing on him when he made the tragic decision to take the boat out in a storm."

During this brief speech, Bea's emotions were a tumult of hope and disappointment. His admission that he'd known nothing of Clara and Braxfield's relationship indicated an ignorance of their membership in the English Correspondence Guild—which, she thought, could have led to a simple misunderstanding. Unaware of their association, he would inevitably mistake the camaraderie of allies for a romantic connection. He would assume their visits to unfashionable parts of town were to conduct salacious trysts rather than to attend society meetings.

The poor confused Earl of Wem, seeing so much and comprehending so little.

For a moment, Bea believed it—that the defining tragedy of her life was the product of a grave misunderstanding between friends—and it lifted her heart as thoroughly as it dashed it against a rock. For would that not be worse: *My father killed my mother and himself for no reason at all.*

And yet she longed for it, for the respite of horrendous acts done in error, and even that brief fantasy was immediately denied to her, for Wem was no nodcock to hurl an accusation without confirming it first. It was not idle speculation.

"Very good, my lord," she said, weary from the whirl of emotions and lack of sleep and dread at what new awful things she would discover about her mother. "That is precisely the information the dowager hoped I'd gather. Now, let's discuss the others."

"Of course," the earl said as he placed the coffee cup on the table beside him.

Bea leaned forward in her chair and waited with a thick sense of dread for him to list the other men with whom her mother had dallied.

Wem did not say anything.

Instead, he scoffed with annoyance and withdrew his pocket watch to look at the time. Bea had a moment to admire a jeweled gold chain as it caught the bright color of the walls, blinking blue in the sunlight, before he returned it to his fob pocket.

"I have already explained to you how highly I value my time and urged you not to waste it," he said with his first display of temper. "Now, please, before my patience runs out, tell me the next name and I will report what I know."

Bea felt as if the world had tipped sideways. "I apologize, my lord, for the misunderstanding. I was under the impression you had more names."

"I?" he asked aghast. "You come into my library requesting my help, which I have given freely, and then assume I will supply you with additional names in order to make your work easier? If you need help finding further evidence of the woman in question's depravity, then I suggest you hire yourself a lackey. *I* supply *you* with more names. What impertinence!"

As he took her to task for her bold imprudence of trying to manipulate him into doing her job, Bea felt a host of emotions swarm through her, including outrage that he would dare call her mother promiscuous and a harlot for taking a single lover. 'Twas absurdly prudish and extremely moralistic, and she didn't doubt for a moment that he himself had trysted with a half dozen women in the same span of time.

Buffle-headed hypocrite!

Mulish rod-eater!

Oh, she was very angry indeed.

From behind the protection of her disguise, Bea toyed with the idea of venting her spleen on the sanctimonious rotter. He would never know who she was, and if he tried to call upon her firm with the intent of ensuring she suffered the consequences of her actions, he would have the frustrating displeasure of discovering it did not exist. Perhaps in his need for satisfaction, he would call on the dowager to voice his disgust of her associates and she would browbeat him for daring to suggest she could engage in such low behavior.

As gratifying as it would be, Bea knew it was foolish to burn her bridges, for she never knew when the need for something would reappear.

Plastering a smile on her face, she took a deep breath and stood up. "You are right to berate me, your lord. Entirely right. As you have noticed, aspects of this assignment are challenging for me and I was hoping you could supply me with another avenue of investigation. I fear the trail ends here, and the dowager will be so cross if I don't amass enough disqualifying information. But I see I have taken up enough of your time, with which you have been so generous. Obviously, I'm not worthy of your benevolence, but I'm grateful for it nonetheless. Truly, I cannot thank you enough and am so dreadfully sorry for relying on you for additional knowledge. I hope you can forgive me and by extension the dowager for imposing my presence on you."

Appeased by the extravagance of the apology, Wem softened his expression and assured Bea that he had told her everything he knew about Mrs. Hyde-Clare. "Whether that makes her daughter unfit to be the Duke of Kesgrave's wife, I leave to the dowager to decide."

Bea bowed and thanked him again before departing the residence to return to Portman Square. Curiously, her heart was a little lighter now as she slipped into the house than earlier when she'd sneaked out, for, as ludicrous as it was, the fear that her mother had consorted with hordes of men had made her oddly content with the fact that it was only just the one.

CHAPTER TEN

Returned to her room after the distressing encounter with the Earl of Wem, Beatrice could not stop thinking about the bracelet.

Having accepted that his lordship's conclusion was valid, for there was no quarreling with a confession from the viscount himself, she had nothing else to focus on. When she let her mind wander, she was immediately back beside the river, next to her mother as she frantically sought to reach her husband through the madness that had overtaken him. It amazed her how fresh the fear felt twenty years after the fact, as if her mother could feel it still.

As if her mother would feel it always.

No, she thought, the bracelet.

Denied the opportunity to think the best of her mother by Wem, she allowed herself to think a little better and decided Clara would never have ceded a family heirloom to a rake of Braxfield's reputation.

Perhaps if the piece had come to Clara through her own line, she might have been somewhat cavalier about its disposal. But it had been handed down through the Hyde-Clares, from one generation to the next, and she must have been fully cognizant of the fact that she was merely its custodian. Eventually it would be handed down again, presumably to Beatrice. She could not believe her mother would be so infatuated with Braxfield and so lost to decency as to betray that trust.

There were only so many things she was willing to condemn her mother of: conducting a scandalous affair and destroying her husband's sanity, yes; stealing an heirloom from her daughter, no.

Furthermore, Bea could not reconcile the submissiveness required to yield the bracelet to her lover's demand with the unsentimental attitude toward romantic liaisons displayed in her treatise. In the section discussing the equality of love, Clara quarreled with the accepted standard of treating women as "mere playthings" while carefully minding their purity and argued that women would be harder to dismiss if their experience was commensurate with a man's.

The woman who had written that manifesto would never have handed over a treasured heirloom merely to gratify a man's ego. She would have recognized the request as the exercise of male dominance it was and laughed.

Oh, how Bea needed to believe she had laughed.

If the bracelet wasn't among her parents' things and Braxfield was in possession of it, then he could have attained it only through devious means. Given the intimacy of their relationship, she thought it was likely he'd slipped it off her wrist while she slept.

The vain scoundrel!

Bea found the prospect of her mother's cherished bracelet lying among the tawdry artifacts from the viscount's other affairs—Miss Embury-Dennis's plume, the fan of a woman named Delia—intolerable and vowed to retrieve it.

She understood the decision was not entirely rational and stemmed more from a desperate need to focus on an activity than an actual desire to hold the bracelet in her hands. The sense of helplessness that had dogged her footsteps since discovering the truth about her parents could only be staved off with occupation. Plotting to meet Wem had kept it at bay; scheming to retrieve the bracelet from Braxfield would hinder it further.

The first step in recovering the heirloom was confirming that it was indeed gone. She knew it was not among the belongings in the chests in the attic room because her aunt had thoughtfully had them delivered to her bedchamber, where she could look through them at her leisure. Naturally, she'd hurled herself at the cases the moment the footmen had left, opening them with barely contained impatience and examining each object with minute interest.

It was extraordinary after all these years to have these memories of her parents, and when she found her father's pipe and inhaled deeply, she was instantly transported to the library at Wellsdale House, her body curled next to his as he read Benjamin Franklin's autobiography.

She'd forgotten it, she realized, her father's habit of reading aloud to her from whatever book he was currently enjoying. The words themselves had never mattered, for it wasn't the story she'd loved but the rumble of his voice under her ear, the sensation of having him close, of being safe and cherished.

It staggered her—that he could go from nurturing her sweetly to orphaning her cruelly in a matter of days.

There was some consolation, she supposed, in finding the stocks Lady Abercrombie had mentioned, a tidy bundle that included certificates for the Phillips steam engine. Her father had not left her entirely unprepared for the world.

To confirm the bracelet was not returned with her parents' other possessions, Bea sought out her aunt, who was reviewing menus with the housekeeper in the breakfast room.

"I see the color has yet to return to your cheeks," Aunt Vera said in greeting. "You should get a little more rest, and I will have Annie bring up some food in a little bit."

"Thank you, yes, I would appreciate that," Bea said, although she wasn't at all hungry. The tray her aunt had sent up for breakfast had contained more than enough food for a second, afternoon meal. "I did not see my mother's sapphire bracelet among the items in the chest. As it is a Hyde-Clare family heirloom, I wondered if you perhaps had it or Flora."

As there was an implied accusation in the question, Beatrice was fully prepared to incite her aunt's anger and receive a chilly reply. When the other woman barked, "Good gracious!" she tensed for a tirade.

But Aunt Vera surprised her by adding with exasperated amusement, "Can you imagine the ruckus it would cause if I gave something that valuable to Flora and not Russell? I expect he would insist we sell it immediately and split the profits among the two of them. Then he would march into Gentleman Jackson's Salon and plunk down the entire pile of banknotes to pay for lessons. No, I don't have the bracelet. When we didn't find it among their possessions, either in the London house they had rented for years or the family seat in Sussex, I assumed she'd lost it. When or how, I don't know, as we'd had minimal contact with them for some time. But I've always regretted the loss of the piece and will admit that whenever I pass through the dining room, I sigh a little bit over it."

Bea could not conceive what the dining room had to do with the topic at hand. "Why is that?"

Her aunt shook her head as if Bea had missed something very obvious. "Because your grandmother is wearing it in her portrait."

Although Bea had known that the severe woman in the emerald silk dress hanging over the sideboard was her father's mother, she had never looked at it carefully enough to notice what jewelry she wore. Indeed, she never looked at it at all, for she found Harriet Hyde-Clare's disapproving scowl to be as effective in paint as it was in person. The artist, a minor talent from France called

Charles-André Lussier, had been a little too honest in his depiction, depriving his subject of the illusion of kindness.

Recalling the stern woman who had demanded obedience and pinched your arm if she did not get it quickly enough, Bea knew she would not have appreciated a sympathetic misrepresentation. She delighted in being feared and no doubt relished looking exactly like the sort of woman who would give an ugly tea set to her new daughter-in-law.

Bea avoided her grandmother's gaze now as she examined the bracelet, with its gold links shaped into delicate hearts whose points were punctuated with small sapphires. It was beautiful and unique, and she could easily understand why it had caught the dowager's eye. Bea had never desired adornment, and yet she felt her wrist tingle with a strange longing to wear it.

Having seen it, she was more resolved than ever to retrieve it.

Invigorated with purpose, she dashed to the stairs and was promptly detained by her aunt, who informed her that while she had been secluded in her room, Lady Abercrombie had called.

"She asked me to remind you that she expects to be kept apprised of your progress," Aunt Vera said, her brow furrowing in distaste. "I can only assume by that she means your betrothal to Kesgrave, but surely she knows how intrusive it is to try to wrangle an invitation to the wedding breakfast. Presumptuous woman!"

As it had not occurred to Bea to provide her ladyship with timely information about her investigation, the reminder did not go amiss. "Thank you," she said, resuming her climb up the stairs.

"And Kesgrave sent a note inviting us to dine tomorrow at Kesgrave House. Naturally, I'm eager to be received there, as the architecture is said to be magnificent and the interiors monstrously lavish, but I do not think it is fair to expose you to the rigors of a social outing while you're still reeling from the painful revelations of your parents' moral failures. You have scarcely been able to step out of your room today, which is the only suitable response and it comforts me to see you acting in an appropriate manner. Do not despair, my dear," Aunt Vera said in a bolstering tone, "we will get through this. In the meantime, I will tell Kesgrave you are under the weather and advise him to ask again in a week. I trust that meets with your approval."

Now that the truth about her parents had been revealed, Bea suspected there would be many references to their so-called moral failures. She didn't blame her aunt for either raising the specter of the brutal murder-suicide or employing a euphemism to describe it. She firmly believed her relatives had done the best they could with their limited resources, both material and intellectual, and as awful as they had been to her, they had done better by her than her own father, who had orphaned her without compunction.

"Yes, that does, thank you," Bea said gratefully and returned to her room.

In truth, however, she felt a fissure of alarm, for a message meant to put off the duke would surely draw him in, and she braced for another surreptitious late-night visit.

She had no idea what she would say to him when he arrived, for she feared the truth would lodge itself in her throat. But she couldn't lie to him either. He had a right to know what her family was capable of.

Her parents' catastrophic moral failures lived inside her.

Banishing this upsetting thought from her head, Bea changed back into her cousin's clothes and left the house through the servants' entrance for a second time that day. She waved down a hack and directed it to take her to Hallam Street, where Braxfield's town house was situated. It sat on the corner of Duchess Street, near Cavendish Square, its graceful white facade gleaming pristinely in the waning March sun.

Thanks to her outing with Nuneaton and his sister two nights before, she knew the viscount would be attending the theater on the morrow and then enjoying a late supper at his club. That would be the perfect time to steal onto the premises and search for the bracelet. Gaining entry, she decided as she strolled around the corner to dip her head discreetly into the mews, would not be impossible, for a collection of well-manicured evergreens shaded the windows on the ground floor. They would provide some protection from passersby and carriages while she surreptitiously pried open the window. Once inside, the only challenge would be in evading the servants, but she felt confident they would be mostly in their quarters, grateful to have some time off while their employer was out.

Ah, but first she would have to figure out how to unlatch the interior shutters without breaking them. She was too far away to examine them carefully, but if they were anything like the ones in the dining room in Portman Square, they would have a thin space between them where they met.

Too thin to insert a bodkin or needle?

It was impossible to say from this distance, but she thought it was a promising scheme. And, she decided as a team of horses clattered loudly by, she could always force them open if necessary. The rattle of the traffic would hide the sound of the breaking wood.

It was not the most elegant solution, but it certainly had more to recommend it than her other option: impersonating a maid to gain employment in the household. The utter absurdity of assuming a new identity over a period of days, weeks or months caused her to smile for the first time all day, and she spent the ride back to Portman Square listing her qualifications for the position. No, her family had not treated her exactly as a maid for many years, but most certainly as an unpaid companion, and she imagined there were many ways in which the two positions were alike.

Returning to her home, she discovered her presence was not missed, including by Flora, who claimed to have checked on her and was pleased to have noted she had been resting. Presumably, the girl had not opened the door and merely assumed from the lack of response that she was sound asleep.

Although Flora had yet to be informed of the moral failures of Bea's parents, she had recognized for herself that all was not well and did not press her to attend Mrs. Mayhew's rout that evening.

"You must not worry about Kesgrave," Flora said as she gave her cousin a gentle kiss on her cheek as she bid her good night. "I will assure him of your health and will explain that you are simply not feeling quite the thing this evening. As you have recently suffered a dreadful cold, I'm sure he won't be surprised to discover you haven't fully recovered. And you've had so much excitement of late."

With every offer of comfort Flora gave, Bea felt herself growing more and more apprehensive, for Kesgrave knew her recent cold was all a hum and that she was not the fragile flower her family believed her to be. He would again perceive her attempt to avoid him and come to her home demanding answers.

The thought at once terrified and excited her.

While she waited, she applied herself to perfecting her unlocking technique on the windows in the dining room. None of the servants noticed her, but she felt stern disapproval emanating from her grandmother's portrait. Her biggest challenge was finding a bodkin slim enough to slip into the space between the shutters. Once she had the right tool, it took her only forty-five minutes to master its use in the dark. Then she hid the needle in the top drawer of her clothespress and devoted her energies to composing a letter to Lady Abercrombie. She apologized for not contacting her sooner and explained she'd been silent because her investigation had yet to bear fruit.

Bea lied because it felt like a betrayal of her mother's wishes to tell the countess the truth. Clara told Lady Abercrombie everything, even breaking her word to her husband to relate the details of his work for Mr. Pitt. If she'd wanted her friend to know about her affair with Braxfield, she would have told her about it herself.

She wrote the missive at the escritoire in the drawing room because she expected Kesgrave to call at any moment. The last time he visited after seeing her family at a social event—in that case, the opera—he had arrived a little after ten and it was approaching that hour now.

After she finished the letter, she was too anxious about the duke's imminent appearance to do anything but pace the room and try to figure out what she would say. Obviously, he had a right to know exactly what he was leg-shackling himself to—that fact was undeniable. The problem was, she couldn't tell him *exactly what* because she herself did not know. She had changed so much in the past six months that she bore naught but a passing resemblance to the woman who had arrived at Lakeview House to spend a tedious week in the country listening to her cousins squabble. That Beatrice would gawk in horror to see her challenging a duke and deciding to vandalize a pair of shutters to gain unlawful entry to a house.

Perhaps if she'd known exactly what she was before the unsavory revelations about her parents she wouldn't be as confused. But she had begun the investigation into their murders already worried that Kesgrave would not accept that aspect of her personality now that they were betrothed and been unable to decide if she needed that part of herself or not.

And now there was this fresh horror to absorb.

But how could she take it in when the shame and humiliation consumed all the space inside her? All she had room for was this essential truth: Her father chose to kill his wife and himself rather than be forced to raise her, the misbegotten reminder of his worst mistake.

She had not been worth living for.

Beatrice was so consumed by her thoughts that she didn't realize until the clock sounded that it was already eleven o'clock.

Eleven o'clock and no Kesgrave.

On a sigh, she returned to her bedchamber to retire but didn't immediately change into her nightclothes. She checked on the bodkin to make sure it was still there, which of course it was, for only three hours had passed since she placed it in the drawer. Then she straightened the contents of her parents' three chests, organizing the items by size and carefully refolding the fabrics.

Although she wouldn't let herself think it explicitly, she knew she was dawdling in expectation of Kesgrave's arrival. Surely, he had just been waiting for the house to grow dark.

But as midnight neared, she could fool herself no longer and finally conceded that he was not coming.

It was, she discovered as she slid under the covers, a crushing blow because it could mean only one of two things: that he hadn't noticed her efforts to avoid him or he was relieved by her efforts to avoid him. The former seemed inconceivable, for only four nights ago he had sat on this very bed and revealed how thoroughly he understood the workings of her mind. In the space of a few days, he could not have lost that knowledge. No, he knew something was wrong and chose not to discover what it was. He knew as well as she that every time he'd pressed her for information, she had given it.

If he didn't press her for it now, it was because he didn't want to have it.

It was a heartrending thought, and she was simply too exhausted to do anything but submit to the pain and sadness. Lying on her side, tears sliding gently down her cheeks, she turned her face toward the door because some foolish part of her nurtured the hope that he might still saunter in. She'd done this before—this very exact same thing once before— when they were in the Lake District, and she fell asleep now, as she'd fallen asleep then, waiting for the duke to appear, and felt a curious emptiness at the realization that she had somehow found herself back at the beginning.

CHAPTER ELEVEN

Beatrice, dressed the next evening in Mr. Wright's reliable brown suit, could not make herself climb out of the hack in Duchess Street. As the driver told her once, then twice, that she had arrived at her destination, she remained strangely rooted to her seat, as if her muscles had frozen in place like tree branches encased in ice.

It was an unexpected development because every other aspect of her scheme had gone according to plan. After another day of wallowing in despair in the privacy of her room, emerging only in the late afternoon to pick half-heartedly at a tea cake in the front parlor with her aunt and cousin, she'd waited until the house was empty at eight o'clock before donning her cousin's clothes. Then she'd retrieved the bodkin from the drawer, sneaked out through the servants' entrance and hailed a hack to Duchess Street.

Now that she was there, her intentions were as fixed as ever.

And yet the terrifying sense that this was wrong, all wrong, was too strong to resist, and she sat there overcome by helplessness. The problem wasn't that she didn't want to break into the earl's house to find her mother's bracelet.

No, it was far worse than that.

The problem was, she didn't want to break into the earl's house to find her mother's bracelet without Kesgrave.

Kesgrave, who, over the course of three investigations, had become as integral to her as breathing.

She'd never invited him into any of her schemes, but there he had been, over and over, seemingly every time she turned around. His ability to appear wherever she was—at the British Museum, at the snuff shop—as if by fiat had given him an unsettling omniscience that she had found incredibly insufferable at the time.

And yet here she was, on the corner of Hallam and Duchess Streets, pining for his sudden arrival.

Waiting for it.

She knew from recent experience that she could wait all night and he still wouldn't appear, but acknowledging that did nothing to help her climb out of the hack.

The driver repeated himself for a third time, impatience coloring his tone, and still she remained unmoving. Images of Kesgrave, however, darted through her head—Kesgrave by her bedchamber's fire in Lakeview House, Kesgrave next to her on the Strand, Kesgrave across from her in the research room at Montague House. She remembered his bemusement in the carriage after their interview with Lord Taunton when he wondered what indignity she would subject him to next and recalled the pleasure on his face, the utter glee in his voice, as he volunteered his services.

That speech.

Oh, that speech.

It had been a declaration of love had she been clever enough to understand it. Despite his displays of devotion, she had doubted him endlessly, again and again, and had stopped only when she was sitting on the chest of a murderer on the Larkwells' terrace during the come-out of their daughter.

No, that wasn't true.

She had merely paused her doubt for a few hours.

Almost immediately, certainly by the time Aunt Vera had progressed to the eighth footman, she'd begun to doubt him again, as if her mistrust were a machine of sorts, producing more and more fear and uncertainty until she did not quite know who she was anymore.

Even now it was spouting doubt like smoke from a chimney.

She had to destroy the machine before it destroyed her.

Her heart thrashing painfully in her chest, she regained just enough mobility to direct the driver to take her to Berkeley Square. A mere ten minutes later, she was alighting from the carriage in front of Kesgrave House, and it was a measure of her anxiety that she did not pause to admire the beauty of the stately home, with its front gardens and Ionic columns flanked by airy pavilions, nor shrink in fear at its intimidating grandeur, for it was quite the most stunning house in London. Had she been more cognizant of its opulence, she would have surely thought to present herself at the servants' entrance, for no steward would dare knock on the front door of such an edifice and demand to see the duke.

No, Bea thought as the butler glared at her with contempt, she had not demanded anything. Slightly breathless with apprehension, she'd politely requested an opportunity to speak with Kesgrave.

Unimpressed by the courtesy, the butler coldly and precisely informed her that his grace was abroad for the evening.

Of course he was, for what gentleman was not?

Undeterred by this minor setback, Bea asked the butler to send for him immediately.

Her tone, she thought, was more imploring than commanding, but Marlow, a physically imposing man with a barrel chest and heavy black brows that seemed to pulse in disdain, took exception to it. Naturally, he did, for who was this Mr. Wright but an upstart steward of indeterminate employment and little status? Such a person was beneath the duke's notice.

As much as his fingers itched to slam the door in her face, Marlow restrained himself and calmly suggested she send a note in the morning—if she did in fact have business to discuss with the duke, a development he doubted very much, as nobody the duke had dealings with could be so ill-bred as to present himself at *this* hour possessing *that* attitude.

Bea, whose horror at having to soon oversee this supercilious man was only slightly more than her amusement at this supercilious man having to be overseen by her, assured the butler that he would not regret sending for Kesgrave.

"There will, I fear, be grave consequences if you do not," she added ominously.

She meant only, of course, that the duke would be very upset to arrive home at whatever hour and find her sitting on his doorstep, for now that she had resolved to trust him wholly, she refused to be dissuaded from the task. But the butler took the comment as a threat to do physical harm to his person and assured her with all his dignity that the duke did not have any business dealings with street brawlers.

Bea laughed, slipping briefly into her regular voice and coughing immediately to cover it up.

"Let alone a street brawler with a pernicious cold. Now do be off before you make the entire household sick," he added, trying to close the door.

Naturally, Bea was compelled to insert her foot, for she was not yet done making her case, and an undignified scuffle ensued. Noting the fracas, someone in the hallway asked the butler if he needed help, and Marlow rushed to assure his colleague that he had the matter well in hand.

Nevertheless, the other man stepped into the doorway. As soon as he did, he gasped in horror. "Mr. Wright!"

It was Kesgrave's steward, Mr. Stephens, who resented Mr. Wright because he thought the other man was trying to usurp his position with the duke. He thought this because Bea had introduced herself as Kesgrave's steward to gain entry to Lord Fazeley's town house. Naturally, she had done it as a matter of expedience, for she was not actually a steward and therefore not in need of a post, but that could not be explained to Mr. Stephens, so the duke had fired her on the spot to appease him.

"You know this…man?" the butler asked with a devastating pause that indicated that *insect* was the word he would have found more accurate.

"He was employed for an infinitesimally small duration of time as the duke's second steward," Mr. Stephens explained.

"I don't recall," the butler said.

Mr. Stephens's lips curved in triumph. "You wouldn't. It was *that* infinitesimally small. Now what can we do for you, Mr. Wright? If you've come looking for employment, we have nothing available."

Grateful for the familiar face, Bea requested again that a message be sent at once to Kesgrave requesting his return. When Mr. Stephens insisted that was impossible, she asked to see Jenkins and was tersely informed by the butler that the groom had driven the duke to his destination.

"Which was where?" she said, knowing a direction was unlikely to be provided but feeling compelled to try.

In response, the butler gave her an ant-squashing glare, and she decided she would rather supervise eighteen footmen than this one disdainful behemoth.

"Very well," she said. "Send a message to Jenkins that a Mr. Wright would like to see the duke immediately at his residence, and I promise you they will both return within the hour. Now I will wait in the drawing room. I assume you will want to send someone to keep an eye on me. Mr. Stephens will do because he already has a deep suspicion of me and won't have to cultivate the proper tenor of mistrust. Come, Mr. Stephens, let us make ourselves uncomfortable. I do not require refreshment but would not turn it away if you insisted."

As brusque and matter-of-fact as her manner was, Bea's purposeful stride could not help but falter as she stepped into the vast entrance hall, with its soaring ceiling, classical statuary and marble staircase. Somehow the large house, which preened confidently over the southwestern corner of Berkeley Square, was more daunting from the inside, and by the time she had taken a seat in the drawing room, she was thoroughly horrified at the prospect of being its mistress. As unnerving as Aunt Vera's talk about the duke's large staff was, it bore no resemblance to the stunning reality of Kesgrave House.

How could one soul bear so much splendor?

For the first time in her life she thought her aunt was correct: Hyde-Clares did not reside in a place like this.

On the settee, Bea pressed herself against the arm, as if to make herself smaller as she examined the lovely room, which was adorned with gilt and intricate plasterwork. Scenes from Greek myths stared down from frescoes on the ceiling.

It was impossible to sit there and imagine Marlow efficiently delivering a pot of tea to her. All she could picture was his heavy black brows pulsating with derision as he advised her to fetch her own tray from the kitchen.

The image made her laugh lightly, and Mr. Stephens, whose beady gaze remained focused on her form, narrowed his eyes at the sound.

He thinks I'm plotting to steal the silver, she decided as she strove to keep herself from fidgeting anxiously. Staying in one place was intolerable, but she feared any attempt to move around the room would unduly alarm her companion.

Ultimately, it made no difference because it was the waiting itself that was intolerable, not the sitting still.

It was all very well to bravely resolve to speak openly and honestly to your betrothed when you were more than a dozen blocks away, but fearlessness was effervescent and she could feel it fizzing and fading within her. As if she'd moved her gaze from light to shadow, all she could see were her own dark spaces and they hollowed her out. Sitting there, in the magnificent drawing room at Kesgrave House, under Mr. Stephens's withering stare, the clock ticking mercilessly, she was Beatrice Hyde-Clare, drab spinster at every social event she'd ever attended, desperately scrambling for something to say.

And then he was there, the Duke of Kesgrave, his expression torn between pleasure and concern, as he strode into the room in his evening clothes, his blond hair glimmering, his blue eyes curious as they met and held hers. His lips curved slightly, twitching in that way, so familiar, so endearing, and he seemed barely to notice his steward, who had jumped to his feet the moment he'd entered and strove to make some explanation for the unusual circumstance.

Bea had no idea what Mr. Stephens said, for the sight of Kesgrave had robbed her of thought and she could only stare into his eyes with a visceral feeling of relief.

The look on his face—'twas not the look of an indifferent man.

Indeed, it was the very opposite of apathy.

Eventually, Kesgrave interrupted the steward. "You were right to be wary, Mr. Stephens, for Mr. Wright is a highly unreliable fellow, but I will handle it now. Please thank Marlow for sending the message to Jenkins."

Fear was an effervescent thing too, she discovered, and could dissipate in a flash. One look and it was gone.

Bea heard the door click and knew she had no time to waste. Minutes were passing, as the clock ruthlessly attested, and there was still a scheme to implement and so many questions to answer.

Unaware of the relentless passage of time, or merely impervious to it, Kesgrave said amiably as he stepped deeper into the room, "If you are going to persist in avoiding me despite our betrothal, a circumstance that will make the wedding tricky but not impossible, then I suggest you come up with a list of specific illnesses because these vague ailments from which you continually suffer aren't very convincing. As always, I am happy to assist you and would suggest a methodical approach, starting at the letter A and working forward alphabetically."

Bea smiled.

No, she grinned broadly and wondered what she'd ever had to be afraid of.

Although Kesgrave had drawn closer, he was still standing, so she rose to her feet as well. She felt curiously exposed, so she positioned herself behind an armchair and rested her forearms against its top. Then she said, "I've been conducting an investigation into my parents' deaths, which I originally suspected was at the hands of the founder of a defunct radical reform organization, but have since learned it was the result of my father's own action. My mother was having an affair with Viscount Braxfield and found herself *enceinte* by him, which caused my father's mental faculties to fray to such an extreme he killed her and her unborn child, then himself. I believe that during the affair Braxfield obtained my mother's bracelet through underhanded means, and you and I are going now to Hallam Street to break into Braxfield's residence and steal it back."

She spoke quickly and straightforwardly, in a tone that struck her as dispassionate, but even when it was relayed simply, as if items on a list, the tale was still sordid and she saw him wince. Because her eyes were focused exclusively on his, she couldn't miss it.

Calmly, she waited for the barrage of questions. She felt confident if they talked through it slowly, if she addressed his concerns and supplied much of the information she had left out in her rush to tell him the worst, he would understand and agree.

"All right," he said.

She assumed he was teasing her by indulging in another moment of uncharacteristic concision to calm her nerves. It was, she thought, a moment of levity before they burrowed into the wretched sordidness of her past.

But then she realized it wasn't.

No, it was a statement of consent.

His faith in her was that complete.

The revelation was so staggering she could barely breathe. How was it possible, she wondered, that he was somehow better than all her best thoughts put together? It simply was not feasible that someone with his imperious nature and ostentatious pedantry and firm belief in the superiority of his own ideas could have so much conviction in her.

Bea was too overwhelmed to speak immediately, and she had to take several deep breaths before she felt in control of herself. Then she said, "I must warn you, your grace, if you continue in this manner of concision instead of returning to your usual verbosity, I will be compelled to throw you over for a longer-winded beau."

Kesgrave strolled over to where she stood behind the armchair, which, she could now admit, she was clutching like a shield, and took one of her hands in his own. Then he directed her to the settee. He sat down next to her, pressed a kiss against her forehead and, taking her other hand in his, said, "Given that the act of breaking into a residence is a pursuit that typically requires careful planning and precision, I assumed we had no time to spare. But I do have things to say on this topic and would do so now if it complies with our schedule."

Her heart clenching foolishly at his use of *our schedule,* as if this plan and all the others were to be jointly owned, she explained that Braxfield was out for the evening. "He's at the theater with his niece Mrs. Palmer and will then take a late supper at his club with Nuneaton. As it is only ten-thirty now, I think we can spare a few minutes to talk. You must have questions."

"I do, yes," he said, smiling, "quite a few, for I'm curious what you thought of Lord Pudsey's salon, as it's a gathering most notable for its assemblage of politicians who pontificate knowledgeably on any number of arcane subjects. I have been given to understand from personal experience that you have little appreciation for such displays."

"Ah, so you own that you *do* pontificate," she murmured, not at all surprised he had learned of the outing. If Nuneaton himself had not mentioned her presence, then inevitably one of the other guests had. As her aunt was fond of lamenting, she was a person of note now—not because she had managed to snag a duke but because she had managed to overcome a blistering roster of disadvantages to snag one.

"Pontification is in the eye of the beholder," he said.

"No, it's in the ear of the beheld—or, rather, the captive, for that more aptly describes your audience," she replied before explaining that she'd found the evening to be both entertaining and elucidating. "Which was due entirely to Mrs. Palmer's charming belligerence. She cuts a swath through a political salon like Wellington in a Belgian field. But come, your grace, that can't be what you really want to know."

"You are correct," he conceded. "I'm also intrigued by the call you paid on Lord Wem and the information you required from him, and by your visit to the Addison, for I find it to be a most pleasant establishment and would like to accompany you if you have need to return."

Although he spoke without emotion, as if he were delivering nothing more interesting than a report on the weather, his eyes glowed with mirth and triumph, his delight at having shocked her radiating off him like heat from a fire.

"I'm going to refrain from asking how you know all that because Braxfield's late dinner with his nephew will not extend far past two and I know your detailed explication of your brilliance will," she said. "Additionally, I've discovered in the past week that I've come to rely on your omniscience and feel oddly lonely without it."

Naturally, such an admission required a response, and despite the fact that she was dressed as Mr. Wright and one of his servants could enter the room at any moment, the duke pulled her into his arms and kissed her ardently.

Bea, who returned his fervor despite her concern for their situation, realized she would never get used to the sensations he created: the racing of her heart, the pounding of her blood, the inexplicable and impossible yearning to disappear into him so that she slid her hands inside his tailcoat in a hopeless attempt to draw nearer.

The duke pulled away slowly, raising his head as if determined to stop, then lowering it again for one more kiss, brief but still satisfying, then another and another. Finally, he groaned with resolve and said, "Now, *that* is what will make us miss our two o'clock deadline. We should prepare to leave. If you will give me but a moment, I must retrieve something from my bedchamber first."

"Damien, I just told you that my father killed my mother, who was pregnant with another man's child, and himself as well," Bea said, unable to understand how he could blithely dismiss it to fetch an item from his rooms. "It's inconceivable that you don't want to discuss the matter further."

Although he had just separated himself from her, he immediately regained her hands and said, "It's a horrendous thing, and my heart breaks for the child you were then and the woman you are now. I can only assume it is very painful for you, and I would like to discuss that. But I don't need to know anything more, and furthermore, you don't owe me anything more. I want to know only what you want to tell me."

Once again, she was stunned by his acceptance. Whatever she had imagined love to be, especially as a young girl in the heady early days of her first season, never in her wildest dreams did she think it would be this sort of unconditional faith in her person.

Seeing her astonishment, the duke smiled and said, "Do you know what I've been doing for the past four days?"

"Being browbeaten by your butler?" she suggested.

"Waiting," he said cryptically.

"Waiting," she repeated flatly.

"Waiting for you to trust me," he clarified, loosening his hold on her left hand to caress it softly with his thumb. "I knew something was amiss that day in the carriage when I drove you home from tea with my grandmother. You had the most abstracted air and barely seemed to hear a word I said. I even launched into a five-minute lecture on the history of the clerk of the hanaper, an office of the chancery charged with sealing patents, charters and writs, in hopes of earning your scorn."

Although Bea remembered feeling quite confused during that ride, she was surprised to discover the depth of her distraction. To make amends, she said, "I have heard only a fraction of your speech, but I'm prepared to bestow my scorn now."

"Your generosity is humbling," he said dryly.

She bowed her head in acknowledgment.

"Knowing something had upset you," he continued, "I wanted to steal into your bedchamber again and discover the cause so that I could put your mind at ease. It was then, when I felt that impulse, that I realized the familiarity of the pattern: my running you to ground somewhere and cajoling the truth out of you. You, in contrast, had never sought me out to reveal your thoughts. And I decided that wasn't how I wanted our marriage to be, with my always cajoling the truth. I wanted you to come to me. Or, rather, I wanted you to trust me enough to feel comfortable coming to me. And you did. Although, brat, it took you four days—quite possibly the four longest days of my life, thank you very much. You can have no idea how close I came last night to barging into your room and demanding you trust me, especially after your aunt claimed you were feeling under the weather. The only thing that kept me away was the knowledge that trust cannot be demanded. It must be freely given or it's meaningless."

Bea, who had passed a miserable night convinced that the duke had come to his senses at last, smiled wryly at this observation and assured him if he had given in to the impulse, he would have been well satisfied with the results. "By midnight, I was despondent over your seeming lack of interest in my welfare and would have denied you nothing if you had only appeared. Indeed, I fell asleep waiting for your visit, which was the second time I have done so. I devoutly hope there is not a third."

"The second time?" he wondered aloud. "When have I failed you before?"

"Lakeview House. After that dreadful scene in the library and the Runner had taken away Lady Skeffington," she said. "I thought for sure you would climb up the tree so we could have a private conversation. I had assumed, you see, that you would be as eager as I was to review the events with a colleague who'd shared in the endeavor. Alas, you were not."

"Ah, but I was," he insisted, grasping her hand again and raising it to his lips. "I was particularly interested in hearing more about your ordeal in that appalling shack. But invading your room without the urgency of a murderer remaining at large seemed like a gross breach of etiquette. I can also see—with the clarity that comes with retrospection—that I'd wanted to be closer to you so I deliberately took a step back. Though I could not understand it yet, you were irresistible to me even then."

Naturally, Bea could not let such a confession pass without showing proper appreciation, and the kiss she pressed against his lips, originally intended to be perfunctory, quickly turned searing.

"No, no, no," Kesgrave said softly between kisses before finally breaking away and rising to his feet. "No, my love, if we miss our opportunity to break into Braxfield's residence tonight, the consequences will be grave, for I'm convinced you would never let me forget it was my fault. Then you won't invite me to help the next time you break into a gentleman's apartments and I will be forced to sneak up on you whilst you are hiding in a dark corner, and your shout of alarm will alert the butler, which will cause a great ruckus involving Runners and magistrates. And *that* must be avoided at all costs. Now do give me a few minutes to procure my device and we will be on our way."

"Learning that you would have the poor judgment to sneak up on me in the middle of a burglary makes me rather inclined to slip out while you're gone," she said.

"You must do what feels right," he allowed, "but the device I'm about to retrieve allows me to unlock any door I want, so I will find the bracelet while you're still trying to break open the shutters at the back of the house."

"The side," she said ruefully.

"Excuse me?"

"I was to enter by the side of the house, not the mews," she explained, "and my intent was to shimmy open the latch with a bodkin. I'm not a vandal, your grace. Now please fetch your lockpick so we may be on our way."

True to his words, the duke returned within minutes, and as Jenkins drove them to Braxfield's house, she described the bracelet and explained why she thought Braxfield had it.

Kesgrave confirmed Mrs. Ralston's estimation of Braxfield, adding that the gentleman's methods had scarcely changed in two decades. "He is more discreet now. Age, I believe, has made him not as eager for a fight, so he's less inclined to deal with irate fathers and incensed husbands, but he still likes to collect tokens. Nuneaton informs me he recently divested Lady Wishaw of a particularly beloved Indian shawl."

By the time they arrived at the house, it was almost eleven-thirty and only a few candles were lit inside. Silently, they climbed up the front steps and Bea watched with curiosity as the duke withdrew a small iron instrument that looked like a two-headed key and inserted one end into the lock. Then he moved the tool from side to side with light, nimble movements.

As he worked, he quietly explained the mechanism, which thrilled Bea, who adored him for being a victim of his own pedantry even whilst engaged in illicit activity.

"Most locks are imprecise devices and will give way at even the general hint of a fit. There are exceptions, of course, as some locks are so precise they respond to only one key. In my experience, the best locks are manufactured in Switzerland. This one, however, was probably made by a local locksmith, skilled in his trade but by no means a Swiss expert, which is why I am already in," he said, opening the door slowly.

Inside, the house was silent, which was hardly surprising as most of the servants were in all likelihood abed. When Braxfield returned, a steady pounding on the door would quickly rouse the house and bring a footman to the door.

A single candle burned in the hallway lamp, lighting the way, and Bea followed the duke to the staircase. It too was lit with just enough brightness to ensure safety, and Bea climbed the stairs with careful deliberation, painfully aware that anyplace she laid her foot had the potential to creak.

They made it to the first floor landing without causing the slightest peep.

Kesgrave indicated that they should proceed to the second floor, and as this had been her plan as well, she nodded in agreement. Then she stepped forward, and the floorboard creaked so loudly it sounded like a violin screech in an empty ballroom.

She froze in place and waited to see the response. The size of the house and its pervasive darkness made her feel relatively secure. If someone did come bounding up the staircase to look for them, they could find a place to hide easily enough.

But there was no bounding up the staircase or anywhere, and they resumed their ascent to the second floor. Braxfield's bedchamber was across from the staircase. Kesgrave took a candle from the bed table and lit it using the lamp at the top of the stairs. Then he returned to the room, shared the flame with another candle, which he handed to her, and quietly shut the door.

"I'll start in here," he whispered. "You look in the dressing room."

Beatrice nodded and, holding out the light, got immediately to work, searching the large cabinet pressed against the far wall, then the shelves along the one to her right. It was an easy enough space to explore, even in the near blackness, because everything was so neatly arranged. All the waistcoats were hung together. All the cravats were folded together. All the shoes were lined up together. On the vanity, his lordship's brushes, combs and razor were arrayed neatly. There were a few boxes in the room—a small one containing watch fob ribbons, a larger one with stockings—but nothing was large enough to hold twenty years' worth of romantic mementos.

Wherever Braxfield was keeping her mother's bracelet, it wasn't in this room. She rejoined the duke in the bedchamber, where she found him on his knees looking under the bed. Returning the candle to the table, she leaned down and followed his gaze. There, only a few inches from the edge of the mattress, was a low wooden trunk of a moderate size, perhaps three feet long. Decorated in painted flowers, it was, Bea thought, an appropriately pretty box for the storage of love tokens.

"Nothing in the dressing room?" he asked softly.

"Only evidence of a well-ordered mind," she said, her own voice just louder than a whisper.

"I've had no success either," he said, handing her the candle so he could reach for the trunk with both hands. "But I remain optimistic."

Once the case was clear of the bed, Kesgrave pulled his tool from his pocket and applied it to the lock.

"I grew up in a castle full of locked things," he explained as he worked, his fingers spry as they moved side to side. "Locked cabinets, locked doors, locked trunks."

"Was this castle designed by Mrs. Radcliffe?" she asked.

Kesgrave chuckled. "I see now that came out as more nefarious than I'd intended. I meant merely that I grew up in a large home with lots of locks. The larger a house is, the more locks it has. That is how I became so adept at opening them. I found it galling to be locked out of anything."

"How dare people desire privacy," she said sarcastically.

"Yes, how dare they," he agreed as the lock slid open. "Now let's invade the viscount's, shall we?"

He did not have to open the trunk all the way before Bea knew it was the correct one, for her eye was immediately greeted by Lady Wishaw's Indian shawl—a lovely silk scarf in pale Ceylon ruby and edged with delicate blue, green and yellow flowers. She lifted it from the trunk, noting at once how fine the material was, and carefully placed it on the floorboards so that she may see what else lay within.

It was a varied collection, with some items indicating a clear monetary value and other, less costly objects harboring, perhaps, a deep sentimental appeal. The vast majority of the tokens were small and dainty—rings, brooches, gloves, ribbons, lockets, earrings. One woman had surrendered a miniature, presumably of herself, although the powdered wig suggested the portrait was from the middle of the last century, which made Bea wonder. They found a book of handwritten poems in French by a Mlle Elodie André and a porcelain perfume bottle in cobalt blue with painted birds and plants. Empty now, it still smelled sweetly of roses.

Although several pieces in the trove clearly signaled that the collection had been amassed over a long period of time, such as the scent and the miniature, Bea was glad to have it confirmed in the form of Miss Embury-Dennis's plume. As Miss Embury-Dennis was her mother's contemporary, it meant that her bracelet had to be here among the other items, not stored away in another trunk of objects from an earlier period.

As the bracelet was thin and delicate, she assumed it had slipped to the bottom, and it was only when Kesgrave removed a fragile fan—French brisé with horn sticks—that she began to worry it wasn't there.

Only a few things remained.

"Could we have missed it?" she asked. "Perhaps it slipped into or between something else?"

Kesgrave conceded the possibility and methodically handed each item to her so she could examine it thoroughly before returning it to the trunk.

It was not there.

"Maybe it fell to the floor," she said, "around the trunk or something."

Dutifully, he lifted it up while she looked under it and around it and behind it. Because it was so dark, it seemed like the easiest thing to overlook, and she slithered under the bed, sweeping her arm back and forth in an effort to examine every inch of floor.

Nothing.

She had no idea what it meant.

Bea was about to express her confusion to Kesgrave when he suddenly blew out the candles, bathing the room in blackness, and slid under the bed with her.

"What is—"

But she heard it too, the creaking on the staircase as someone climbed higher and higher, and broke off midsentence. In the utter darkness, she reached for Kesgrave, locating his hand with surprising ease. He was right next to her, and she heard him breathe in her ear, "It's just the valet airing out the room before Braxfield returns. It will take only a minute. I must admit, I feel oddly at home hiding under a bed. I did it constantly when I was a child."

Although Bea felt none of his sanguinity, she appreciated his attempt to make even furtive concealment under a heavy piece of furniture a pleasant experience. "That would be home at the Castle of Otranto?"

"Different architect," he said. "Otranto is Walpole."

She was about to tease him about his deplorable reading habits when his hand tightened on hers and the door opened. The valet's heavy steps filled the room as he crossed to the far side and opened the window exactly as Kesgrave had said.

Only he did not immediately leave. Rather, he took

several steps to his left, entering, Bea realized with apprehension, the dressing room. Had she left it in the same pristine condition she'd found it? She closed her eyes as if to picture it and knew it was impossible to say, for it had been so dark and she did not have the opportunity to inspect it as a whole.

She was reasonably confident she had moved carefully throughout the room, lifting only a few items at a time and replacing them gingerly. And even if a shirt collar was a little bit out of place, the valet wouldn't instantly assume an intruder was responsible. He'd think he'd left it a little off-center by mistake. And if he did think an intruder was responsible, he wouldn't naturally conclude she was still in the room under his master's bed.

Far too many thoughts would have to align for the viscount's valet to lower himself to his hands and knees and inspect under the bed. Surely, the odds against it were greater than—

"He is preparing for Braxfield's return," Kesgrave said, "so we must leave now while he's absorbed in his task. No, my love, don't tense up. You have the great good fortune to be trapped under the bed with a conspirator who has been trapped under many beds during his career. Just think what a pickle you'd be in if you had broken in with another accomplice—Nuneaton, for example. He would be completely useless to you in this situation."

Although Bea's heart was pounding madly at the prospect of being caught in such a damning position, she could not resist teasing him for the illogic of his observation. "The nephew of the man who owns this house would be *completely* useless in this situation?"

"Perhaps not this particular situation but every other muddled stew you might get yourself into, yes," he said. "Now, as the door is in front of us, I suggest we carefully switch around our positions so that we slide out feetfirst because you have more agility when you can pull yourself free by your legs, rather than push yourself free with them.

It's also a lot easier to leap to your feet and run in that position, a lesson I learned the hard way."

Beatrice swallowed the giggle that rose to her throat, unable to comprehend how she could be trapped under a viscount's bed and still be capable of laughter. More than that, she could not comprehend how the Duke of Kesgrave could be trapped under a viscount's bed and still be capable of frivolous comments. Nothing in his breeding or disposition—stodgy, pedantic, stubborn, smug—hinted at such irreverence.

Turning around in the confined space was no easy task, but nor was it impossible and she managed to shift into position without making noise or kicking the duke. He performed the rotation with greater speed and agility.

Side by side, they slid out from under the bed. Bea, concluding that staying below the line of the valet's sight would aid in the escape, raised only to her knees, a movement Kesgrave mimicked. Together, they crawled to the door and into the hallway, only standing when they reached the top of the staircase. Then proceeding at an insufferably moderate pace, for she desired nothing more than to bound down the steps as swiftly as possible, she slowly followed him down the two sets of stairs until they were finally on the ground floor. Gratefully, her eyes sought out the front door in the murky light, and unable to bear the suspense of caution, she ran to it as fast as she could. It opened immediately, for the duke had not locked it behind them, and they stepped outside into the March night.

Bea breathed in the cool air but did not slow down until she was a full block away, and although she knew it was not wise, dressed as she was in her cousin's coat and trousers, she threw herself into Kesgrave's arms with unrestrained exuberance. Kesgrave, who could usually be relied upon to keep a cool head, seemed just as relieved as she was, and there was no telling what scandal they might have set off if Jenkins had not driven up at that moment to take her home.

CHAPTER TWELVE

Aunt Vera could not make sense of Beatrice's rosy cheeks the next morning at breakfast. The high color in her face was certainly unusual, and she assumed it indicated a good night's sleep. But she had no sooner complimented her niece on appearing so well rested than she began to wonder if perhaps the girl didn't look a little *too* well rested.

"Too well rested?" Bea asked as she added a lump of sugar to her tea. "I'm not sure what you mean."

"Perhaps you are sleeping so much because you are excessively tired, which would suggest an illness," her aunt explained. "Now that I think about it, your cheeks are unduly red. You must be suffering a fever. Return to you room at once, and I will have Mrs. Emerson send up some restorative jelly."

Bea laughed. "I appreciate your concern and understand why you feel it, as my usual complexion is quite pale and wan. I'm perfectly fine and not the least bit warm. I am merely happy."

This piece of information also puzzled Aunt Vera, whose brow wrinkled in confusion as if she were trying to solve a complex mathematical equation. "Happy? How can you be happy with all that you have discovered about your parents?"

Flora, who had been immersed in buttering a piece of toast, raised her head at this intriguing comment. "What about her parents?"

Although Bea had expected her relative to be pleased by her rebounding spirits at best and indifferent at worst, she knew her far too well to be surprised by any strange turn. "Am I to be miserable about it forever, then?"

Aunt Vera was instantly contrite. "No, no, of course not. How wretched that would be. But it hasn't even been a whole week. Surely, something a little longer would not be outside the bounds of propriety. Perhaps a month?"

Bea could not suppress the gurgle of mirth that bubbled inside her. "I'm sorry, Aunt Vera, but am I correct in understanding that we are negotiating the length of my misery?"

The other woman managed to look outraged by the question and chastised her niece for being so absurd. "Negotiating the length of your misery! As if such a preposterous thing could be done. No, we are merely discussing the mourning period for the death of…the death of…your illusions. Indeed, so many of your illusions have died. You need time to heal. That is my only concern."

This information was also interesting, and her cousin put down the knife as she said, "When did Bea lose her illusions? Was it when poor Mr. Davies was struck dead by a carriage? Bea, I though we were all over that sad business. Has Kesgrave not knitted together your broken heart?"

The utter ubiquity of the fictitious Mr. Davies never failed to astonish Bea, and knowing how deeply invested her cousin was in the tragedy of his death, she rushed to assure her cousin that the duke had indeed mended her heart.

"I did try so hard to protect you," Aunt Vera said before adding with a hint of rebuke, "but you made it so difficult. If you had just let matters rest! But no, you had to dig and dig until you uncovered the truth."

Given that she had questioned nothing about her circumstance for twenty years, Bea thought this was a rather unfair accusation. But before she could object, Russell entered the room and sat down next to Flora. Having overheard part of the conversation, he asked, "What truth?"

"I have yet to discover that," his sister said as she lifted the slice of toast. "They are being decidedly closed-mouthed about it, but it seems to have something to do with Bea's parents. Mama is displeased that Bea is so cheerful this morning."

"Not displeased," her mother murmured. "Disconcerted."

Russell filled a teacup and looked at his cousin. "What do you have to be so cheerful about? Did your mother finally provide the promised funds to pay for your lessons at Gentleman Jackson's?"

His sister glared at him in disgust. "Your ability to see the world through only the prism of your own interests is deeply troubling. Obviously, Bea is excited because today is the Stirling ball."

Amused by their antics, Bea explained that she was in a good mood because the duke was taking her for a drive. As true as it was, however, his imminent arrival did not wholly account for her happiness.

Much more of it was owed to their inability to find her mother's bracelet among Braxfield's tokens the night before. It was foolish to hope, of course, but she could not suppress the glimmer of excitement that beat within her. Possibly, though improbably, the dismal tragedy of her parents' deaths as relayed to her by Aunt Vera might not be the correct story. If her mother did not have an affair with the viscount, then the child she was carrying might have in fact been her father's, which meant he would have no cause to have killed both his wife and himself in a murderous rage. Perhaps her parents had been mercilessly set adrift on a hacked-up rowboat in a driving rainstorm by someone else entirely, like one of Jeffries's lieutenants at the English Correspondence Guild.

O, wonderful world of possibilities!

Bea knew it was inanity itself to celebrate such a thing, but that was the depth to which she'd sunk. All she wanted now was a less sordid death for her parents and perhaps a little more joy at the end of their lives. Whatever terror her mother suffered, she dearly hoped it wasn't at the hands of her beloved husband.

Kesgrave, who had discussed the matter with her late into the night in his coach while Jenkins patiently waited, suggested their next step should be a frank conversation with Braxfield.

He added, "That is to say, a conversation in which you explain to the other person openly and honestly all that you're thinking and allow them to do the same. I'm defining the term because I know it must be a strange one to you, as you've never had a 'frank conversation' before."

Then, not content to have defined his term with exquisite condescension, he went on to explain the many benefits of the straightforward approach. It was a detailed list, to be sure, and although she assured him that an extended catalogue was not necessary, he ceased his lecture only when she resolved to enlist Nuneaton's help in arranging the interview posthaste.

"That is not necessary," he said hastily. "I will send around a note to Braxfield in the morning."

Bea was happy for other reasons as well. The midnight dash from Braxfield's house, their daring escape from under his valet's nose, still thrummed in her veins. How terrifying it had been, how tense and dreadful, to listen to the heavy footsteps pass right by her head, threatening with each step the possibility of discovery.

It was an experience she never wanted to repeat, and yet there was a tiny piece of her that regretted that it had to end at all, for how remarkable it had been—Kesgrave's hand in hers, his voice in her ear, keeping her calm and making her laugh, creating intimacy where there should have been only fear.

Her love for the duke had already been huge. Before they'd entered the viscount's house, it had already consumed every inch of space inside her. And yet somehow, last night, it had grown a little bit bigger. And while she doubted Kesgrave had found their turn under the bed to be equally transformative, the thought did not plague her. Their bond, which had felt to her as fragile and fraught as a twig, had revealed itself to be as solid as a tree trunk, and she no longer feared that his feelings would flicker out like a candle at the first strong gust.

"Don't worry," Bea said to Aunt Vera now as she noticed disapproval sweep across her face. "I've already informed Annie and she will accompany us, so the proprieties will be observed."

"Don't worry?" her aunt echoed as she leaned forward in her chair, both arms resting on the table as she contemplated the impossibility of her exhortation. "But you're in mourning."

"Is she?" asked Russell baffled. "What for? Not Mr. Davies. I'm sure Kesgrave would object."

"No," Flora said, although her tone lacked conviction. "I believe for her parents."

Understandably, this answer brought no illumination and Russell said, "I thought they died twenty years ago."

"The *idea* of her parents," Flora clarified.

Unable to contain her amusement a single moment longer, Bea burst out into gales of laughter, which caused her aunt, who was already annoyed by her cavalier disregard for her dead illusions, to renounce all responsibility for her. "You are Kesgrave's problem now."

"Mama," Flora said reprovingly. "Don't say *problem*, say *joy*."

But such a thing was beyond her meager abilities, and she excused herself from the table. Unconcerned, her daughter launched eagerly into the pleasures that were sure to await them at Lord Stirling's ball, her first complete one as a soon-to-be cousin-in-law to a duke.

Bea listened to her ramble excitedly, and although she thought her cousin was putting a bit too much stock in the advantages of being in close approximation to a duchy, she offered nothing discouraging.

Kesgrave arrived a short while later to take them to their meeting with Braxfield, and Bea felt much of her giddiness fade as she contemplated the information she was about to learn. She could not say why the prospect of having the viscount confirm the affair unsettled her more than having Wem do it, but it did, excessively, and as they waited on the doorstep for the butler to answer, she felt a perverse compulsion to run away.

Instead of fleeing, she brushed her hand against Kesgrave's, and he, perhaps sensing her apprehension, held it warmly in his own until the door opened.

The hallway took on a different cast in the morning sunshine, and Bea was surprised to see the walls were a cheerful yellow. The distance to the staircase was altered as well, revealing itself to be much shorter than she remembered. Running from the steps to the door had felt as long as an entire Mayfair block.

Braxfield greeted them in the drawing room, which was also bright and sunny, and after ascertaining what his guests would like for refreshment—tea would be lovely, they said—launched into praise of Bea, who had made an excellent impression on his niece.

"I saw her last night, you see, at the theater," he explained as the butler delivered the tray. "We saw *Othello*. Ordinarily one of my favorites, but the production was flat. The actors did not seem entirely present, for which I blame the director, as it is his duty to hold his cast together. But no matter. As I was saying, Katie quite enjoyed your company, Miss Hyde-Clare. She said you made salient arguments, which is high praise, as my niece has little patience for any argument that is not her own. I hope you will come to the salon with us again. Although you might think it gets a little tedious, with the same people attending month after month, but the topic changes constantly, which keeps things lively."

Bea felt some of her anxiety fade as she recalled his niece's enthusiastic performance at Lord Pudsey's. "I cannot believe Mrs. Palmer will allow the subject to change from income tax repeal anytime soon, my lord. But I understand why you would hope otherwise."

Braxfield chortled. "No, no, she has really kicked up a fuss on that one. Can't say why she has such a bee in her bonnet over it, other than she has the soul of a contrarian. It would be just like her to find something that has almost universal support and then take the opposite view. I'm surprised she did not root for Napoleon during the war."

It was on the tip of Bea's tongue to make a teasing comment about Mrs. Palmer's loyalties, and although some part of her wanted to spend the rest of the visit in trivial conversation with the viscount, she was too stubborn to give in to the cowardly impulse. Having failed to discover his secrets under the cover of darkness, she had no choice but to do it in the light of day.

With a fleeting glance at Kesgrave—for support or approval, she did not know—she took a deep breath and said to her host, "At the salon you confirmed that you had worked with my parents to infiltrate the English Correspondence Guild."

"Confirmed?" he asked, taken aback by the term.

Bea knew that her tone implied calculation, and she made no attempt to shy away from it. Kesgrave had suggested a frank conversation, so a frank conversation she would have—no manipulations, no maneuvering, no sidling up to the information she wanted to discover and hoping it was revealed.

"Yes, confirmed," she said matter-of-factly. "I went to the salon in expectation of meeting you and asking about my parents. I had recently discovered some troubling things about their last months and had hoped to find out more. I learned of your association with the group from Mr. Jeffries, whom I interviewed earlier this week. Now, if you don't mind, I would like to ask you a few questions as well."

This honest declaration of intent did not sit well with Lord Braxfield, who raised his narrow chin so high it seemed almost to point at Bea accusingly. His slight nose twitched in annoyance, and he looked at Kesgrave as if shocked he would condone such behavior.

Bea, who found very little surprising in his reaction, thought the duke might revise his positive view of frank conversations if he were forced to conduct them as a woman.

Kesgrave returned his lordship's indignation with an impassive stare of his own, and finding himself without an ally, Braxfield asked his guests if they would like some port.

"I would like some port," he explained, "for suddenly I feel as though I'm about to get a drubbing from my steward for mismanaging the accounts or, worse, a lecture from my brother on the importance of investing in modern water closets. I cannot say which is worse, but both arouse a strong desire for port."

Braxfield rang for his butler, who promptly delivered a bottle with three glasses, which he filled before leaving the room without comment. The viscount distributed the glasses to his guests, then nodded his head in salute and took a deep sip. As he lowered the glass, he said, "Very well, young lady, I am fortified. You may begin your interrogation."

She wanted to protest his description of the frank conversation but decided it was apt. "I am interested in your relationship with my mother. Could you please describe your relationship with her?"

He took another sip of the wine before answering. "I found her charming and beautiful. She was always an amusing supper partner, a little more outré in her humor than other women, not quite *comme il fault,* which is why she disguised herself as a man to join the guild alongside your father. I thought it rather shocking that he let her, but I soon realized he could not say no to her. He was wonderful company but lacking in backbone. I supposed that's why he was so easily swayed by the guild's revolutionary fervor. He thought their goals were entirely reasonable. Richard remained cognizant of his duty, I'm pleased to say, and continued to send reports to Pitt. He stayed loyal to the Crown in action, however treasonous he was in thought," he said, raising the glass to his lips again. "I believe I told you much of this the other night. I'm not sure what more information you hope to gain."

Bea acknowledged his point as her hand tightened around the glass's stem. She had no desire to drink port—or, indeed anything—but it felt good to have something to do with her fingers. "You did, yes. But I would like to know more about your interactions with my mother. I know there was more between you than what you have described."

His beady nose twitched again, conveying his annoyance, and his pointy chin tipped up as if he was going to angrily deny the claim, but when he spoke, his tone was mild. "A light flirtation, of course. She was a remarkably beautiful woman, and I have never been able to resist a beautiful woman. I have always found myself most comfortable surrounded by a coterie of lovelies."

Although he delivered this speech with convincing insouciance, Bea could plainly see he was hiding something. His pose was evasive and his tone was aggressively reasonable. Perhaps if she hadn't already known about the affair, she wouldn't have noticed the signs of prevarication, but she had and she did.

Now, as she observed his discomfort, she felt a sense of dread settle in her stomach. It was apprehension, yes, at the prospect of having the affair unequivocally confirmed by one of its participants, an especially heavy blow after the giddy hopefulness of the morning. But more than that, she was unnerved by his uncharacteristic reluctance to admit to the relationship. A man of his history and inclinations would have no compunction about admitting publicly to an adulterous liaison. What had Mrs. Ralston said about his penchant for seducing married ladies? *He loved to flaunt their allegiances in the face of their husbands.*

That he was reluctant to do so now—that he, in fact, looked almost guilty at the prospect—indicated something else was at play.

The missing bracelet was key, she thought, the thing that set apart Braxfield's dalliance with her mother from all the others in which he'd indulged. It should have been among the cache of tokens, and the fact that it was not indicated something.

Was it shame, she wondered, at the way he'd attained it?

If Clara had refused to hand over the sapphire treasure as proof of her affection, would Braxfield have responded in anger?

It was possible.

He was, after all, a man unaccustomed to the sensation of failure and would inevitably resent the woman who'd caused him to feel it. How furious it must have made him to have his will thwarted, his desire denied, the proof of his virility withheld.

Violence was an indelible part of him. Jeffries, her mother, the dowager—even Braxfield himself—had all testified to his pugnacity and aggression. They described his attempts to incite members of the English Correspondence Guild to riot. He could not stand how peacefully they gathered to formulate their arguments and write their treatises.

Of course a man with such brutality in his soul would not allow one slightly stubborn disenchanted lover to refuse him, to tarnish his pristine record and his perception of himself as an accomplished lothario.

Clara Hyde-Clare was probably the first woman to ever say no.

Bea's heart thrashed wildly and her fingers twitched to squeeze Kesgrave's hand, but she did nothing to reveal her distress or anxiety. Instead, she forced a smile to her lips and said gently to the man who she believed murdered her mother, "But it was much more than a harmless flirtation, was it not?"

For a moment, Braxfield looked trapped, as if he had nowhere to run, even as he sat in his own drawing room, but then he shook off the fear and stared at her with faintly amused contempt. It was an effective look, as intimidating as it was disdainful, and Bea instantly recalled Lord Taunton at the Larkwells' ball, playing his cards with the same sort of derisive mirth, so confident he held the upper hand and so quick to choke the life out of her when he discovered he didn't.

Bea felt a quiver of fear, sharp and fierce, but refused to succumb to it. She was in a drawing room, not a deserted terrace on the edge of a ball, and Kesgrave was beside her.

Determined, she returned his gaze with an unwavering disdain of her own, aware that she was seeing him clearly for the first time, as her father had seen him from the very beginning. Richard had known Braxfield was dangerous, for it was there in Clara's letters: *Richard finds his pugnacity worrisome and his temperament dangerous, but I'm convinced it's only talk, for no gentleman could be so unprincipled."*

The contest drew on for several riveting seconds, Bea's own eyes resolutely unblinking, before the viscount turned away. "All right, all right, I admit it. Yes, I did it. I helped your mother write a treatise on the topic of female equality. It went against everything I believed and I could not approve of any of her points, but, damn her eyes, the writing was brilliant and her arguments impeccable, and I did everything I could to help her improve it."

Bea lived an entire lifetime in the space between his admission of guilt—*all right, all right, I admit it, yes, I did it*—and the revelation of his crime. Inside her, relief blossomed like a hundred flowers all at once and just as quickly withered. In its wake all she could do was stare at the viscount with dumbfounded incomprehension.

Next to her, Kesgrave shifted and suddenly his right

hand was holding hers while his left hand removed the glass of port from her fingers before she dropped it. He placed it on the table.

Bea struggled to organize her thoughts. If Braxfield knew about her mother's book then he was familiar with her views on female equality. Had he exploited her unconventional ideas to maneuver her into an affair? It was still entirely possible that the events had happened exactly as she'd imagined them.

But the person sitting across from her was not wearing the expression of a brutal man or even a guilty one. Rather, he looked sheepish and embarrassed.

Calmly, Bea took a deep breath and said forthrightly, "You were not having an affair with her?"

Braxfield found the question uproarious and laughed as if he had just been told the greatest joke in the English language. "An affair with a woman who touted equality?" he asked, his amusement abating just enough to make room for his scorn. "Who wrote treatises? Who thought her own ideas were so important they should be published? My dear Miss Hyde-Clare, I said your mother was beautiful. I never said she was attractive. Where did you get such a ludicrous idea?"

For Bea, his laughter was a tonic, and no denial, however strenuous, could have been as persuasive as his hilarity. "The Earl of Wem said—"

"That fool!" he interjected. "He came here one day, ranting and raving about my affair with Clara, demanding that I put an end to it at once. Like a lunatic, he was."

"You didn't deny it," Beatrice said softly.

He pinned her gaze with an appalled look. "Of course I did not. He came into my house, making accusations and demanding obedience. He did not deserve the dignity of my denial. Kesgrave, you would have done the same thing."

"Perhaps," conceded the duke.

"There is no *perhaps* about it," Braxfield insisted. "I don't know where the slow-wit got the mutton-headed idea in the first place."

"You were working with my mother on her treatise," Bea explained as the weight of the truth began to sink in. The Earl of Wem was wrong. Aunt Vera was wrong. "Perhaps you were spending more time together, or perhaps you started to interact with each other differently, like colleagues."

He looked horrified by the idea of being colleagues with a woman and then conceded the very thing was possible. "Richard had read it, of course, but he adored your mother and thought everything she did was wonderful. She couldn't get a single coherent word of criticism out of him."

If Bea never heard another favorable thing about her parents for the rest of her life, this image, of her father being too enamored of her mother to offer a critique of her work, would be sufficient. After the relentless turmoil of the past few days, it was a beautiful gift.

"Thank you," Bea said with heartfelt gratitude.

Now that the interrogation was over, Braxfield was gracious and kind. "Of course, of course. Anything for a friend of my niece's. I'm genuinely sorry Wem got you worked up over the thing. Damn fool," he said again but without the heat. "I understand, of course, for no man wants to see his oldest friend made a cuckold, but if he had only applied what little sense he had to the matter, he would have realized the charge was without merit. Clara and Richard had just left to spend the rest of the summer in the country, and any woman with whom I was favoring my attentions could not have borne to leave town."

At the boast, Kesgrave gently squeezed Bea's hand and she returned the pressure, indicating that, yes, she was ready to leave. They made their goodbyes quickly, with Bea promising to attend Lord Pudsey's next salon and the duke revealing the limits of his jealousy of Nuneaton by firmly refusing the pleasure.

The bright sunlight hurt her eyes as they stepped outside, but when Kesgrave suggested they walk to

Portman Square, she promptly said yes. With Annie a few paces behind, they strolled down Duchess Street, their hands close but not touching.

"I'm very happy for you, Bea," he said, warmth suffusing his voice. "It must be a huge relief to know your father did not kill your mother or himself."

"So massive I want to scream and cry at the same time," she revealed, "and I have lived with the horror for only three days. My aunt and uncle have lived with it for twenty years. This truth, as wrong as it was, shaped my whole life. I'm not sure how much compassion Aunt Vera has within her soul—already, this morning, she was blaming me for forcing her to tell me the truth—but I think she would have been a little kinder if she hadn't felt a terrible pressure to make sure I didn't turn out promiscuous like my mother or homicidal like my father. If nothing else, she would have at least let me have the solace of their memory."

"I hope you can take some comfort from it now," he said gently.

She sighed softly, for she hoped the same thing too. "I have three chests filled with their items now. That is more than I had a week ago."

"And your mother's treatise, which I would like to read if you are comfortable sharing it," he said.

"It might not be to your liking," she cautioned.

"My notions of equality are not quite as antiquated as Braxfield's," he assured her as they walked toward Cavendish Square.

"As your future wife, I find that very reassuring, but I meant the writing style. My mother is succinct and makes her points cleanly," she explained. "You will find none of the loquacious self-importance that you value so highly in a persuasive argument. I say that only as a warning, not a criticism, you understand. I personally love loquacious self-importance."

Kesgrave laughed, and careless of the public setting, took her hand in his own. "Just you wait until we are married, brat. Then I will show you how I can win an argument without saying a word."

Her stomach fluttered in anticipation. "When will that be?"

"Whenever you want," he said. "I got the special license days ago."

"And were just waiting."

"Yes."

Bea nodded, surprised at the human heart's ability to continually expand, and said she would love to get married tomorrow if that complied with his ducal schedule.

"It does," he said, "as the only thing I have marked down is to shine my coronet, and I can do that in the morning. I will let my grandmother know. She would like us to have the ceremony in her drawing room."

At the mention of the dowager, her thoughts turned to the bracelet, and she knew she could not let the matter rest. She would get married the next day and resume her investigation the day after. Haltingly, she explained this to Kesgrave, for every man had the right to his new bride's undivided attention and she felt a little bit guilty at not being able to provide it.

"But only a little bit, you understand," she said as they turned right onto Barrett Street, "for your self-worth is already high enough without my consuming interest increasing it."

He decried the abuse and swore his self-worth had long been trampled under her feet. "I understand, however, your need to continue your investigation and will help in any way I can. I assume our first step is to find the men Jeffries describes as his lieutenants…what were their names?…Berks and Thorpe and interview them. You think it's possible they found out your parents' true identities, followed them to the country and killed them?"

It sounded, she conceded, remarkably unlikely when he outlined the sequence of events that would have had to occur, but it was the best place to start. "I would also like to talk to jewelers. Whoever killed my mother must have stolen the bracelet, for it was worth a very great deal. Berks or Thorpe or any other member of the guild would have sold it for the money, as a gold bracelet dotted in sapphires would not feed their family," she said, aware that she should have realized this sooner. It was the simplest explanation for the missing heirloom, and the simplest explanation was almost always the correct one.

The duke agreed with her reasoning and said he would send Mr. Stephens to speak to jewelers that very afternoon.

"And you can ask your butler who fixes your clocks," she said, "as that is Berks's profession. I'm convinced that there are only a small number of clockmakers in London and that they all know each other."

They turned right into Portman Square and Kesgrave agreed to her request before pointing out with mild pedantry that in less than twenty-four hours Marlow would be *her* butler.

Bea blanched in terror.

CHAPTER THIRTEEN

Although Bea could detect no appreciable change in Flora's popularity as a result of her cousin's pending nuptials, the girl insisted her dance card was twice as full as usual. As every dance card had a finite number of slots for gentlemen's names, this was demonstrably false, but Bea was too kind to mention it.

Flora's brother, of course, was not, and the argument that ensued, conducted with the brightest possible smiles so as to appear amiable, made Bea particularly glad that that night would be the last one she would spend under her relatives' roof. Even the thought of subjecting herself daily to Marlow's disdainful sneer could not dim her delight.

"Must you grin so broadly?" Aunt Vera asked as she observed the bright expression on her niece's face. "A duchess should have dignity, an aloof sort of charm that intimidates people. You must cultivate a lofty demeanor or I fear you will be a very bad duchess."

Bea further upset her aunt by laughing. "My dear, I'm *sure* I will make a very bad duchess, and my only consolation is I'm confident Kesgrave won't mind. He had years to find a very good duchess and respectfully declined."

Aunt Vera had no choice but to agree with this observation and conceded that perhaps her niece would prosper quite well as his wife. "Your parents would be very proud."

The words came out stilted and unsure, but Bea, who knew how difficult it was for her aunt to utter them after twenty years of suppressing all thoughts of Richard and Clara, was deeply touched. It meant the world to her that her aunt was trying to right an old wrong.

When Bea told her the truth—along with Uncle Horace in the drawing room as soon as she'd returned from her outing with Kesgrave—her aunt had grown very agitated. Her face had turned white and her body had started to shake and tears had streamed down her cheeks in great torrents as she murmured to herself over and over, "Honest mistake, honest mistake. It was an honest mistake."

Yes, Bea thought now, it *had* been an honest mistake, and she harbored no ill will toward her relatives or Lord Wem. On the eve of her wedding to Kesgrave, she could afford to be philosophical, and she doubted that if she'd gotten the childhood she'd deserved—the honest love and affection denied her—she would be on the verge of making him a very bad duchess.

Try as she might, she could not regret anything that had led her to that point.

How strangely fate worked, she thought, remembering the moment all those years ago when, standing on the doorstep of 19 Portman Square as an orphan, she'd felt as if the trajectory of her life had veered off course. Nothing would ever be right again.

Now she wondered if that wasn't the moment her future straightened itself out.

"I'm not sure how you can consider yourself an arbiter of anything related to dancing when you have two left feet," Flora said snidely to her brother. "I wouldn't be surprised if your clumsiness is the real reason Mama won't let you take lessons at Gentleman Jackson's."

Russell's cheeks turned a bright pink color at this accusation, and he huffed angrily that any ungainliness he may or may not possess—to be clear, he was *not* conceding the accuracy of the charge—could be overcome with a few dancing lessons, whereas the deficiencies of her nose were beyond repair.

Flora screeched at the insult.

Unable to bear her children's bickering, Aunt Vera asked Russell to fetch her a glass of ratafia. "I am suddenly quite parched."

Her son looked put out at having to perform an errand for his mother, and Bea, taking pity on him, slid her arm through his and volunteered to escort him to the refreshment table. She'd been planning on crossing the floor anyway, for she wanted to find Lady Abercrombie and provide her with an update on her investigation.

"Let us discuss the merits of fencing," she said cheerfully as she led her cousin through the crowd, "as it will aid in your coordination and I'm sure my aunt could be persuaded to allow you to take up the sport. I understand it's not as exciting as boxing, with its opportunities to plant a facer or have your lip bloodied, but consider what a romantic figure you would cut, wielding a blade."

He owned himself not entirely repelled by the idea.

Bea laughed at his deliberately evasive reply and advised him to think about it. Then she turned to secure her own glass of ratafia and found herself standing next to Lord Wem. She felt the spark of familiarity before remembering that they had never officially met and coolly looked away.

But he'd recognized her too and responded to the warmth he'd seen in her expression.

"We have never been formally introduced, Miss Hyde-Clare," he said with a tentative smile, "but I knew you as a baby and was good friends with your parents. Indeed, your father was my closest friend. I hope it's not too forward of me to say how pleased I was to hear of your forthcoming marriage to the Duke of Kesgrave. I'm sure your parents would have been pleased as well."

Considering the revelations of the day, Bea found it perfectly fitting that they meet just then and she thanked him for his kindness. Then she said, "Of late Lady Abercrombie has been gifting me with remembrances of my mother, and I wonder if you would be willing to share some memories of my father. You would have known him in a different way from my uncle."

His whole face lit up. "Oh, my dear, nothing would make me happier. All these years later and I still miss him dreadfully."

"Wonderful," she said, fully aware that at some point during their meeting she would have to reveal the actual nature of her mother's relationship with Braxfield. She recalled the bitterness with which he'd spit out the word *harlot* and suspected he would find the truth difficult to hear, for it was obvious that he'd been deeply affected by the supposed infidelity of his oldest friend's wife. Perhaps he had seen the couple as a romantic ideal, and the ugliness of their rupture convinced him never to marry. She hoped he would ultimately find comfort in knowing his original estimation of their relationship was accurate. "I will send a note to your house to arrange a time."

"Very good," he said with a nod of approval. Then he looked around furtively and gestured to an area away from the table that was not as crowded. "Do you have another moment for a brief conversation? There's something I would like to tell you in confidence."

"Yes, of course," she said, accompanying him several feet away until he found a spot near a corner that he deemed suitable.

"This must seem very mysterious to you," he said with a self-conscious laugh. "I'm sorry for that. It's just that I did say I wouldn't tell anyone, but I did not swear an oath, so there is no vow to be broken. And you are lovely and kind, asking me to tell you stories of your father, so I thought you should know." He looked around again, then leaned in closer and dropped his voice. "The Dowager Duchess of

Kesgrave is gathering information on you and your parents in an attempt to end your engagement to her grandson. I know because she sent a solicitor to me to ask questions."

Coming face to face with her own trickery—Bea wanted to laugh, for it was so preposterous how easily and effortlessly the lie had rebounded onto herself. 'Twas like the story about Mr. Davies, a harmless fiction concocted to elicit confidences from an Incomparable that somehow changed the course of her life. If she hadn't been in the *London Daily Gazette* offices when Fazeley dropped dead....

How capricious fate was, she thought.

Out of respect for Lord Wem, whose revelations deserved a properly horrified response, she opened her eyes wide and said, "No, I can't believe it!" She drew out the amazement as she tried to think of an insult to fling at the dowager that was mean but not too mean, for she had already done the poor woman a grave disservice by enlisting her in her plot.

"That underhanded schemer!" Bea said with simulated anger. Then, worrying the slight didn't slice close enough to the bone, she added, "That manipulative scoundrel! How dare she think I'm not good enough for her grandson!"

Wem nodded eagerly and cautioned her to keep her voice low as he quickly surveyed the area to make sure she had not drawn attention to them. "Obviously, you cannot tell the duke, for interfering in family relationships never goes the way one plans. But I wanted you to know so you may be on your guard. Even if she doesn't succeed in ending your engagement, she is not to be trusted."

"Yes, yes, of course," she said, surprisingly moved by the warning, even though it had been completely unnecessary. "You are right. I must take the long view of the situation. Thank you, my lord, for telling me. I'm grateful."

"Nonsense!" he said with a dismissive wave of his hand. "What kind of friend would I be to your father if I didn't warn his daughter that there was a plot afoot to harm her? You needn't worry. I didn't tell the solicitor anything."

Now her astonishment was real, and her jaw dropped slightly at the boldness of the lie.

"Well you stare," Wem said with satisfaction. "Did you think I would be intimidated by a duchess? Not I. I flicked her man my most haughty look, glanced at my pocket watch in the most supercilious manner, told him not to waste my time and ordered him to be on his way. I am nobody's gossip."

As he spoke, commending himself on his integrity, Bea felt her anger grow. It took a particular sort of audacity to paint yourself as a high-minded objector when you were in fact an unprincipled informant. 'Twould not be so bad had he been even a little bit reticent. But he had not shown any hesitation in sharing all he knew about Clara. He'd defamed her character swiftly and bitterly. If only he had stared her down and then taken the fob out of his pocket with all the finely wrought contempt he described now.

Underhanded schemer!

Manipulative scoundrel!

He was trying to have it both ways—the indulgence of venting his spleen to the duchess's man and the pleasure of winning Beatrice's goodwill.

It was, she thought, an especially distasteful type of moral weakness, the compulsion to contort yourself into any shape to earn the approval of whomever you were speaking to. She would have been more sympathetic to this flaw if he had been only a little kinder. If he had not spit out the word *harlot* quite so viciously, as if he were the one who had been betrayed, not her father, or implied with his careless choice of words that Clara had taken a legion of lovers, Bea's patience might have been greater. Alas, she remembered all too clearly the scorn he'd heaped on her head when she explained she was waiting for further evidence of her mother's promiscuity.

The scoffing sound he'd made as he withdrew his watch to look at the time with barely contained impatience still rang in her ear, and she readily recalled the waspishness with which he'd slipped the chain back into his pocket, the sunlight glinting…the sunlight glinting….

Her mind stopped there and refused to go further. It was staring at the sunlight that glinted off the chain. It was gaping at the flicker of blue.

The flicker of sapphire blue.

Not gold catching and reflecting the vivid blue of the walls.

Sapphires.

Her heart began to pound furiously as all at once the piercing bitterness with which he'd spat out the word *harlot* made a terrible sort of sense. His response to Clara's betrayal felt personal because it *was* personal. In dallying with Braxfield and perhaps countless others, she'd sinned against him, not Richard, and, having gained his confirmation, he'd struck out in fury.

What had sparked the wrath? Love for Clara or jealousy of Richard? Wem had met her first, she thought, unable to recall who had told her that. But she remembered clearly a line from one of her mother's letters: *Wem swears he will settle for nothing less than my eternal devotion.* The timing worked out, she realized, for Wem's confrontation with Braxfield happened after her parents had left town for the summer. Maddened by the viscount's seeming confirmation, the earl dashed to Wellsdale House to rage at Clara.

To rage at her and then what?

"My dear girl, you've gone white," Wem said, brushing her arm lightly in concern.

She flinched as the hand that killed her mother touched her.

Gather your wits.

"Delayed reaction," she said, her voice a little breathless, which rendered the claim all the more believable. But too much blood was thundering in her head, making it difficult to think. She had to calm down.

Take a deep breath. "The dowager. Her sending an investigator. I just…it just occurred to me how vicious she is to do something like that. To destroy two people's happiness. I knew she did not love me, but I didn't think her distaste was so…"

Bea let the thought hang there to take another deep breath, and she felt the noise in her head start to subside.

Wem nodded solemnly. "Of course, it's a lot to take in. Would you like to sit down? Shall I find us some seats?"

She shook her head no as she stared at him, still quite handsome with his brown eyes and dark lashes and bottom lip that protruded just a little too much. How calm he was, so cool in his concern over her welfare, so composed as he offered to help.

Oh, but something terrible simmered beneath. Another snippet from her mother's letters darted through her head: *They are rough men but do not appear to be brutal, and yet sometimes, just below the surface, I feel the roil of anger.*

That was Wem—the brutality seething beneath the cool appraisal.

She knew she had to pierce the façade, deprive him of the lie he'd been telling himself for twenty years. Clara was not a harlot. She did not deserve it.

Now Bea held one hand to her chest as she made a great show of trying to calm down. "I'm so grateful to you, my lord, for telling the dowager nothing, for I know you could have told her a terrible story about my mother and Lord Braxfield."

Wem stiffened at once. "I cannot believe you know about that unfortunate event."

It was a good start, she thought, noting the way the viscount's name unsettled him. "Do not be cross. Aunt Vera thought it was important that I know so that I may guard myself against a similar moral failure."

He nodded vigorously, applauding the practicality of the decision, although he still could not approve. "It was not a suitable topic for innocent ears. And a daughter should think the best of her parents, not that her mother was…morally weak…with men who were not her father. I'm sorry you had to go through that."

It should have sounded empty and false—the remorse for her suffering when he was the one who'd caused it. And yet he remained wholly convincing.

Again—always again—her mind flitted to the riverbank in the driving rain, and she pictured her mother, terrified and confused, denying every word he said, struggling to explain the truth, pleading with him to listen, only this time it was Wem, not her father. But just like her father, he was too filled with rage to hear it.

He would hear it now.

"I understand your concern and will own that I share it, but if Aunt Vera had not told me, I would never have discovered the truth," she said gently, forcing herself to touch his arm until he raised his head and looked her directly in the eyes. "It was a mistake."

"Of course it was a mistake," he assured her, his tone sympathetic as if offering comfort. "It was a dreadful mistake, for Braxfield was and is an unscrupulous snake. If her base desires were so difficult to control, there were plenty of men with decency she could have chosen."

"No, no," Bea said, smiling with deliberate brightness. "The belief that she was having an affair was the mistake. That's the news I'd hoped to share with you when we met again. It was all a dreadful misunderstanding. You see, Braxfield was not engaging in inappropriate relations with my mother. He was helping her write a treatise on female equality."

Although she hadn't expected this revelation to unsettle him into confessing, she was much taken aback when he laughed.

"My dear child," he said, shaking his head and looking at her with something close to pity, "somebody has been telling you Banbury tales, and I understand why you would want to believe them. But that doesn't make them true."

His condescension was pitched perfectly, and Bea, grateful for it, responded with treacly appreciation. "Lord Wem, you are so kind to be worried that someone is trying to dupe me, but you must put such thoughts from your mind. Nobody told me about the treatise. I found it myself when I went through my parents' belongings. It is written in Clara's own hand. I promise you, if you saw it yourself, you'd recognize it."

He seemed more confused than comforted. "Clara was not a writer," he murmured softly as he tried to understand. "And female equality, you say? I don't see...I cannot grasp what that would have to do with her. You are saying extraordinary things."

"No, my lord, here's the extraordinary thing: There are notes on the manuscript, suggesting ways it can be improved and they were written by Lord Braxfield."

Far from seeing his lordship's involvement in the project as a vindicating factor, Wem found in it confirmation of what he already knew. "Braxfield! He encouraged her to write it. I cannot pretend to comprehend his motives, but I don't doubt this...this...this *treatise*—absurd word for a piece of writing by a woman—served his lascivious purpose."

He was getting agitated, Bea thought. His color was rising, and he didn't seem to know what to do with his hands. He fidgeted with the ribbon that attached to his watch. He had not dared to use her mother's bracelet as the chain tonight, for many of the guests had known her and someone might recognize it.

"Naturally, you are cynical," she said with exaggerated understanding, "for you have thought something to be true for twenty years and it's very difficult to reevaluate a longstanding belief in light of new information. But I assure you it's not so implausible. It will make more sense when I tell you this: She was a member of the English Correspondence Guild."

Now it entered his eyes—a sort of bewildered fear, an insidious foreboding that he might not know as much as he'd thought.

"I know, it sounds like another Banbury tale, but it's the truth. Both my parents were members," she explained, her attention divided between the distress in his eyes and the hand that fiddled with the ribbon. "It was a favor for Mr. Pitt. He asked my father to infiltrate the guild on behalf of the government and to report back on its activities. Clara insisted on going along for a lark. When you know that, her interest in matters of female equality doesn't seem as unlikely. You never knew this. My parents never told you. They didn't want you to worry about their safety. My mother even wrote exactly that in her letter to Lady Abercrombie. She said you didn't know about the assignment because if you did, you would cluck over them like a mother hen."

How wrong she had been.

The earl made no response, but the color in his cheeks deepened and Beatrice wondered what he was thinking. Was he sifting through his memories, examining events in a new light, or growing more entrenched in his beliefs?

"And that is why she asked Braxfield for his opinion," she said as if one thing logically led to the other. But of course it did not for Lord Wem, whose mouth opened briefly as if to speak, then closed abruptly. "As he was also a member of the guild. The three of them were in it together, working at the direction of Pitt. Together. And when my father proved to be too much of an adoring husband to be of any use as a critic, she turned to Braxfield, whom she considered to be a colleague of sorts. So you see, their relationship was entirely aboveboard. A little unconventional, I will grant you, but nothing morally weak or questionable. Is that not wonderful news, my lord?"

He did not answer or appear to have even heard the question. He had a vacant look about him, as if he'd disappeared inside his own mind. Bea would not allow him the refuge.

"I said, my lord, is that not wonderful?" she repeated as she drew closer to him and raised her voice a little.

Although he seemed to see her now, he could not muster a reply, only nodding his head slowly.

Bea continued in her assault, employing the same tone of excessive consideration. "I can only imagine how difficult this must be for you to absorb, as I know Braxfield confirmed it. It must have felt like a settled thing—your worst suspicions corroborated by the blackguard himself. But Braxfield was only tweaking you for storming into his home and lodging a vile accusation against him. He didn't so much as confirm the affair as not deny it," she said, tut-tutting disapprovingly as if exasperated by a thoughtless prank, then adding to further provoke him, "He knows now he gave my aunt and uncle a few very bad moments, and he's apologized to them."

The hand by the fob pocket ceased its motions and clutched the ribbon in a fist. The color in his cheeks had begun to lessen, Bea noted, as Wem found a new equilibrium. Whatever the new story he was telling himself was, it was having a calming effect on his nerves. He had too much control. She had to shatter it.

Smiling sympathetically, Bea took a step closer to the earl so that she could feel the heat of his breath on her cheek. "It has been so horrible for you—and my aunt and uncle—to have to imagine Clara yielding to Braxfield."

His entire posture changed at the word *yielding*. His body didn't stiffen with rage, it snapped with it, and his eyes glimmered hot and fierce.

Undaunted, she continued her assault. "To have to imagine her lying with him, his hands roaming her body while his mouth lay fevered kisses on her skin. To imagine her eager response, her seeking his attentions, her craving his touch. And you knowing she belonged to your friend, not Brax—"

Suddenly his hands seized her shoulders, clasping them tightly, his fingers digging into her skin through the silk of her gown. Even as the pain seared through her, she smiled in triumphant satisfaction. Rage—finally!

"*She belonged to me!*" he screeched. "She was never Richard's. She was always mine. *Mine!* And then Braxfield...and then Braxfield—" But he could not finish the thought and only shook his head while tightening his grip on her shoulders. "I don't know why you are doing this. Why you are telling me these lies. Lies, lies, lies, such awful lies. She was a whore—I *know* it—spreading her legs for Braxfield. Then she could damn well spread them for me!" Then, for a moment, his face flickered with calm and he said in almost a reasonable tone, "You're trying to trick me, that's what it is. You want me to think I killed her for nothing." And then it was gone and his eyes seethed with rage and he shook her violently. "*It was not for nothing!*"

Bea ignored the pain in her shoulders.

No, not ignored. Delighted in it, for it was proof that she'd demolished his control.

"Oh, but it was for nothing," she said gleefully, taunting him mercilessly in hopes that he would crumble, that he would cave into himself, that without the lies to hold him up he would collapse. "It was all for nothing. You killed her for nothing at all. What happened? Did you propose something sordid and indecent, and Clara, rightfully horrified, turned you down flat? Did you throw Braxfield at her? Did you call her promiscuous, a harlot? Did you *tell* her how it was going to be and refuse to take no for an answer?"

"It wasn't like that!" he screamed. "She wanted me. I could tell. It was obvious from everything she did and said. She wanted me desperately, but I was her husband's closest friend and she couldn't reconcile it with her conscience. I meant too much to her, so she gave herself to Braxfield. To that lout and that scoundrel and that rake who could not appreciate the beautiful creature she was. But she wanted me! She just couldn't say the words because she loved me too much. I didn't need the words.

No, I didn't need her to say anything at all. But she kept saying no. I wanted her silence and she kept saying no. I had to stop her from speaking. That's all it was. That's all that happened. I stopped her from saying no in that desperate voice, as if she was terrified Richard would walk into the drawing room and discover the truth about us. I had to stop her, for she was punishing me as much as herself."

Bea felt dizzy, as if the ballroom were swirling around her, but she kept her eyes focused on his, on the madness she saw there. And she pictured the scene in the room where her father had read Benjamin Franklin's biography to her while she was curled up against his body, warm and safe and happy—Wem stifling her mother's cries as he tried to smother the truth, as if brute force could give form to his wildest fantasies.

"And Richard found you," she said softly to urge him on.

But it wasn't necessary, for he said at almost the same moment, "And Richard found us, and he was so angry at me. He thought I'd hurt her on purpose. I never wanted to hurt her. I only wanted to love her. I loved her so much and she loved me, but we never got a chance to be together. It was a tragedy. But Richard didn't understand that. No, he kept yelling at me, saying these vile, *vile* things, and I had to silence him too. There was so much noise, so much noise and clatter and clamor. I *had* to silence him so he would stop saying such awful things."

Bea could feel the silence. Having imagined one wretched scene after another at the riverbank in the torrential rain, she could feel the pervasive silence of the drawing room after he'd pressed the life from their bodies.

Wem fell silent too, perhaps consumed as well by the horror of the memory.

"You had to do something, though, didn't you, because nobody would understand," she prompted. "Anyone who walked into the drawing room and found the two dead bodies wouldn't understand that you had been forced to silence them. They'd think you'd done it on purpose, and they would get very angry at you and say more vile things. So you brought them to the river and chopped a hole in their boat."

He smiled, and the smile was serene. "They were always happiest on the water."

Horrified to the innermost heart of her, she wrenched her shoulders from his grip and took two steps back. She had nothing else to say to him. There was nothing else she needed to know. She waited for the relief, she craved the relief, but none came. All she had was the horror in her heart.

Wem snarled and clasped her shoulders again, but when he spoke it was in torment, not anger. "Why must you keep doing this, Clara? Why must you keep judging me? Why can I not close my eyes without seeing that look on your face? Why must you condemn me? Why can you not leave me alone? Why, Clara, why?"

She wanted to see a monster when she looked at him, a raging beast with a child's heart who would deprive the world of something beautiful because he couldn't have it, but he was just the weak, stupid, selfish man who had destroyed her family without even thinking about it. It was all so ugly, and fearing the horror was permanently lodged in her heart, she broke free of his grip and turned away.

There, standing not a full step behind, was Kesgrave.

Now the relief poured through her, flooding her senses like a river overrunning its banks and soaking the surrounding acres. It filled up her heart and emptied it of the horror.

She met his gaze, so steady and blue, and she knew at once he'd seen everything. He might have missed the first few moments of the exchange, the soft opening volley, but he'd been there for enough, for the important part, for the end. It was a gift beyond measure to know she wouldn't have to go through it again, word for word, grappling for a way to convey the ugliness.

Staring into his eyes, she took her first deep breath,

and with the slow exhalation of air she felt the pressure inside her release. A teardrop slid down her cheek, followed by several others, and as she tilted her head to wipe them away, she perceived for the first time the breadth of her audience.

'Twas not just the duke.

Seemingly, the entire ballroom, every guest of Lord Stirling's, was staring at her, their astonishment varying by the person. Her host appeared on the verge of an apoplectic seizure, and Nuneaton looked as though he had a few questions. And it was silent, she realized, the orchestra having ceased. Why had it stopped? Was it time for supper?

It was unsettling to turn from the horror of Wem and find herself the target of so many stunned looks, and Bea shrunk from it for a moment, for it had the unreal feel of a nightmare and that pervasive fear of suddenly being exposed. But then she saw the absurdity of the moment—drab little Beatrice Hyde-Clare causing such an uproar—and felt herself calm, soothed, she thought, by the irrepressibility of her sense of humor. It was actually funny, for only a week before she'd created a fracas on the terrace at the Larkwells' ball, and not content with offstage theatrics, she had mounted the drama in the ballroom itself.

Now that was a thought she longed to share with the duke, she thought as her eyes swung back to his. And she noted then the strangeness of it all—the way Lord Stirling was standing at Kesgrave's elbow, next to Uncle Horace, whose face was pure white.

He'd held them all back, she thought—her host, her uncle, even Lord Braxfield.

Kesgrave had known that she needed to finish the confrontation with Wem on her own, so he stopped everyone from interceding, even himself.

And now he was waiting, just waiting.

It was another gift, a remarkable one, she thought, to love a man who did not need you to explain the minutiae of a situation to him, however eager he was to explain it to you.

The silence stretched, and Bea, feeling its heft, realized how weary she was. Her bones suddenly felt as though they weighed hundreds of pounds. She wanted to be gone and knew the duke would take her, but she could not simply walk out of the ballroom without saying a word. Some remark had to be addressed to her host.

Striving for what she hoped sounded like cool detachment and not thinly veiled hysteria, she said, "Lord Stirling, I believe confessing to the murder of my parents has overwhelmed Lord Wem's faculties, and I think he should be removed to ensure the comfort of your other guests. I would suggest taking him to Bedlam, but of course I leave it to your discretion."

There were audible gasps at this speech—certainly, a cry of horror from her aunt—and a whir filled the room as onlookers overcame their astonishment at the events to begin commenting on them. The scene she had enacted would be well more than a nine days' wonder. The gossips would feast for weeks on the fodder she'd provided, and she was just enough of the self-effacing Miss Hyde-Clare to regret how that would reflect on the duke.

But Kesgrave did not flinch as the whir became a hum and the hum became a buzz and the buzz became a roar. Indeed, he showed no response at all, waiting, just waiting, for her.

Although Lord Stirling had been slow to grasp what was happening, he stepped forward now with a bow and an apology, as if Wem's destructive obsession with her mother and murderous tendencies were in some way a fault of his hospitality.

"It pains me to see anyone treated so horribly in my own home," he explained with a sincerity Bea could not doubt. He made no mention of the earl, who was now sitting in the corner with his legs pressed against his chest, and she was grateful, for there was nothing left to be said, at least not for her.

"I am fatigued, my lord, and will take my leave of you now. Thank you for your generous reception," she added without irony, for she was truly grateful for the opportunity the ball had presented. If she had not encountered Wem quite by happenstance at the refreshment table, she would have spent weeks tracking down erstwhile members of the English Correspondence Guild. She might never have discovered the truth, or worse, she might have spent the rest of her life searching for it.

Kesgrave deserved better.

A lightness overcame her as she turned to the duke and looked at him with a world of expectation in her eyes. "Your grace?" she said.

He needed no further prompting and finally closed the distance that separated them. "Miss Hyde-Clare," he said softly, holding out his arm, which she gratefully accepted.

The duke bid good night to their host, nodding absently to a few others—Nuneaton, she noted, and her aunt—and led her toward the staircase. As they walked across the dance floor, the crowd parted to allow them to pass, simply too stunned, she thought, to try to detain them. Only Mrs. Ralston made the attempt, beaming with voracity and predation as she begged for a minute to compliment Miss Hyde-Clare on how well she had handled her…um, just to be clear…her parents' *murderer*? But the couple merely stepped around her as Bea begged the question by explaining she could not linger a moment longer, for she must return home to rest, as she had something very important to do on the morrow.

ABOUT THE AUTHOR

Lynn Messina is the author of more than a dozen novels, including the Beatrice Hyde-Clare mysteries, a series of cozies set in Regency-era England. Her first novel, *Fashionistas,* has been translated into sixteen languages and was briefly slated to be a movie starring Lindsay Lohan. Her essays have appeared in *Self, American Baby* and the *New York Times* Modern Love column, and she's a regular contributor to the *Times* parenting blog. She lives in New York City with her sons.

Made in the USA
Middletown, DE
01 June 2023